Hope's Haven

A Smoky Mountain Retreat

SAGE PARKER

ISBN: 9798856578118

To you. For picking up this book.
I hope you have a wonderful day. .

CONTENTS

CHAPTER 1

It was blisteringly hot, and Tessa wiped the sweat off her brow. She only had a few more items on her to-do list before she would finally escape the heat of her tiny office for the sanctity of her air-conditioned car. She was desperately crunching numbers that just wouldn't add up and hoping to leave her hot office when the shrill sound of the front gate's bell made her jump.

Annoyed, she glanced up at the enormous clock over her desk. *Almost 6:30,* she thought. *Much too late for a salesman or a delivery.* She turned her computer monitor to the cameras, locating the camera facing the front gate.

At first, she couldn't see anything, but then a young girl popped into her view. The girl was testing the gate to see if it was locked and looking to see if there was a way around it or over it. As she scrambled about, a well-worn duffel hung forlornly on her shoulder, clearly devoid of many belongings. Tessa could see that her blond hair was unkempt, she was not well dressed, and she was clearly underfed.

As she watched the girl darting around and peering over her shoulder at the road, Tessa sighed audibly, fearing this was going to turn into a long night. She was supposed to be at Stephanie's house for a birthday party in less than half an hour, so she was already running late. Stephanie was Tessa's best friend since childhood, and also her business partner in running the shelter she had founded. She hated making her wait, but the young girl outside her gate needed help. She switched on the intercom and saw the girl jump in surprise as her voice came through.

"Yes, can I help you with something?" Tessa asked politely, hoping against hope that maybe the girl was looking for a different address than hers, and she might still make it to the party relatively on time.

"Ummm, yeah. I really hope so. I'm looking for someone. Can I come in for a minute and talk?"

The girl's voice was timid and unsure, and she kept looking around her as if she were afraid of being seen or heard.

"I'm afraid we're closed for the evening, honey."

Tessa saw the girl's face fall in disappointment, and she wondered if the girl even knew she was at a shelter.

"Please, I don't have anywhere else to go. I'm looking for Tessa Graves. If you just tell her I need help and a place to stay, I'm sure that she'll let me in."

Tessa hated to turn anyone away when they asked for help, especially a young girl. However, Hope's Haven was already near capacity and Tessa knew that her first responsibility was for the safety and well-being of the women already here. All the women that were admitted had to go through a vetting process before they were admitted.

"Is there anywhere else you can stay for the night, or someone you can call to come and get you? I can call a ride for you if you need one or even put you up in a hotel for the night. I'll be happy to pay for it."

The girl had finally located the intercom speaker and was looking at it in desperation.

"No, please, there's no one else. I just really need to talk to Miss Graves."

Tessa chewed her lower lip in consternation, looking closely at the young girl, who was still fidgeting and darting around in front of the gate, trying to see if she could recognize her. This girl clearly knew who she was, but Tessa didn't recognize her at all. She was certain that if she had seen her before, she would look at least a little familiar.

"What's your name, honey?" Maybe the girl had been here a few years ago with her mother. Tessa hoped she would recognize the name.

The girl straightened her shoulders, relieved to be asked a question that she had an answer to.

"My name is Susan Smith," the girl said confidently, standing still for the first time and looking directly at the intercom where Tessa's voice was coming from.

The all-too-familiar buzzing in her head started immediately, and Tessa shook her head sadly. Ever since the horrible night when she received the blow to her head that had been meant to kill her, she had had an uncanny ability to know when someone was being deceptive.

She's lying, she thought, and of course, she didn't recognize the name at all.

It had taken Tessa months to recover from the head trauma she had sustained in the attack, and it was almost a year before she could even consider continuing with her life.

But it had been the unexpected windfall in her bank account from an anonymous donor that had prompted her to come up with the vision of opening a shelter for abused women.

Tessa had opened Hope's Haven five years ago, hoping to use the money to shelter women in need of help. She had envisioned the large house overlooking the valley below as a refuge for anyone in need of some love and sustenance.

Unfortunately, she had quickly realized that the number of women who needed help, and the dangers the men who were often chasing them posed, were far greater than her spacious mansion could accommodate or handle.

With Stephanie and Carter's help, she had devised a set of rules on who would be admitted. They had set it up to help protect the women who were already in residence, as well as the women trying to be admitted. Since many of the women looking for help were abused and looking to escape their abusers, Tessa was determined to make sure that the security at Hope's Haven remained unbreached and the women remained safe. But now, as she watched the young girl darting and looking around, clearly trying to stay out of view of the road, Tessa couldn't help but be reminded of another young girl who had needed her ten years ago. She had almost turned that one away as well, but the decision to help her had turned out to be life-altering for Tessa.

Frustrated, Tessa expelled a huge breath of air and jammed down the button on the intercom again.

"Okay, I'm opening the gate. Come straight through the gate and follow the path until you see the house, then wait by the front door. I'll come down and meet you."

She hit the remote that opened the gate, watching as the girl walked in to make sure that no one else darted through before the gate closed again. When she was satisfied that the girl had entered alone, she got up and made her way down the wide hallway. The hall was hot and stifling, but she could feel cool air escaping from the rooms lining the hallway where she housed the residents. *At least I could get the air conditioning in the rooms done in time for the hot weather,* she thought to herself, remembering the bitter complaints she had received from previous residents about the heat in the years before.

As she reached the door, Tessa steeled herself for what she would find on the other side and then cautiously opened the door.

She looked into a pair of large brown eyes that seemed to be too big for the tiny, peaked face they were in. She also noticed how the girl's slender shoulders visibly slumped in relief when she saw Tessa.

"Oh, thank goodness, it's you, Miss Graves. I knew you would help me. Please, can I just stay here for a while? I only need a little time to get some money together and figure out where to go next, and then I'll be out of your hair, I promise."

The girl spoke quickly, and her eyes never left Tessa's face as she spoke.

Tessa squinted her eyes, looking at the girl in front of her critically. The buzzing in her head continued, and she knew that there was something that the girl was not telling her.

Clearly, the young girl knew who she was, but Tessa still didn't recognize her. Examining the slight frame standing in front of her, she tried to envision the child with a darker hair color. The platinum hair on the young girl's head was clearly a poor dye job, but she still came up empty.

"What did you say your name was?" she inquired again.

The girl's hand flew to her throat, and she stammered, "Oh, it's Susan Smith." She was obviously finding it harder to lie when looking Tessa directly in the face.

"I'm not sure that I recognize you or that name. How do you know who I am?"

Tessa watched the girl's face and mannerisms carefully for any more signs of deception.

This time, the girl seemed to relax, more confident in the answer that she was about to give.

"You helped my mom a few years ago when she was trying to get away from my dad. I was with her."

Tessa nodded, satisfied. The buzzing diminished, so the girl was telling the truth about that, but she was certain there was more to the story that she wasn't telling her.

"I see. And where is your mom now?"

"I, ummm… I haven't seen her in a while. We, ummm… We got separated about a year ago. I haven't seen her since."

The girl was being very evasive, but Tessa could tell that Susan was not outright lying.

"You must have been very young when I helped your mother. How did you find me on your own?"

Again, Tessa watched the girl intently as she planned her answer.

"Oh, I guess I just remembered it from when you helped my mom. I didn't know where else to go for help. You just naturally popped into my head."

Tessa was disappointed. The buzzing was back. The girl was lying again.

"I see. So, you were staying here with your mom then?" she asked, remembering how Susan had been looking around the gate. It was obvious she had never been here before.

Susan smiled at Tessa brightly. "Yeah, that's right. I stayed here with my mom and my baby brother."

Tessa absently shook her head. The girl was still lying, and Tessa believed that she would not get the truth about how Susan knew her and about the shelter any time tonight.

She glanced down at her watch and winced. Even if she left right now, she had no hope of making it to Steph's party on time. It was a birthday party for Stephanie's youngest son, Charly, and she hated to disappoint him, but she still had the problem of what to do with Susan Smith before she had any hope of leaving the shelter.

Sighing, she glanced down at the disheveled girl. Tessa wasn't overly tall, but the girl was extremely tiny and haggard-looking. Tessa wondered when she had received her last meal.

"Okay, listen, we don't usually admit residents right off the street without a proper background check, but I can't really toss you out on the streets by yourself tonight, can I? You can't be more than fourteen or fifteen years old."

The girl drew up her tiny frame and looked at Tessa defiantly. "I'm eighteen."

Tessa looked at her reproachfully.

"No, you're not even close to being eighteen, Susan. Look, if I'm going to help you, you need to tell me the truth. If I don't know what's really going on with you and what you're running from, then I can't help you fix it, can I?"

"Who said that I'm running from anything?" Susan flashed her another angry look. "I just need somewhere to stay and get my thoughts together, and then I'll be fine."

Tessa looked sternly at Susan.

"We are a shelter for women in need of help, Susan, not a free hotel for people who are down on their luck. If you really are eighteen and just need a little help and money, there are places I can direct you to that will be able to help you better than Hope's Haven."

She watched while the girl gnawed her lower lip, clearly trying to process what Tessa was saying and what she should say. Tears were welling up in the girl's eyes, and Tessa could see that Susan was trying hard to keep herself composed.

"Look, there's no reason to cry." She tried to sound reassuring.

"I will not turn you out tonight. Let's go on into my office, and I'll get some paperwork started on you, and then I'll see if I can find a room for you to stay in tonight. We can figure out the best place for you to go in the morning."

Tessa turned and walked down the hall towards her office, listening to the steps of the young girl following closely behind her and already wondering if she would regret her decision to help the young girl.

When she opened the door, the stifling, hot air in the tiny room immediately engulfed them both. If the temperature in the hallway had been warm, the heat in her office was physically oppressive. As her hair plastered itself to her forehead, she once again lamented that she wasn't already in her nicely air-conditioned car heading to the pool party where Stephanie and her family were waiting.

"It's kind of hot in here, isn't it?"

The girl looked at the tiny but neat little office and wondered why the woman who owned such a large house wouldn't air-condition her own workspace.

"Only in the summer," Tessa joked, sitting down at her desk and starting a quick text to Stephanie, explaining that she was going to be late and why.

Almost immediately after hitting send, her phone dinged in rapid succession. Tessa knew it was Stephanie replying to her. Steph had a unique way of hitting the send button as soon as she finished a thought and then writing more. Anytime Tessa's phone dinged multiple times, Tessa could count on it being Steph.

Looking down at her phone, she could tell that Steph wasn't happy. The texts were written in complete capitals and finished with exclamation marks. Tessa frowned. She knew that her friend wouldn't be overjoyed at her decision, but she hadn't expected such a powerful reaction.

Before she could even finish reading the last text, her phone rang with the custom ring she had assigned to Stephanie, and Tessa sighed, knowing she was about to get an earful from her friend. She looked over at the girl sitting across from her, who looked bored and was busy examining her fingernails as if she didn't have a care in the world.

"Excuse me, I think I'd better take this outside," she said, walking to the door and shutting it behind her. As soon as she answered the phone, she heard Steph's voice, and it didn't sound happy.

"Are you crazy!?" Steph's voice was loud and clear, and Tessa hoped that the shut door was enough to muffle her voice. "Have you learned nothing in the years that we've been in business? If I remember correctly, you were part of setting up the procedures and protocols for admitting residents, which you are clearly choosing to ignore once again. I assume you have a good reason?" Steph's voice fluctuated between aggravation and concern as she chided her friend.

"Calm down, Steph. She's just a young kid. She can't be more than 14 or 15 and doesn't weigh more than 90 pounds soaking wet. I don't think that the poor little girl poses any great threat to me or to anyone else. You should see her. She looks dirty, desperate, and pitiful. I can't just leave her out on the street tonight. You would have taken her in too!"

Stephanie sighed heavily. "Okay, I get it. You had to help. But you could still call her an Uber and put her up in a hotel for the night, Tess. We've done that before."

Tessa frowned thoughtfully. "I thought of that, but the girl specifically asked for me, and when I suggested I send her to town, she just looked so sad and forlorn that I didn't have the heart to turn her away."

"That soft heart of yours always gets you into trouble, Tessa. Besides, how did she know you, anyway? Have you met her before?"

Tessa shook her head absently, even though Steph couldn't see her.

"I'm not sure. She claims that we've met before when I helped her mother, but to be honest, I don't recognize her or her name. I do know that she's lying about her name. Her hair is clearly a dye job, and she says she was much younger at the time, so it's not really surprising that I don't recognize her."

"She's lying about her name, and you let her in? For heaven's sake, Tessa! It's quite a gift you have to know if someone is lying, but what good is it if you will not use it to stay safe and help yourself?"

"People lie all of the time about their names for various reasons," Tessa defended herself. "That doesn't make her a criminal or up to no good. It's more likely that she's a runaway who doesn't want to be found."

"Exactly! And we don't deal with runaways who don't want to be found. Our job is to help women who are abused get away from their abusers and start a new and safer life." Stephanie huffed in exasperation on the other end of the phone.

"Look, Tessa, I know you want to help everyone who comes to our door, and believe me, so do I, but we don't have the space or the funds to do that. There are other agencies that she can turn to if she's a runaway who needs help."

"I know, I know, and you're right, Steph. I'll call Jack first thing in the morning and see if he can look in his database for any reports on missing girls. We can get her some help from a proper agency. In the meantime, let me just get her settled in for the night, and then I can head on over to the birthday party for my godson before he goes to bed."

Jack was the local police chief, and Tessa and Stephanie had met him shortly after they opened the shelter. An irate husband of one of their residents had found out where she was staying, and Jack had been among the officers who had answered their call for help. He had won the respect and admiration of both women with his professionalism and helpfulness, and over the years had become an important part of keeping the shelter safe.

"All right Tessa, have it your way then. I guess since she's already there, you may as well set her up for the night. We can talk about what we'll do with her tomorrow. Just be careful and stay alert. Oh, and Tessa, please hurry. Charly is already asking why his favorite auntie isn't here yet."

As the phone call disconnected, Tessa smiled at the mental picture of the cute little blonde-haired boy waiting anxiously for her. *I really need to hurry and get over there*, she thought, hating to disappoint him and knowing that he had been looking forward to this party for weeks.

"Sorry about that," she said, rushing back into her office. She stopped short when she saw the girl standing at her filing cabinet. As soon as she saw Tessa, she quickly slammed it shut, turning around and trying to look nonchalant.

"Oh, umm, sorry. I was just so bored sitting here that I thought I'd look around." The girl's face was red and flushed, and she was clearly embarrassed at having been caught. Tessa would have known she was lying even without the buzzing going on in her head.

"You looked around in my filing cabinet?" Tessa queried, curious what the girl's response would be.

Tessa watched as a multitude of thoughts and emotions ran across the girl's face. She was obviously searching for a feasible explanation.

"Well, I thought maybe I could find the file on my mother," she finally said, her relief at having found a plausible explanation apparent.

Does this girl ever tell the truth? Tessa thought, irritated. She was regretting her rash decision to take her in, and her head was aching from the incessant buzzing, but she still wanted to give her the benefit of the doubt.

"I thought you said that your name is Susan Smith. Why were you looking under B in the cabinet?" Tessa narrowed her eyes at the girl, hoping to get at least one truthful answer tonight.

"Oh, was I?" Susan glanced nonchalantly at the file cabinet she had just been rifling through. "I guess I'm not very good at knowing how these file things work."

She came over from behind the desk, and the rickety little chair that she had been sitting in earlier squeaked as she sat down.

"Could we just get on with the admission paperwork?" Susan asked impatiently. "I'm kind of exhausted and really ready to just lay down somewhere."

Tessa felt herself bristling at the girl's tone, but she bit her tongue when she looked down at Susan's face and saw the red-rimmed, clearly stressed-out eyes that were looking up at her.

She sat down behind her desk and pulled out the admissions paperwork that she had stashed in the front drawer, always at the ready for anyone who needed her help.

"Okay, then let's get started. I know that you've already told me the answers to some of the questions I'm going to be asking, but let's just go through them again and get it down on paper this time."

Filling out paperwork only took about 15 minutes, in large part because the girl was being very vague about many of the questions that Tessa was asking. She wouldn't disclose her last address, next of kin, or where she had been staying since she had left her mother. She claimed that her mother had remarried and that she either didn't know or couldn't remember her mother's new married name.

Finally, Tessa realized Susan wasn't going to disclose any factual information about herself, and so she stacked the admittance papers together with a resigned sigh.

"All right, Susan. Maybe in the morning you'll be able to remember a little more than tonight. Let's just get you settled into a room, get some food into you, and then you can rest."

Susan stood up eagerly and followed Tessa out of the hot and stuffy office into the hallway, which felt at least 10 degrees cooler.

"It really is hot in there. Are the rooms a little cooler at least?" she asked, looking around her as they walked.

Tessa grimaced slightly, wishing the girl could at least be grateful she had a roof over her head tonight and wondering if it was any cooler under the bridge she claimed to have been living under.

"The rooms all have air conditioning. I just haven't been able to afford to put it in my office yet."

"Oh, sweet!" Susan looked pleased at the prospect of a nice, cool room to sleep in. "Do you sleep here too?" She looked over at Tessa. "I sure hope you put some air in your room as well."

"Thanks for the concern," Tessa answered wryly, highly doubting that Susan was concerned for her comfort. "But no, I don't live here. I have an apartment in town, and thankfully, it does have air conditioning."

"Oh, I see."

Tessa noted Susan seemed to be mulling something over in her head, and she decided it would be prudent to let Angela, a longtime resident of the shelter, know about her new housemate and ask her to keep an eye on the young girl.

She took Susan to a nice, clean, airy little room. It was the last room she had available, and thankfully, it was right next to the suite that Angela shared with her three children.

"Get yourself settled, and I'll go next door and let Angela, one of our more established residents, know that you're here. She's been at Hope's Haven for a while, so she can help you get settled and show you where everything is."

Tessa walked next door and knocked softly. She was immediately greeted by a beaming, heavy-set, and boisterous woman.

"I thought I heard some commotion at the front door," Angela remarked after Tessa had explained the situation with Susan to her.

"Didn't you tell me earlier that you have a party to get to for that sweet little cherub of Miss Stephanie's?" she asked.

"You just leave this little lady with me, and I'll see that she gets fed and put to bed. You go on and get to that party before that little boy misses you too much."

Tessa smiled at the friendly woman gratefully, glancing down. She was already running almost an hour late, and she knew that Charly would wait impatiently for her so he could cut his cake.

"Thank you, Angela. You're such a help around here. I don't know what I'm going to do without you when it's time for you to leave!"

The older woman just smiled and gave her a gentle push.

"You just run along now and leave everything to Angela," she said.

"I'll see that the girl gets fed and put to bed. I have your number programmed in this new phone you helped me buy, just in case I need to get hold of you. Don't you worry about a thing and just enjoy the party."

Tessa gave Angela a spontaneous hug and hurried off to her office to collect her purse and car keys, stopping only quickly at Susan's room to let her know Angela would be helping her get settled and fed for the night and that she would be back in the morning.

When she finally settled into her car, she let the air conditioner blast on her hot and tired body for a minute, sighing in relief and trying to clear her mind of the day's troubles. She hated to take her problems with her when she went to see Stephanie's two boys, Daniel Junior and Charly, and she always tried to go through a mind-clearing ritual whenever she was going to see them.

Finally, feeling slightly better and looking forward to celebrating Charly's seventh birthday party, she started her car and pulled slowly out of the carport and through the front gate, making sure that it was securely closed behind her before driving off along the quiet lane that led to the main road.

She was so engrossed in her thoughts, already humming Happy Birthday and looking forward to the hug she was going to get from Charly, that she didn't notice the dark sedan slowly coming up behind her.

The heavier-set man looked over at the slightly built, younger man sitting next to him. "Can you follow the tracker? Is it still working?"

The younger man glanced over at the older man and nodded, grinning in satisfaction. "I see it, and it's not moving. She's not in the car." Planting the tracker on the girl had been his idea, and frankly, he was proud of it.

"Looks like she could talk her way in, after all. I knew we could count on her." The older man took his eyes off the road just long enough to give him a stern look.

"Don't get too excited. She may be in, but she still has some work to do before we can say she succeeded, and I sure hope for her sake that she does succeed."

The younger man frowned and glanced at the compact car ahead of them.

"Just don't lose the woman. We need to figure out where she lives in case the girl doesn't find what the big guy wants at the shelter. I have a Plan B if things don't go as planned."

Despite being the younger of the two, it was becoming apparent that he was going to have to take the lead in this.

"You mark my words; I don't have any intention of letting her fail." He announced.

CHAPTER 2

As soon as she walked into the front door of the cute little row house, Tessa was almost bowled over by two exuberant little boys rushing at her, full of excitement.

"Aunt Tessa, you're finally here! What took you so long? Did you bring me a birthday present?" Charly's dark eyes looked up at her expectantly as he fired off his questions.

"A present? Now, why would I have a present for you?" Tessa tickled the little boy and held the gift she was carrying high above her head and out of his reach.

Charly squealed in delight and lunged up, trying to get his gift. "Because it's my birthday, Aunt Tessa! You know that!"

"Easy there, slugger. Let's leave her in one piece, at least until we get some cake in her."

Carter, Tessa's other very best friend, walked over and slung the little boy high over his shoulder, giving Tessa a peck on the cheek as he did and making the little boy giggle happily.

"We were thinking that you would never get here." Carter grinned. His soft brown eyes gazed into Tessa's.

She gave him an affectionate hug. His slight figure felt even thinner. Tessa looked at him, concerned. "You could use some of that cake yourself, Carter. I'm thinking you don't eat at all anymore."

There was a casual sense of comradery and affection between the two of them that Tessa knew could only come from years of friendship, and she smiled at him fondly.

"I was a little afraid that you might not come because you were hoping to avoid me."

Carter set the boy down gently and looked at her reproachfully. "I've been trying to get a hold of you for a few days now with no response."

"Yeah, sorry about that. It's just been so busy, and I haven't really had a chance to get back to you."

Tessa knew the excuse was lame, but she hadn't known how to handle the confession Carter had made the last time they were together, so her solution had been to avoid him and the conversation she knew they had to have at one point.

Carter reached out and stroked her cheek softly. "I didn't want things to get awkward between us, but I had to let you know how I feel. You know we can talk about anything, Tessa. You can always tell me what you're feeling and thinking, and I hope I can do the same."

"I know that, Carter, and of course you can. I'm sorry I've been evasive, and we will talk. Just give me a little time."

She looked over at Stephanie and smiled a greeting at her friend, hoping that Carter would let the subject rest, at least for the evening. Stephanie smiled back, her hands full with the boys at the moment, but her look said that she still had some things to say to Tessa at a later time.

Tessa sighed resolutely. She knew her friends only wanted the best for her, but sometimes they could both be smothering and controlling.

Dan, Stephanie's husband, walked over, giving her a quick hug and a wink. The large man was a true gentle giant who always seemed to know when one of them needed his support.

"I'll run interference for you tonight if you need me to. I'm afraid that Steph is planning to give you an earful after the party."

Tessa groaned. "Is she like that with you too, Dan? I swear that sometimes she acts more like a helicopter mom than the friend and business partner she's supposed to be."

"She's just worried about you, Tessa." His eyes clouded over. "We all worry about you. Ever since the attack, we've all been on edge with Tessa. I guess we will continue to worry until we figure out why and who."

The culprits who had attacked her and killed her family had still not been found. Tessa knew that every one of them still wondered if they would come back and finish what they had started and were overly concerned with her safety.

He glanced over at the boys, who were at the moment bouncing around their mother, begging to open gifts before cake, and turned back to Tessa.

"The boys need you in their lives, and so do the rest of us. We can't afford to lose you, so I guess you'll just have to put up with us all hovering a little."

Tessa looked at the two boys, her eyes shining with love for them, but Dan could see the barely veiled sadness hovering just behind them and wished he hadn't brought it up.

"That was almost six years ago, Dan. If whoever attacked my family really wanted me dead, they would have come for me a long time ago." Tessa shook her head sadly. "They got who they wanted, and now I'm left on this earth alone to cope with it."

Just then, Charly and Daniel Junior attacked her legs to drag her over to the couch.

"Come on, Aunt Tessa!" DJ yelled. "Charly is going to open yours first!" He grinned up at her. "And I'll bet I know what you got him!" Ten-year-old Daniel Junior had been her advisor on choosing a present for his brother.

Tessa opened her eyes in mock surprise. "Well, you had better not tell him or I will have to tickle you as punishment!" She bent down and tickled DJ while Charly attacked his brother from the other side.

"Children, that's enough now. You're going to have the neighbors complaining about all the noise that you're making. And that includes you, Tessa!"

Stephanie was shaking her head and frowning while she was scolding them, but Tessa could see her eyes smiling behind the exaggerated scowl.

"Sorry, Mom, but Aunt Tessa was going to tickle me to death," DJ solemnly explained.

"Throwing me under the bus again, huh?" Tessa threw the boy a grin. "This isn't over yet, young man. Now let's help Charly open those presents."

Charly ripped open the wrapping paper that Tessa had so painstakingly chosen and squealed in delight when he saw the firetruck that Tessa had bought him.

"Look, Mom and Dad. It has lights and sirens that work, and the ladder goes up and down just by pushing the button!" He turned on the sirens and lights, and the entire room was instantly engulfed by the deafening sound of sirens wailing.

Stephanie held her ears. "Oh my goodness, Tessa! What were you thinking!? This will have the neighbors on us for sure!"

Tessa looked over at a grinning DJ accusingly. "I guess you forgot to tell me how loud that thing was when you told me Charly wanted it."

DJ just grinned. "You only asked me what he wanted, not how loud it was."

Dan laughed and hugged the mortified Stephanie. "It'll be fine, Steph. The neighbors will get over it. They had kids at one time, too. You worry too much."

Stephanie scowled at him but pecked his cheek affectionately. "I just wish that we could afford something a little more private than this row house. I always worry that the walls are so thin, and our neighbors are pretty much all older. I doubt they want to hear little kids all of the time."

"You should probably just go over and introduce yourselves. Get to know them and then you'll know what they're like and if they really are bothered by you," Carter suggested.

Tessa thought Carter had a good point. "I agree, Steph," she replied. "You can't avoid them forever, you know. Maybe they'll fall so much in love with these two that you'll end up inviting them to all the parties, and then they can't complain about all of the noise."

Stephanie looked over at her two children, who were at the moment tousling over who would get the bigger squirt gun, and grimaced. "I really doubt that. I think it's better that I just stay incognito. That way they won't know who to complain to."

Carter and Tessa laughed as Stephanie called the boys over to the table to cut the cake and sing Happy Birthday.

After the song was over and the cake was cut, Tessa drew herself away from the table a bit, surveying the cheerful scene in front of her. Carter came over to put his arms around her.

"It's still pretty hard for you, isn't it?"

Tessa nodded, trying to keep her emotions in check before replying.

"I think I need a minute. I doubt the boys will notice. All the grandparents, aunts, and uncles are here right now. They won't miss me if I step back for a second."

Carter hugged her closely. "Okay. Let's just go outside on the veranda and get some air. No one is going to blame you for needing some time every now and again."

They walked through the glass doors and out onto the patio. Dan and Stephanie had set up a huge swing set for the boys in the corner of the yard, and now, as Tessa looked at it, her eyes filled with tears.

"Remember how much Hope loved her swing set, Carter? She would beg me to push her for hours on end, singing to herself and telling me she was heading up to the moon."

Carter pulled Tessa in close, holding her against his chest and caressing the top of her head.

"Yeah, I remember. That was just so Hope. She was always happy and full of life. I know she's up in heaven now, probably still singing and dancing around."

Carter wished his words would give Tess some comfort, but he suspected that for Tessa, the pain would always be just as raw as it had been when Hope was first taken from her.

Tessa nodded, her head still buried against his chest, taking comfort in the familiar scent of the man she had known practically her whole life, knowing that if he could, he would do anything to bring Hope and Luke back to her.

"I just don't understand how anyone could be so cruel as to take the life of someone so precious and so young." She stepped back and looked at Carter, her eyes tormented.

"Will I ever be able to celebrate the birthday of another child without the pain I feel for not being able to celebrate those same milestones with Hope? Oh Carter, she was cheated out of so much happiness and joy!"

Tessa buried her head back into Carter's shoulder, trying to shake the pain and find solace in Carter's arms.

"I don't know Tess. I really don't," Carter answered honestly, not wanting to utter the same cliché phrases Tessa heard from everyone else and not knowing what else to say.

"Sometimes I miss them both so much that I just don't want to go on anymore!" Tessa swallowed the lump in her throat and fought against the clenching grief gripping at her chest.

As much as she loved Stephanie's two little boys, almost like they were her own, special events like these always brought on a wave of sadness and despair that was hard for her to bear, even after all these years.

Carter stroked her back gently, wishing there was something he could do to help alleviate her pain. Fighting his own unfulfilled needs and desires, he breathed in the faint smell of her shampoo and the soft lavender of her perfume.

As much as he longed for Tessa to be his, he knew now was not the time to talk about it. Until she could process the grief that she still felt over losing her husband Luke and her daughter Hope, he would need to be patient and move slowly, no matter how many more years it might take. Carter knew he was willing to wait.

"I wish that there was some way that I could make the pain easier for you, Tessa. You know how much I care for you. I haven't kept my feelings a secret, but believe me, if I could, I would bring Luke and Hope back for you."

His words were whispered and uttered softly into the top of her head, and although she couldn't see them, Tessa could almost feel the wistfulness in his eyes. The soft whir in her head told her that he was sincere.

"I do know that, Carter. You have always been such a good friend to both me and Luke. In fact, I really couldn't ask for a better or more loyal friend than you. I'm just not ready to move on yet."

She looked up at him, smiling sadly through her glistening eyes.

"I know I would be blessed to have a man like you at my side, Carter. I'm just not sure that I'll ever be able to move away from the grief of losing Luke and Hope. It's not fair for me to ask you to wait for me. If you could find someone else, I would be happy for you, Carter. I really would. I don't want you to wait for me forever."

Carter tilted her chin upward, giving her a gentle kiss on the nose.

"I'll wait for you for however long it takes, Tessa. I'm not going anywhere. I'm in it for the long haul."

Tessa and Carter had been standing just outside the house, near the sliding glass door leading to the veranda, when Tessa felt herself being drenched with a stream of water. She jumped back in shock and squealed in surprise, hearing the gleeful laughter of two little boys.

"We got you, Aunt Tessa, and you too, Uncle Carter!" DJ called out from behind the huge squirt gun he was holding.

"I sure as heck hope you have a license for that thing, cuz I'm about to tickle it out of you two!" laughed Carter, sprinting over to where the two of them were still standing and laughing.

With a squeal, the boys split up, each taking off in a different direction, with Carter deciding to chase after the birthday boy and making him giggle uncontrollably as he tickled him.

"He really is a good guy, you know," said Stephanie, walking up to Tessa and putting an arm around her waist.

Tessa sighed. "I know that, Steph. He's a great guy with a heart of gold. He always was the greatest friend to Luke and uncle to Hope."

"You know he is hoping to be more than just a good guy as far as you're concerned, right?" Stephanie gave her a questioning look.

"Yes, I do know that, Steph. He confessed it to me the other night, although, to be honest, I've suspected his feelings for a while now. You know that it's almost impossible to keep secrets from me since the attack." She smiled ruefully at her friend.

Steph looked at Tessa, her brow wrinkled in concern.

"I probably should have warned you, but he confided in me a few weeks ago. The three of us have been best friends since grade school, and I think he just needed to get some advice from someone about what to do. I told him to let you know how he felt."

"I see." Tessa couldn't help feeling a little guilty, almost wishing she had the same feelings for Carter that he had for her.

"I'm honestly not trying to lead him on, Steph. I know I do rely on him a lot for support and comfort, but until a few months ago, I truly thought that he only felt a plutonic friendship as well."

Stephanie nodded. "I know that, Tessa. I think that's what Carter has been trying to convince himself of for years. But I know that he's had a secret crush on you since grade school, and now that you're available again, those old feelings he had buried have more than likely come up again."

Tessa shuddered. "I'm not exactly 'available' again, Steph. It's not like Luke and I separated or divorced." She gave Stephanie a pained look. "He was murdered, Steph! He was wrenched away from me in the prime of our lives. We still had so much to do together and so many plans. I don't know if I will ever be able to get over that and move on. Luke and Hope were my entire life, and that's all gone now."

Tessa shook her head slowly. "I'm not sure I'll ever be able to let another man into my life, much less into my bed again. That wouldn't feel fair to Luke or his memory."

Stephanie looked at her friend sternly. "Look, Tess, I know that what happened to you, Luke and Hope was a horrible, tragic, and evil act. It was unthinkable, and we also all lost a good friend and a precious angel that day." She shivered as the events of that day came flooding back to her. "We almost lost you too, Tess, and I thank God every day that we didn't." Reaching over, she drew Tessa in and hugged her close before continuing. "But that was six years ago. As much as everyone misses them, you can't just give up your life and your happiness forever. Luke would never have wanted that for you. He would have wanted you to continue living."

Tessa smiled sadly, the thoughts of Luke's smiling face flashing in front of her. "I know that you're right, Steph. I know he would want me to go on. But I didn't just lose a husband that day. I lost my entire life. Whoever took my precious little Hope destroyed any chance I would ever have of living a normal life again."

Tessa looked over at Carter and the boys wrestling on the ground, pointing at them.

"I can't even just enjoy the sight of children playing anymore without my heart wrenching in my chest. I wish I would have been killed that day as well. A part of me is dead anyway, and it would be so much easier than trying to go on without them." She sobbed.

"Don't you ever say that again, Tessa Graves. We all need you in our lives," Stephanie shouted so loudly that a few people stopped talking and looked over, curious at what the two women were arguing about.

She caught herself and calmed her voice, reaching out to take Tessa's hand.

"Look, Tess, I can only imagine how hard it must be for you to come and celebrate the milestones of my boys, knowing that you will never have the chance with Hope, and I don't know if I could even do it."

Stephanie dabbed at her eyes. "The boys love you so much, Tess. I don't think their lives would be the same without you, and I really do appreciate that you are a part of our lives."

Stephanie gazed lovingly at her two boys, now laying exhausted on the grass, still laughing from their tickling session.

"The boys loved Hope as well. She was such a happy little girl, and she would want her mommy to be happy too. You know Hope wouldn't want you to give up on life either, Tess.

Tessa nodded, remembering her little girl and how joyful she had always been.

"I know you're right, but it's just so hard to feel happy when they're not here." She sighed, trying to regain her composure.

"Maybe if I had some kind of closure, it would be easier. If only I could get answers to why this all happened. Knowing that whoever murdered my family is still out there makes me crazy." She looked at Stephanie, but this time her eyes were glistening with determination.

"I'm going to find them, Steph, and I'm going to find out why they did this, even if it takes the rest of my life."

Stephanie smiled in encouragement. Tessa's obsession with finding the murderers of her family probably wasn't a healthy thing, but she would rather see a determined Tessa than the desolate Tessa she had just seen.

"That does bring me to my next point, though," said Stephanie, facing Tessa squarely, her hands on her hips. "I thought we agreed we were going to follow the protocol for admitting residents into the shelter without exceptions. It seems like you certainly didn't follow that protocol tonight."

Tessa looked at Stephanie remorsefully. "I know I didn't, Steph, and I'm sorry. But you should have seen that poor girl. She looks so skinny, so young, and desperate. I couldn't just leave her out in the cold."

Stephanie snorted. "I don't think you could have left her out in the cold, Tess. We're going through a heatwave right now. The girl would hardly have frozen to death even if she had stayed outside. Besides, we have a fund set up to help people we can't admit, so we can get them a hotel, and they don't need to stay outside."

"I know that too, Steph, but she asked for my help specifically. She knew who I was. There's just something different about this girl, something intriguing." Stephanie looked at Tessa critically.

"She reminds you of Hope's birth mother, doesn't she?" she asked. Tessa winced and looked down. "I thought I was the truth seer around here. I'm not the only one with the gift to look into people's hearts."

"I don't need to be hit over the head to see what you see in most of the young girls that show up at our shelter. As I recall, she was just a young and desperate child as well. This isn't the first time you've insisted on helping someone because they remind you of Hope's birth mother."

"No, I guess it isn't the first time. I just can't help but remember how I almost turned that young woman away, and that if I had, if I hadn't helped her, I would never have been able to adopt my precious Hope." Tessa's eyes clouded over again. "Of course, if I hadn't had Hope in the house that day, she would probably still be alive."

"Tessa, you need to stop blaming yourself for what happened," Stephanie chided her friend gently. "No one can look into the future, not even you. Hope had the most wonderful mother that a child could ever have in you, and she had a wonderful life. You're not to blame for what some evil men did. None of what happened is your fault, Tess."

Before Tessa could respond, Dan walked over to the two women.

"Sounds like things are getting a little heavy over here. Remember, this is Charly's birthday, and we are here to celebrate." He gave Tessa a quick hug of support but was determined to keep his son's birthday a happy occasion. "We all appreciate you being here to celebrate with us, Tessa, even though we know it brings up a lot of memories for you. But let's try to concentrate on the wonderful memories we have of Hope, instead of one horrible event. She loved coming to parties and playing with the boys. Let's focus on her life, not just her death."

Tessa smiled at Dan, grateful for his ever-calming and practical words. He was right, of course. It wasn't fair to remember just one horrible moment and forget all the fun Hope had shared with them.

"You know, for a contractor, you sure have a lot of insight. Maybe you should be in social work, and I should become the builder?" she joked.

"Good lord, no!" Dan threw up his hands in mock horror. "We could never unleash you on the world with a saw or a hammer. You are bound to destroy everything you touch. I don't think I have ever seen you hammer in a nail straight."

"Well, you may be right," Tessa grinned. "But you really would make a good social worker."

Tessa heard the ding of her phone and reached into her purse, puzzled. "I wonder who's texting me at this hour. I don't usually hear from anyone this late except for Carter or you, Steph, and you're both here."

She read the text and looked at Stephanie, her face concerned. "What is it?" Stephanie asked, alerted by the look on Tessa's face.

"It looks like you might have been right once again." Tessa held up her phone. "It's from Angela. I left the girl in her care and asked her to keep an eye on her."

Stephanie frowned. "And? What happened?"

Tessa rubbed her forehead. It was promising to be a long night after all. "Angela thought she heard someone or something making some noise and she followed the sound to check it out. Apparently she caught Susan snooping through my office again."

CHAPTER 3

"What do you mean, 'again'?" Stephanie asked.

"Oh, that's right, I haven't had time to catch you up on everything yet. When I stepped back into the office after I called you, I caught Susan red-handed looking through the files in my file cabinet."

"And you admitted her into the shelter, even after that?!" Stephanie looked at Tessa astounded. "Did you at least ask her what she was looking for?" she asked, clearly annoyed.

"Of course I did," Tessa said indignantly.

"Aaaand? What did she say?"

"Well, she said she was trying to look for the records from when her mother had been there, but she was lying. I would have known that even before the blow to my head. She was looking under B instead of S."

Stephanie shook her head, exasperated. "Oh Tess! Sometimes I really wonder about you! You are much too trusting for your own good."

"Don't worry," Tessa tried to sound reassuring. "She probably is looking for her mother or a relative of some kind, and their name more than likely starts with B and not S. I mean, I know she's not telling the truth about her name." She sighed. "She's still just a young, harmless little girl, but I guess I had better head back to the shelter now anyway and sort this out."

Carter had been standing close and listening to the conversation.

"I'll go with you, Tess," he said. "I don't think it's a good idea for you to go alone until we figure out what is going on with that girl."

"That's very sweet of you, Carter, but the shelter is in the complete opposite direction of where you live. And I happen to know that you have a very early meeting tomorrow morning. Besides, I won't be alone. Angela is there, and she has told the girl, in no uncertain terms, to stay in her room for the rest of the night."

Tessa smiled as she pictured Angela reprimanding the girl, hands on her broad hips and using her stern voice. "I don't think I'd have the courage to disobey Angela when she puts on her 'mom' attitude. I doubt that Susan, or whatever her name is, will dare to disobey her either," she joked.

Carter frowned. "I would still feel better if I could look around with you. Sometimes it's just better for a man to take a look. I sometimes worry about the two of you over there all by yourselves. You have nothing to defend yourselves with."

Stephanie gave him a scathing look. "Really, Carter, that's about as sexist a remark as I've ever heard, even coming from you. We are not two little shrinking violets, and you well know that. Both Tessa and I have taken many self-defense courses, and we can handle a young sixteen-year-old girl."

Dan was standing close by, holding an exhausted little Charly in his arms. He grinned at Carter. "Don't underestimate these two women in clearing out the riffraff. They are two tough gals." Then he stopped smiling and gave Steph a more serious look. "I do agree with Carter, though. I don't think Tess should go alone, and one of us should go with her."

He looked down at the sleeping child in his arms. "I think that you'll need to take two exhausted little boys to bed soon. It's been a very long and exciting day for them, and they'll need you to get them settled. You know that I'm no good at that, so I'll go with Tessa."

Steph sighed. "No, you're not good at that, that's for sure." She looked at Tessa. "Dan's right. He should take a ride with you. That way, Carter can go home and get some sleep before his big meeting, and we'll all know that you're safe."

Tessa let out an exasperated breath of air, looking at her three friends in mock disgust.

"You three are being absolutely ridiculous. I can take care of this myself. But if it makes you all feel any better, Angela said she already called our new neighbor, Beau Reeves, and asked him to look over the grounds for us. His place borders right on ours, and he has offered many times to come over and help monitor things."

Stephanie smiled knowingly. "That's right. I forgot all about him." She looked at Carter and Dan, explaining, "He seems to be home a lot since he moved in, so I'm guessing he must be retired, but I got the impression from the little I talked with him he knows something about security and stuff like that. Maybe he was a security guard or something once?" She glanced at Tessa, "I'm surprised that Angela has his number, but he does seem like the perfect person to have around tonight."

Tessa nodded, relieved that Stephanie seemed to give up on the idea of sending poor Dan with her. "Yes, I don't think he works anymore. Angela said he gave her his number shortly after they met. Like you said, he seems to be around and working on his property all the time. I'm sure he wouldn't mind taking a quick walk around our place tonight."

Carter raised an eyebrow. "He's the really tall, well-built, dark-haired guy that I always see walking around close to the property line, isn't he? He seemed pretty aloof and standoffish to me. When did you two have time to talk to him?"

Tessa smiled at Carter's description of Beau and nodded. "Yes, he came over and introduced himself a few weeks ago when I was walking outside. He actually seemed very nice and offered to watch our place as well as his. He seemed curious about what we do there, how often we rotate our residents, and things like that. Since he's our neighbor, I figured he should know we're running a shelter. He said that he was more than willing to pop over any time we needed him."

"Hmmm," Stephanie looked at her friend strangely. "That's very chatty, considering that I could barely get him to tell me his name when I met him and introduced myself. He seemed very secretive to me. That's why I figured he was in the security business." She shrugged and looked over at her husband, who was still holding her sleeping son. "Well, be that as it may, if he offered, and Angela already called him, then that might be the best solution. You won't be completely alone in case that girl really is up to something. Carter can go home, and Dan can help me put these two rascals to bed and clean up," she said.

Dan groaned, looking around at the disheveled house with all of the newly opened toys. "I think I'd rather go with Tess, to be honest," he said.

Tessa laughed, looking up from her phone. "Sorry buddy, looks like you're stuck here helping your wife like the good husband that you are. I already sent a text out to Beau, thanking him for coming by."

Carter frowned. "That was fast. Do you have the guy on speed dial already?"

Tessa flushed slightly. "Well, yes, actually I do. I've had to call him a few times about some erosion we were having on the back of both of the properties, and it was just easier than always having to look him up."

Stephanie gave her another weird look. "I did not know that you were so chummy with our handsome new neighbor."

"Do you even know anything about him? He could be a serial killer in his own right. It seems like he is paying an awful lot of attention to you," Carter asked, suspicious.

Tessa wasn't sure if Carter was jealous or concerned with his comment. "He isn't paying a lot of attention to me, Carter," she said. "I've only seen him a few times, and he has as much of a reason to be concerned with erosion on the property as I do. You know how rainy it can get here, and if we're not proactive, we could both lose a sizable chunk of property. He just wants to prevent that from happening. I'm fairly sure he is not a serial killer in hiding."

Just then, Tessa's phone dinged.

"That's him. He said he is on his way over and will look around the grounds to see if anyone is lurking or anything is amiss. He already told Angela he's coming and ready to help with the girl if she needs it before I get there." She looked at her friends. "See, I told you. He's just a nice man being a friendly neighbor."

"Yeah right, I'm sure that's it. He just wants to be neighborly," Carter grumbled.

Stephanie threw Carter an amused look. "You really should be grateful to him, Carter. At least you don't need to drive out of your way to check on things at the shelter, and you'll be able to catch your beauty sleep before your meeting tomorrow."

"Besides," Dan chimed in, "I'm fairly sure that Jack Lewis would have let us know if there was something wrong with him. As soon as Stephanie told me that a single man moved in next door, I called him and asked him to check him out. You really can't be too careful about anyone, you know."

Dan and the local sheriff had forged a friendship of sorts over the last few years, and he trusted the man to keep the women safe.

Carter chortled. "I sometimes think we need to watch out for Jack just as much as anyone else when it comes to Tess."

"Oh honestly, Carter, now you're just being ridiculous!" Tessa shook her long dark hair in aggravation. "Jack is an excellent police officer. He would never have been elected Sheriff if he didn't have a stellar reputation. Steph and I trust him implicitly, and he has been very helpful to us in the past."

"It seems like he's taking advantage of your help in questioning his suspects as well, so I guess it doesn't hurt for him to check out some of your residents now and then," Carter countered.

"Careful, Carter, your green-eyed little monster is showing," Stephanie chastised her friend gently. "As long as Tessa somehow has developed this uncanny ability to read people and know when they are lying, there's no reason she shouldn't help local law enforcement sometimes. It certainly benefits all of us to get the bad guys off the street," she continued.

Carter put up his hands defensively. "Okay, okay, I guess that Jack Lewis has quite the fan club in all of you. I didn't mean to take anything away from his talent at solving crimes. I just don't think that it's necessary to involve Tessa all the time. She has enough to deal with already."

"You know, I don't mind helping him, Carter. I've already told you that. Besides, it helps keep me in the loop about the investigation into Luke and Hope's murder. I'll keep any info that I can get with the police. That way, I can make sure they keep looking for the person responsible for destroying my family." Tessa bit her lip pensively and looked at her friends. "I keep hoping that one of these days, the culprit will just walk in, and I'll recognize him and find out why he would have murdered my family."

Stephanie walked over to give Tessa a gentle hug. "Oh Tess, I really hope that happens, but let's face it, after five years, the chances of that happening are pretty slim. You may have to learn to move on with your life, understanding that we might never know why any of this happened."

Tessa shook her head vehemently. "No, Steph. I won't stop searching until I find out who and why. Don't forget, they also wanted me dead, and I'm still alive. Maybe someday they'll come back to finish the job, and if they do, I plan to be waiting and ready for them."

Stephanie shuddered at the thought. The idea of losing her friend was more than she could bear. They had been best friends forever and had done so much together. Stephanie knew she wouldn't be able to carry on without Tessa.

"No one is after you anymore, Tess! Don't you even think or say such a thing!" Stephanie said.

Tessa looked at her friend compassionately, but before she could say anything more, her phone pinged again. "That's Beau. While we've been chatting, he's been busy looking around the property. He found nothing unusual, but Angela asked him to come in and stay with her until I come. I'd better get over there fast. I don't want to take advantage of his kindness for too long."

Tessa stuffed her phone in her purse and hustled to the door.

"Are you sure you don't want me to come with you?" Carter asked uncertainly, shuffling from one foot to the other. He really did have a very early morning meeting that he still needed to prepare for, but the thought of Tessa hurrying off to the shelter and having her neighbor playing the hero, instead of himself, didn't sit well with him.

Tessa leaned up as she passed him and gave him a quick peck on the cheek. "Don't worry about me, Carter Williams. I have Angela and Beau to help me wrangle in the fifteen-year-old if she gets unruly," she joked.

"Just be careful, Tessa," Stephanie warned, giving her a quick hug as well.

"You're assuming that she's just a naive teen. She really could be much older and much more cunning than you're guessing. We've certainly run into that before as well."

"I know, I know," Tessa said over her shoulder as she breezed through the door and hopped into her car.

"Do you think I should go?" Carter asked Stephanie uneasily. "She really does have a knack for getting herself into trouble."

Stephanie sighed heavily. "She does have that knack, that's for sure," she agreed, but she gave Carter a reassuring look. "I think she'll be okay this time though. She has Angela and our new neighbor to help her, and you need to focus on your career as well, Carter. I know how hard and long you've struggled to build your business."

Dan walked in from putting little Charly to bed and clapped Carter on the shoulder. "She'll be just fine, don't worry. This isn't the first time that Tess has broken protocol or had to go running off on an emergency to the shelter."

Carter furrowed his brow. "I know, but I can't shake the feeling that this time something is really wrong," he said.

After speeding down the highway and risking a ticket, Tessa finally reached the shelter. She opened the automatic gate carefully, scanning her surroundings, and once again checked to make sure that no one snuck in after her before the gate was fully closed. She knew she was probably being overly cautious, but she had had a strange feeling of being watched ever since she had left Stephanie's house.

The uneasy feeling persisted as she walked to the door, and she jumped as a figure appeared out of nowhere just as she reached it. "Oh my, you scared me!" she exclaimed, putting her hand to her chest to calm herself.

"Sorry, I figured I would stay outside and keep my ears and eyes open for anything unusual until you showed up. I didn't mean to scare you."

Tessa looked at the tall, handsome man standing before her. *Carter was right; he really was well-built,* she thought, her heart skipping a beat, just like it always did whenever she saw him. His dark eyes remained calm, betraying no emotion, but she thought she could detect a slight air of amusement in them. She wondered if he had indeed intended to startle her.

Six years ago, the blow to her head was intended to kill her. Instead, she now had a remarkable ability to read people, their emotions, and tell if they were being deceitful. Even during her recovery in the hospital, she had known immediately when anyone was lying to her or trying to hide the truth. No one had told her that her family was gone, but she had known it immediately, as soon as she had questioned the doctors.

Her unique talent had since become so much a part of her that she had come to rely on it, much like she relied on the rest of her senses. It was a source of contention for her friends, who, in the beginning, had tried valiantly to protect her feelings by hiding the details of the crime from her, only to find their efforts futile.

The problem with Beau Reeves was that she couldn't read him like she could everyone else. No matter how much she concentrated or tried, the man remained just as unreadable and mysterious as the first time he had walked over and introduced himself. Now, as she watched his strong, tanned hand brushing back the dark hair from his face, she wondered again what he was feeling and why she always felt so out of sorts around him.

"Angela is trying to contain the young lady in your office. We should probably go in and see what is going on," he announced finally, as she wasn't making a move to open the door.

Tessa dropped her eyes from his face and turned quickly, her face slightly flushed. She fancied herself a very self-assured businesswoman, but when it came to her dark and mysterious neighbor, she seemed to act like a giddy young high school girl again.

"Yes, of course. I'm sorry that I kept the two of you waiting for so long. I was at a birthday party, and it took me a minute to leave, and then I had such a slowpoke in front of me, I thought I'd never get here." As Tessa fumbled with the door, she wished she could just stop herself from rambling on like a fool.

Beau reached around her, his body covering hers and causing her to gasp. He took the key from her shaky hands and opened the front door for her. When he had it fully open, he stepped back and waved her in.

"Please, go on in first. I'll follow you and make sure that the door is securely locked behind us. We wouldn't want anyone to walk in and surprise us."

His smile seemed mischievous, and Tessa strode ahead of him towards her office, her heart hammering in her chest, wondering if he had meant anything further with his comment, and if she even wanted him to, while reminding herself that they were not alone in the house.

Angela was waiting with the young girl just up ahead. "There you are, Miss Tessa!" Angela was sitting at Tessa's desk, looking every bit like a principal who had brought in her disobedient student and was about to dole out punishment. "I'm so sorry I had to disturb you. I know you were trying to celebrate that sweet little boy of Miss Stephanie's birthday. Believe me, if I didn't think this was important, I would have never called you."

Susan, who was sitting slouched in the chair across from Angela, threw her a heated look, trying to look as tough as a tiny, skinny little teenage girl possibly could. "I don't know why this woman dragged me in here to make me sit like a schoolgirl in front of her for hours. All I want to do is get some rest, like you told me I could."

Angela looked at the girl sternly. "I didn't exactly have to drag you in here, now did I, dear? You were already in here snooping around in files that are none of your concern."

The girl looked up at Tessa, her eyes wide and innocent-looking. "I wasn't snooping for anything, honest. I walked in here looking for you. I thought I heard someone in the office, and I saw the light was on, so I just wanted to ask you a question. Next thing I know, as soon as I walked in, this woman comes storming in accusing me of stealing and spying."

Angela gasped and stared at the girl. "That's not true! I saw you go in and waited a full ten minutes before I came in after you. And you were clearly shuffling through those files right there." She looked at Tessa with stricken eyes. "That's the God's honest truth, Miss Tessa!"

Tessa's head was once again buzzing, and she walked around the desk and put a comforting hand on Angela. She already knew that the girl was lying without Angela saying anything. She just wanted to reassure the distraught woman.

"Don't fret, Angela. I believe you. I'm just sorry that you are caught up in any of this. It's entirely my fault for breaking our usual protocol and letting this young woman into our house without the proper vetting." She gave Susan a stern look. "I believe I asked you to stay in your room and not to cause any trouble tonight. It looks like I may have misjudged your intentions and in doing so, I put our other residents at risk as well."

Tessa turned back to Angela. "Thank you for helping tonight and making sure the house and everyone in it is safe. I know I can always count on you to do the right thing." She gave the distraught woman a hug and urged her to the door. "You'd better get back to those darling little children of yours and see that they're asleep. I know they fret when you're not close by, and you need to get some sleep as well. Remember, I had asked the trauma counselor to come by tomorrow to speak with you, so you'll need your rest."

Even though Angela's family had been at Hope's Haven for several months, the children were still very traumatized and hated being alone without their mother close by. Tessa hoped that the counseling she had arranged for them would help the family work through the trauma, but the sessions always seemed to take a mental toll on Angela and the children.

Angela threw her a grateful look. She had ended up here several months ago, bloody, beaten-up, and hoping to escape from a very abusive husband. Having put up with his drinking and constant beatings for 10 years, even bearing him three children throughout the abuse, she had finally drawn the line when he beat on their oldest son.

She had packed what she could carry and ran for the nearest bus station. It wasn't until she was there that she had realized the money in her pocket wouldn't be enough to get her and the three children out of the city and to safety.

In desperation, she had tried to steal a purse from a sleeping woman, hoping to take just enough money from it to cover the rest of the fare they needed. However, the woman had woken up and seen her before she succeeded, and the police had been called. Angela had been terrified that she would be thrown in jail and the children returned to her husband. But instead, the kind officer, Detective Jack Lewis, had listened to her story patiently and then called Tessa Graves, asking her if she could take Angela and her children into Hope's Haven until they could find a way to safety.

Even though it was late at night, Tessa had rushed over to the police station to meet with her. As soon as she heard Angela's story, she had packed her and the three kids into her car and driven them straight to her shelter. Once there, she had given them a warm room, food, and safety from her abusive husband. Jack Lewis had paid her husband a visit and somehow convinced him it would be better if he left town for a while.

Ever since that night, Angela had come to look at Jack Lewis and Tessa as true angels from heaven, and she would have done anything they asked of her to help return the kindness they had shown. Right now, she was looking at Tessa adoringly.

"Thank you so much for believing me, Miss Tessa. You know I would never lie to you."

"Of course, I know that, Angela. Now go back to bed and check on those sweet little children of yours. I'm sorry you were disturbed. I know they still get frightened when they wake up and you're not there." Tessa gave her a reassuring smile.

"I guess that's a trauma that they'll have to bear for a while yet." Angela shook her head sadly. "I just hope that all of those years with that man haven't ruined them forever." She turned to look at Susan sternly. "You just take my advice, little girl. I'm sure that you've had your share of hardships, or else you probably wouldn't be here, but second chances are a rare thing in this world. Don't you do anything to ruin this chance that was just handed to you. This is your opportunity to change where your life is taking you. You make sure you listen to what Miss Tessa has to say, and you tell her the truth. Lying is only going to hurt you in the long run. You have an opportunity to get some real help here. Don't mess it up."

She gave Tessa another quick hug and smiled up at Beau as she squeezed her broad frame past him. Then, she hurried off to her children. As Susan watched her bustle out from under her downcast eyes, a part of her wished she could be taken in by those big arms. Angela would take care of her in the way that she imagined a mother like Angela protected her own children. It was something she had never experienced, and she imagined it would feel good.

She slouched down further and closed her eyes completely, wondering if the two men who had brought her here tonight were still close by, or if they too had abandoned her. She couldn't help but wonder if Angela was right. Could a girl like her actually have a real chance at a decent life?

Just down the street, the young man slunk down in his seat and closed his eyes almost at the same time as Susan had, sighing tiredly.

"What do you think you're doing?" the older man barked at him gruffly. "We're here to monitor things, not sleep like a fairy princess."

The younger man opened one eye and looked at him lazily. "You keep watch. I'm getting some sleep. Clearly, the boss had some wrong information, and the woman lives here, not in town. Otherwise, she wouldn't have come back here so late. We've been following her for hours, and after all that, this is where she ended up."

The older man glowered at the young man, who was clearly ready to sleep, and resisted the urge to punch him. He was tired too, but he was wiser and had been at this longer than the young punk next to him. He knew better than to question his boss or to fall asleep on the job.

Angrily, he picked up his phone and punched in some numbers.

"Yeah, it's me. Sorry to bother you so late boss, we've been following her, but she came back to the shelter. Look, me and the kid have been at this all day. We're tired, and we're hoping it's ok to break off for now and get some shut eye. It looks like she's alone in there with a few women, so maybe we can storm the place a little later tonight when everyone's sleeping. We can find what you're looking for then."

CHAPTER 4

Alright Susan. I think that it's time that you told me the truth. Why are you really here and what is it you're looking for in my files?"

Tessa had taken the seat that Angela had just vacated and was doing her best to put on a stern face, but it was hard for her. It just wasn't in her to be harsh or tough, and she was fairly certain that she really wasn't fooling anyone, especially not Susan.

"I am telling you the truth. My name is Susan Smith, I'm eighteen, and I just need some help to get a fresh start."

Tessa was tired. It had been a very long day, as well as a very emotional one for her. Anytime she went to a function that involved important milestones for Stephanie's boys, there were just too many memories, and her heart always felt like it was being ripped open all over again. Besides that, the constant buzz in her head was giving her a headache.

"I know your name is not Susan Smith, you are definitely not eighteen, and you must have a reason to be looking through my files. If you really want my help, then you have to give me the true story, or I'm going to have no choice but to call the police and have them come and get you. Hopefully, they will be able to help you, but I can't put the rest of our residents in danger without knowing what is going on with you."

Susan looked like she was ready to cry again, and Tessa could tell that as tired and frustrated as she herself was, Susan was even more desperate and exhausted. As she sat quietly and tried to contemplate what to do about the girl, Tessa saw Beau step over and sit on the corner of her desk, close to the girl, looking down at her compassionately.

"I don't think you're lying, Susan. At least not about most of what you're saying. Maybe your name is not Susan Smith, but I'm sure you have a reason you want to keep your identity to yourself for now. I can see you're afraid of someone or something, but Tessa is right, Susan. We really can't help you unless we know the whole truth and what you're running from."

Susan looked up at Beau, her eyes slowly filling with tears, an anguished look on her face. "I really do wish that I could trust you, Mister, but I've got to handle this myself. There's nothing you can do to help me. And even if I believed that you honestly wanted to help, it's too late for that now." She looked over at Tessa. Her eyes were now pleading with her. "Please, please, just let me stay here for a little longer. At least for the night. I just need to clear my head and figure out what I need to do. I promise I won't cause any trouble, and if you let me stay a few extra days, I promise that I'll help around here as well. I'll do anything you want me to!"

Tessa rubbed her tired eyes. She knew that the right and safest thing she should do would be to send the girl to a hotel tonight. Jack could look into her in the morning, and then they could see how to help her. Unfortunately, the eyes looking at her with such anguish right now reminded her too much of the girl that had come to her ten years ago, also begging for help. There was just no way she could refuse Susan's pleas and put her out tonight.

"Okay, Susan, you can stay here, at least for the night. But you need to stay in your room. No more sneaking around, and you need to help in the morning with whatever Angela asks you to do. Tomorrow, after I get a chance to talk to my partner Stephanie and the local sheriff, we'll figure out what is the best way to help you."

Susan nodded her head emphatically. "I promise. I'll be good, and I'll stay in my room. And tomorrow, I'll help with anything that Angela asks me to do."

Without waiting for Tessa or Beau to say anything further, Susan stood up and headed down the hallway towards the room she had been in earlier. Tessa looked at Beau and shrugged her shoulders helplessly. She followed him and Susan out of her office, making sure that this time she locked the door securely behind her.

After she and Beau had made sure that the girl was back in her room, they walked to the living room.

Beau looked down at her and said, "I'm glad you locked the door to your office, but I think maybe you should really make a habit of it from now. As much as you try to vet them, you don't really know very much about the women that you help, and honestly, the less they can find out about you, the safer you and your partner Stephanie are."

Tessa threw him a suspicious glance. "How do you know whether or not I lock my office at night?"

Beau gave her a half smile. "I asked Angela how Susan got into a locked office, and Angela told me you rarely, if ever, lock the door."

Tessa looked at the man standing before her again in curiosity. She listened to Beau's explanation but was again discomfited by the fact she couldn't tell if he was telling her the truth or not, or even what his intentions were. There was nothing going on in her head, no buzzing and no whirring. Just silence. From the moment she had laid eyes on him, he'd been a closed book to her, and she wasn't sure that she liked that one bit.

"I guess that I'll need to talk to Angela about sharing all of our information with strangers. But you're probably right. It would be better if I lock my door when I leave. I suppose there is a lot of information about our residents, past and present, that someone could be interested in."

At the word stranger, Beau expelled a breath of air, looking down at her with fire glinting in his eyes. "I'm hardly a stranger anymore, Tessa. I'm your neighbor and have been for a few months now. I also know that your friend Jack Lewis ran an extensive background check on me and came up with nothing. Besides that, if I intended any harm, I would certainly have made my move by now." His eyes suddenly changed, and he looked at her slyly. "I'm sure that the diligent Sheriff shared everything he found out about me with you. At this point, I imagine you know way more about me than I know about you."

Tessa had the decency to blush at him for calling her out.

"Jack has become a very close and trusted friend over the years. He respects what we do here, and he just wants to make sure that all the residents, as well as Steph and I, are safe. He's adamant about checking out anyone who gets too close to the shelter, and no, he doesn't always share that information with us. Jack is an extremely discreet man." Tessa then tossed her hair and gave him a haughty look. "So you're really not that special, Mr. Reeves. He runs a background check on all the neighbors and the residents here." Then she looked at him suspiciously. "Besides, how do you even know that we checked you out?"

Beau just grinned at her and shrugged his shoulder indifferently. "Maybe you two are not the only ones with connections."

Tessa was again irked that she couldn't read him or what he was thinking, but she decided it was better to end the conversation and the night for now before she found herself in a battle of wits with her handsome but very secretive neighbor.

"Well, thanks for helping tonight. I really do appreciate it. I think poor Angela was nervous with the girl snooping around like that. These poor women have been through so much, and it's easy for them to get spooked." As she spoke, she was heading for the front door.

"It's really no problem. You can all call me any time you need to," Beau replied graciously, making Tessa wonder once again what he did and why he was so available to them.

She glanced up at him. "I had better get home and get some sleep now. I want to be back here early before the ladies all wake up. I'm sure that Angela will not want to deal with Susan on her own, and I have a bit of a drive back and forth."

Beau followed her out the door, waiting patiently while she locked it, and then following her to her car. As he held the car door for her, he said, "You really do look dog tired. I could come over and check things out early instead. That way you can sleep in, at least for a little longer. And Angela can call me if Susan acts up in any way tomorrow morning as well. I can be over here in less than two minutes to help out."

Tessa abruptly stopped climbing into her car and looked up at him, just realizing something.

"How did you make it over here so fast? And why isn't your car here?" she asked. Angela must have buzzed you in from the road."

He just grinned at her again. "Actually, no, she didn't. I didn't take the road. There's a back path connecting our gardens, and I used that. It's very close to a gardener's cottage that I'm fixing up, and I just discovered it a few days ago. The path is way faster than going all the way to the street and waiting for someone to buzz me in through the front gate, so like I said, I can be over here in less than two minutes."

Frowning, Tessa said, "That could be a big security breach for the women here. If you can get in, so can anyone else. I wonder if any other neighbors can just walk over as well. I thought we had bushes and gates all around the perimeter securing it."

"Don't worry. Anyone using the path would need to get onto my property first, and believe me, my property is better protected than yours. No one is coming through that way other than me. I already checked the rest of your perimeter, as well as my own, when I found the path. I wanted to see if there are any more holes anywhere else. Other than the connection to my place, you are buttoned up nice and tight."

Tessa looked at his face uneasily for another few seconds, not sure if she liked the idea that he could just come and go as he pleased. On the one hand, it was comforting to know that he would be only minutes away if they needed him, but she still did not know if she could trust him or not.

"Well, okay. That's good, I guess. Thanks for checking things out. I'll be here early in the morning, so you really won't need to pop over. I'll call Jack in the morning as well. Hopefully, he can find out something about our Susan Smith."

Beau just nodded at her, saying, "If you don't mind, let me know what he comes up with. I guess I have a vested interest in what goes on over here as well, seeing as we're so close." He shut her door, and Tessa watched as he headed toward the back of her house, still not sure if she should be comforted or alarmed at the thought of the mysterious Beau Reeves being so close.

Tessa pulled through the gate, again making sure that the gate was closed securely behind her. She was chewing on her lower lip and deep in thought as she drove, wondering about the mysterious Beau Reeves and if she could trust him or not. She never noticed the dark sedan that was parked at the corner of her street.

The older man jumped up with a start, roughly elbowing the young man who was snoring beside him. "Get up, you idiot! She's on the move again. Doesn't this woman ever sleep!" he yelled loudly.

The younger man grumbled and then lurched back hard in his seat as the older man gunned the car and sped off, trying to catch the car that had just left the shelter. He cussed and buckled himself in quickly.

"I thought the boss gave the okay to find a way in to get what we're looking for later tonight? You said she'd be staying in there all night."

The older man was frantically looking for Tessa's car and glaring at the younger man as he growled, "Yeah, well, I guess she didn't get that memo then, did she? Where is she going at this time of night? Do you think she has a rendezvous with some dude?"

Now the older man really did glare at his partner. "How would I know where she's going and what she's doing, you idiot? All I know is we better find her and fast, or else the boss is going to have both our heads, so just keep your mouth shut and your eyes open for once."

The young man peered nervously into the dark streets, his bravado faltering as he looked for the elusive car. Unless they found her, his plan would fail, and they would all have to pay a very heavy price. The boss didn't like failure. "There! Up ahead. She just turned left onto the highway!" he exclaimed suddenly.

The other man gunned his car again until they were close enough to follow her without being seen.

"Don't get too close," the younger man cautioned him. "We don't want her to know that she's being followed, and there aren't too many cars out right now. It'll be easy for her to spot us."

"I know, I know. But I don't want to risk losing her again either. Besides, I doubt that she's that good at spotting if someone's following her. She's just a social worker, not a cop or anything."

Tessa watched the car behind her carefully, wondering if it really was following her or if her senses were just on heightened alert because of everything that was going on at the shelter right now. It seemed to stay back just far enough so that she couldn't discern a make or a color, and it would have been impossible to read the license plate in the dark.

She sighed and rubbed her eyes. *I think I'll just keep an eye on it and turn into the street in front of mine, just to make sure,* she thought, fairly certain it was just another late-night traveler but deciding it was wiser to play it safe. "Too bad that my abilities don't extend between car windows," she joked aloud.

She was uneasy but not sure if it was because of the late hour, the car behind her, or her encounter with her handsome neighbor. She thought back to the conversation with the dark, brooding man and wondered again at her inability to be able to read him like she could everyone else. It had taken a few years for her to get used to knowing what people truly meant, but it had become so much a part of her that she was finding it extremely uncomfortable not being able to rely on it with Beau Reeves.

As well as the discomfort she felt around him, she wondered if that was also the reason she felt such a surge of excitement anytime that she saw him. Maybe it was more the mystery and the unknown that made him so appealing, not the man himself. Even now, the mere memory of those intense eyes looking directly at her made her feel butterflies in her stomach.

Easy there, girl. Remember, you're not a teenager anymore. You're a middle-aged woman who's seen more than her share of hardship and heartache. You'd be wise to keep your juvenile excitement under control, she mentally chided herself. She shook her head hard, trying to clear her mind, and noticed she was finally getting close to her apartment.

Glancing in her rearview mirror, she was fairly certain that the car she had seen following her was still behind her. She watched it as she headed off the exit and saw that the car also exited, staying a short distance behind her. Tessa veered onto the first street that came up on her left, instead of going straight, which would have been her usual way. To her intense relief, the car didn't turn behind her but continued on straight. She could feel the knots in her stomach easing up somewhat, and she reproached herself for being so paranoid.

By the time she finally reached the little garage apartment and its private parking lot, the knots were almost completely gone. To her relief, the motion sensor light came on for once, lighting up the tiny lot as she pulled in. She took her apartment key out of her purse before exiting her car and hurried into her apartment, leaning heavily against the door when she was finally inside and expelling the air she had been subconsciously holding in.

Tessa placed her key in the little bowl by the door, turned on the lights, and looked around at the shabby, albeit comfortable, little haven she had created for herself. Paintings in various stages of completion were hanging or leaning on her walls, greeting her like the familiar friends they were. After her family was murdered, she had painted to distract herself from the intense pain of her loss. Over the years, she had found it was one of the best ways for her to cope when her feelings of desperation threatened to overcome her, and she had discovered that she actually had quite a talent for it as well. There were quite a number of people clamoring to purchase her paintings, although so far she had refused to sell any.

She picked up the picture sitting next to the tiny bowl where she had placed her keys on the side table, looking down as she always did when she got home at the smiling faces of her husband and her little girl.

It was her favorite picture of the two of them. She had taken it right after Luke had completed the treehouse he had built for Hope. Sweat had caused his hair to hang limp over his brow, and he was grinning at her camera directly, as if he had just cracked one of his many jokes.

Hope was looking up at him adoringly, her dark ponytail askew on her head, and her cheek smudged with the stain they had used to preserve her little house. Luke had told her they wanted to preserve the treehouse so it would last long enough for Hope's children to play in.

Tessa felt the familiar tears pricking against her eyelids. The treehouse would withstand the test of time. Luke and Hope hadn't. *Oh, how different our life would have been if someone hadn't come in and destroyed it,* she thought in despair. *I wouldn't be coming home to an empty apartment right now, with my heart pounding, and paranoid about a stupid car following me.*

She set down the picture gently in its spot again, deciding that a cup of hot tea and a bath might be just the thing to calm her down after the events of the day. It was late, but she needed to get her equilibrium back, and tomorrow was already promising to be another eventful day.

The two men sat a little way down the street from Tessa's apartment and watched as the lights to the tiny parking lot dutifully came on when her car pulled in. They watched her park and scurry out of her car and into her well-lit doorway.

"See, I told you she had to live around here somewhere, and there she is, pulling right into the parking lot I said she would pull into, just like a good little girl." The older man had a smug and self-satisfied look on his face as he watched Tessa hurry into her apartment.

The younger man looked at his partner with admiration. "I got to hand it to you, Gabe, you sure called that one. I thought for sure that we lost her when you didn't make that turn to follow her."

Gabe was silent for a minute, watching the light in the upstairs apartment go on before he commented, "I wasn't born yesterday, kid. I figured she might have made us, and we needed to throw her off somehow." He grinned. "Besides, she made it pretty easy on me. I know these parts of town pretty well, and when she turned off towards the shopping center, I knew right where we had to go."

He chuckled maliciously. "I didn't think the dame was going to shop at this time of night, so she had to be coming to the only residential area around this part of town." He looked at the young man with his eyes narrowed. "You've got to wake up pretty early in the morning to outsmart old Gabe, kid."

"Like I said, Gabe, you've been making the right calls all night. I guess I sure can learn a lot from you. The boss will be happy that we finally found out where she lives."

The younger man decided that the best way to keep Gabe happy, and clueless, was to flatter him, letting him think he was in total awe of his abilities. He knew he would need to spend a few more days with the man and figured it was best to keep things as peaceful as possible, so he and the girl could carry out their plan unhindered.

"We couldn't have asked for a better location either. It's nice and quiet around here, and it looks to me like the woman lives by herself. It should be pretty easy to get in and out without being noticed." The younger man scanned the area as he spoke.

Gabe nodded his head in agreement. "She's making it a lot easier on us than I could've hoped for. But I'm ready to head on back to bed and get some sleep. I doubt she'll be going anywhere else tonight. Even the boss has to know we need to sleep sometime."

Gabe turned on the car, slowly cruising past the tiny garage apartment as he drove by without turning on his headlights. "Now, if that girl of yours would just finally do her job, we can finish up with the woman and get back to business as usual." He gave the young man a sideways glance.

"I'm sure she'll do what she was told. She's smart, and she'll figure out how to get the job done."

The young man spoke quietly, bristling at the condescending tone of Gabe's voice, but not wanting to get in an argument with him. All he needed to do was bide his time and play his cars right, he would get the last laugh on both Gabe and the big boss man soon enough.

CHAPTER 5

Tessa hung up the phone, looking up at the big clock in her office. *The women were probably finishing breakfast by now,* she thought. If she hurried, she might still get a cup of coffee before it was all gone.

After her late night, she had slept longer than she'd intended this morning and had opted to skip her morning meditation, as well as her morning cup of coffee, so she could get to the shelter early. The lack of her morning routine was not a good way to start the day, but she had wanted to get here before Angela and Susan were up, hoping to prevent a new conflict between the two of them.

As it turned out, both of them were already up and in the kitchen by the time she had arrived. She'd walked into the kitchen and found Angela glaring at the girl, who was sitting at the table sullenly studying her nails and doing her best to ignore the older woman.

"Good morning, Angela. You're up earlier than usual," she'd said, trying her best to sound cheery. Glancing from Angela to Susan, Tessa had wondered where the hostility between the two came from this time. "Is something the matter?"

"It's a good thing I was up early, Miss Tessa. Caught this one sneaking around again." Angela was now glaring back at Susan.

"I was not sneaking around!" Susan fired back. "I already told you; I was just looking around the place, trying to find the kitchen so I could make a cup of coffee."

"Harummph." Angela put her hands on her hips. "In the direction of Miss Tessa's office?" she asked, her frown full of accusation.

Looking back at Tessa, she continued her rant. "And now that I've steered her highness to the kitchen she was looking for, she won't even lift a finger to help make the coffee that she'd supposedly been craving so badly."

Susan never said a word to defend herself. She just sat and stared at Angela defiantly.

"Susan, remember what you agreed to last night?" Tessa tried to keep her voice calm, but the lack of sleep and coffee was making it hard. "You promised to help Angela with whatever it was she asked you to do."

"Fine," Susan suddenly exploded up from her chair like a rocket and raced around the kitchen, banging open cupboards and drawers. "So, where's the coffee? The coffee pot? Give me some eggs and a pan, and I'll scramble you and your brats all the eggs you could want. Just get off my back, will you?" she yelled at Angela.

Angela stepped back and watched her bustle about angrily, wisely holding her tongue until Susan could use up some of that pent-up frustration. She'd been a mother long enough to realize the anger Susan was feeling was not really towards her, and it would do no good to argue with her while she was in this state. Although she felt sorry for her and suspected that Susan had some issues to work through, she didn't want the angry teenager around her children, and she hoped Tessa could figure out what to do with the girl soon.

Tessa did not know how to handle an angry teen and had decided it would be prudent for her to leave the women to work it out among themselves, once again forgoing her coffee, and hurried back to her office to call Jack. She fervently hoped that he would find out something about Susan soon, and she could hustle the girl back to her family before she caused any more trouble for the women here at the shelter.

After telling Jack the entire events of the night before, she waited for him to speak.

"So, you're sure that she is lying about her name and her age?" Jack asked, sorting through the information Tessa had shared.

"Yes, Jack, I'm one hundred percent sure that she's lying. She's also lying about where she came from and the reason she came to me for help. I'm sure of that as well."

She could hear Jack typing on his computer as she spoke, and it was silent for a few more minutes while he worked.

"I don't see any reports of a missing girl fitting the age or the description of the girl at your place, Tess. That means no one has reported her, or it could also mean she just isn't from around here."

Tessa heard his chair creaking through the phone as he moved about.

"I'll call around, but I'm fairly sure if there was a report of a missing teenager anywhere in the surrounding counties, I would have heard about it." Tessa frowned. She was fairly certain that Susan was a runaway, and she'd hoped Jack could find out her true identity fairly quickly.

Jack's voice came through the phone again. "I know you said she's lying about her age, and of course I believe you. You've never been wrong yet. But is it possible that she is making herself younger instead of older? That could explain why she's not reported as a missing child?"

Tessa pondered Jack's question for a moment and then shook her head into the phone. "No, I really don't think so, Jack. This girl looks young, really young."

"Hmmm, okay then. I have a few things I need to take care of this morning, but I'll stop by as soon as I can later on and talk to the girl myself. Keep her there as long as you can, Tess. We'll get this figured out," Jack reassured her. After a brief pause, he continued, "I know that you're busy, but if you have a few minutes tomorrow, I have a suspect in a series of robberies who has agreed to come in. I hoped that maybe you could watch the interview and give me your thoughts."

"Of course, Jack. Just let me know when, and I'll be there." She could tell from the reluctant tone of his voice that he hated to ask, but she also knew he had come to rely heavily on her input whenever he had a tough case to solve. Her senses often saved him days of fruitless questioning.

"Thanks, Tessa. I really do appreciate all the help you are to me and the rest of my officers."

"Of course, Jack. I appreciate all that you do for the shelter as well. I'm glad to help where I can. See you later then. Hopefully, you'll be able to find something about her by then." She hung up and was about to walk out of the office when her phone rang again.

Looking at the caller ID, she smiled. "Hey Carter. Good morning, how's it going? I thought that you'd be in meetings all morning?"

"Yeah, actually I am, but I took a quick bathroom break to see how things went last night and make sure that you're all right." Carter's voice sounded hurried, and Tessa suspected he was talking and rushing back to his meeting at the same time.

"Everything is fine, Carter. You don't need to worry about anything. Like I said, she's just a young girl with some problems, and hopefully we can help her with them." She chuckled, thinking of this morning's encounter in the kitchen. "Granted, she's a bit of a ticking time bomb, but it's nothing I can't handle. I called Sheriff Lewis already to see if he could find any information on her."

"And, did he know anything?" Carter's voice now echoed hollow, as if he were in an elevator.

"No, but he's coming by later this morning or early afternoon to talk to her. I'm hoping that he may have found something out by then. He told me to keep her here until then."

"Okay, well keep me posted and let me know if there is anything I can do in the meantime." Before Tessa could say goodbye, Carter's voice came back over the phone. "Oh, and Tessa, you, me, and Steph need to talk soon. Your finances are looking kind of grim again. We're going to have to figure something out unless you've heard anything from your anonymous donor lately?"

Tessa sighed. She was grateful to Carter for taking care of most of the accounting for Hope's Haven. Neither she nor Stephanie really had a knack for numbers, but she hated that he was always aware of their financial situation. She knew it made him worry and inevitably feel guilty about his own affluence.

"No, I have heard nothing from any of our donors, but I can send out a few flyers to some of our regulars if you think it will help. I donated a few of my pictures to the policeman's fundraiser for next month, and Jack promised to let us put up some advertising for Hope's Haven at the event. That kind of advertising always seems to help bring in donations as well."

"Yeah, that's great, of course," Carter's voice was hushed, and she suspected he was around others and didn't want to be heard, "but you're going to need some money before then if we want to stay current on the payments." He paused for a minute and then continued, "I can always lend you the money to get you through,"

"No, Carter, we've been through this a million times already. Neither Stephanie nor I want to be put in a position of owing you money that we may not pay back," she continued, trying to sound reassuring. "Don't worry, we'll find a way. We always do." She could hear Carter sigh.

"All right then, I'll do what I can to make the most important payments until we can get together and strategize. In the meantime, keep me posted on what you find out about the girl, and do your best to keep her there until the sheriff gets there. See you soon." Carter hung up quickly, and she guessed he was already in his meeting, charming his clients as if they were the only people that mattered to him. Carter had a knack for making all of his clients feel special. That's probably what made him such a successful lawyer.

Keep the girl there until the detective gets there, Tessa thought, wondering if that would be as easy as it sounded.

Susan had looked like she was ready to bolt out the back door when she had left her and Angela alone earlier. She closed the door to her office and headed back to the kitchen, hoping against hope that she would finally get that cup of coffee. As she walked, she sighed, wondering what additional problems the girl could cause before the sheriff came, and if it was even prudent of her to keep her here. So far, she had only caused trouble.

"So where does this one go, Miss Angela?" she heard Susan asking. Tessa walked into the kitchen and watched in awe. Instead of the chaos she had been expecting, she found the young girl and the older woman working together in apparent peace and harmony, calmly cleaning the kitchen.

Angela turned to Tessa with a knowing smile on her face. "Can I get you some coffee, Miss Tessa? I noticed you haven't had any this morning yet, and I know how much you love your morning coffee."

Tessa threw her a questioning look but just said, "Oh, that would be wonderful, Angela. You're right, I really could use a cup."

Angela turned to Susan. "Can you please hand me a mug from the cupboard right above you, honey?"

Susan reached up, pulled out a mug, and handed it to Angela. "Is this one okay?"

"Perfect, dear. Now, why don't you go make your bed and tidy up your room while I get Miss Tessa her coffee? I'll be there in a few minutes, and we'll discuss what you can do to help today."

After Susan had left, Tessa turned to Angela. "Okay, so what gives? Did you beat her into submission after I left? Where is the sullen, stubborn, and angry teenager that I left you with less than an hour ago?"

Angela winked at Tessa. "I have my ways of handling cranky teenagers. I practically raised all of my brothers and sisters alone while my poor mama worked her two jobs trying to keep us fed. There wasn't the time or the money to put up with any of their tantrums, so I may have learned a thing or two."

"Well, whatever you did, thanks. I thought I would have to kick her out, or she would even run away again before Jack got here to interview her."

Angela looked at her with concern. "You aren't really thinking of kicking her out, are you, Miss Tessa? After all, she's just a young girl, and she deserves some help as well."

Well, that was a quick turnabout, Tessa thought, sipping her coffee slowly and looking at the other women still gathered around the large table with their children. She could tell they were all listening intently.

Tessa turned back to Angela and said quietly, "Susan doesn't really fit the profile of our usual residents; you know that, Angela. We're not a hotel or a place for runaways to hide. There are other places that are much better suited to take in a girl like Susan. I owe it to you and to these women to be careful of whom we admit into residence here."

Angela looked down at her hands. "Of course, I know that, Miss Tessa, and earlier this morning I would have probably agreed with you. But there is something about that girl. Underneath that tough exterior and sassy attitude of hers, I sense a very helpless and desperate child that needs help. I just don't want to lose her in the system." She shuddered slightly. "I sure know what that's like. I grew up in it myself before Mama got us back. Trust me, it's tough to break out of it once they have you."

Tessa reached out and squeezed Angela's hand. "Don't worry. Sheriff Lewis is on his way over, and we'll figure out the best way to help her. There's a good chance that Susan's parents are out there somewhere and desperate to find her. Hopefully, with some luck, we can reunite her with her family quickly."

"I pray that's the case, Miss Tessa. I just feel like that girl has potential, and I don't want to see her lost to the streets if I can do anything to help it."

After Angela had left, Tessa spent a few more minutes talking to the women remaining in the kitchen, and then she walked back to her office, a fresh cup of precious coffee cradled in her hand. She saw Stephanie had finally made it in and was busily working at her desk.

"Morning Tess, how did it go last night? I see that there seems to be peace on the home front for now. I checked into the kitchen while you were on the phone, and Angela and the Susan girl seemed to work okay together." As she spoke, Stephanie peered out from behind her cluttered desk, giving Tessa a wave with one hand while sipping her coffee with the other.

"Much to my surprise, yes. Angela clearly has a way with teenagers that I don't have. Last night and this morning I was sure I was going to have to send Susan to the curb just to keep the other women sane, now I'm not so sure anymore."

Stephanie frowned. "You know we can't keep her here, right Tess? I know you feel obligated to help any stray that you find, but remember our mission. Hope's Haven helps abused women and their children. We can't help every wayward person looking for a place to stay. There are other shelters or even foster care for young girls in need."

"Of course, I know that, Steph. But we know nothing about her yet. For all we know, she really is running away from an abusive situation. She hasn't been upfront with us yet or told us her true story. There has to be a reason for that."

"That's exactly my point, Tess. One of our most sacred rules is that the women we admit are honest and open with us. It's imperative they let us know what kind of danger they're in and who is after them. It's the only way that we stand a chance of keeping them, and all the other women here, safe."

"I know, you're right. But let's just wait until Jack gets here and see what he has to say before we decide what to do with her. Maybe he will have some information for us, or maybe Susan will be more open with him than she is with me. Sometimes girls do feel safer with a man than a woman. I still have hope that either Jack or even Angela will have more luck getting her to open up."

They heard the doorbell for the gate ring, and Stephanie looked at her camera. "Right on cue. That's Jack now," she announced while engaging the intercom. "Come on in, Jack. You know the way," she said and pressed the button that released the lock on the gate. They saw him nod through the windshield of his car and watched him drive through the gate and up the front drive.

"Do you want me to let him in?" Stephanie asked, looking over at Tessa.

"No, that's okay. I'll open the front door. I can talk to him while you get some work done. I know you had a bunch of paperwork you wanted to get through today, and one of us does still need to keep the place functioning. There are a lot more things to take care of than just Susan."

Stephanie nodded gratefully at her friend. "I really do have a lot to do. But call me over if you find out anything about our new guest. I'm just as curious as anyone to know where she came from."

Tessa made her way to the front door, opening it just as Jack was about to knock.

Grinning at her, he said, "I thought you could read people's minds, not see through closed doors."

She laughed back at him. "I hate to disappoint you, but there were no secret powers involved here. I just watched you on the camera from Stephanie's office. Besides, I already explained that I don't read minds. All I can do is tell if they're being honest or not. It's really not that spectacular."

"Well, that's spectacular enough for me," he said, stepping through the door and closing it carefully behind him. "Your uncanny senses have certainly helped me and the department more than a few times, that's for sure."

As she led the way to her office, Tessa chatted casually with Jack about the upcoming fundraiser for the police department, thanking him for allowing them to advertise at it. The department had pledged some of the funds raised to help a family that had recently lost their home to a fire, and Jack remarked, "It really is nice of you to offer to auction some of your paintings at the event. That poor family can use all the money we can muster to rebuild. Times are tight around here for everyone, and I know most people won't be able to give too much, even if they want to."

Tessa grimaced. "Well, I'm not sure if my paintings will bring much in either, Jack. I'm just an amateur after all, and my paintings are not all that good. There's a good chance that no one will bid on them at all, so don't get your hopes up too much."

Jack chuckled. "You're underselling yourself, Tessa. I think your paintings are great, and I'm not the only one. Everyone at the department who's seen them has said the same thing. You have a way of capturing faces and scenes around town that really seem to touch people."

Tessa just shook her head doubtfully as she motioned for Jack to sit down. Her paintings were a very private thing for her, and she had painted none of them with the intention for anyone but herself to see them.

She had finally shown them to a few of her friends to get their opinions, and it had been at their urging that she had offered a few of them for sale to the public. She would try anything to help raise money to help keep the shelter functioning. So far, the only people she had sold to had been close friends she loved and respected.

She poured her heart and soul into her paintings, and it had been hard to let them go, but she had convinced herself they were at least going to suitable homes. When Jack had told her about the family and the devastating loss they had suffered, she couldn't help but feel sorry for them and wanted to help. She had decided the only thing she really had to donate to the fundraiser were some of her paintings, but she had experienced pangs of regret ever since. She wasn't sure she was ready to have strangers see them and critique them just yet. Since everything she painted came from her heart, it made her feel like she was selling her deepest feelings to the highest bidder.

Since she was still uncomfortable taking compliments about her talent, she chose to just ignore Jack's praise for now. "So, you still haven't come up with anyone who's missing a young girl?" she asked. "It just seems so strange to me that no one would report it if their young daughter goes missing."

"Unfortunately, it's not that strange or uncommon at all. Kids run away all the time for various reasons, and most of the time they go back home after a few days of cooling off. We usually only get the report if the kid's been missing for a few weeks, and then unfortunately, it becomes harder for us to find them. Sometimes, no one reports them at all." Jack shook his head sadly.

Tessa frowned, knowing that Jack was right, and thinking back to her days as a social worker. She had worked with parents and kids alike, and she knew how hard it was at times to reunite them. Sometimes, the hard feelings and resentments just ran too deep. She had tried so hard with several young girls she had met, and it still pained her that she had failed some of them.

"Tell me more about this Susan," Jack prompted. "Is there anything at all that she is telling the truth about, or is everything a story that she is just making up?"

"Well, she did know about this place, although I don't think that she was actually ever a resident here like she claims to have been. She also clearly recognized me, and she was telling the truth when she says that we met before, but she's lying when she explains the circumstances under which we met. Unfortunately, I can't seem to remember her at all, and I can't find any record of her or her mother ever having been here. At least not under the name Smith, which is not her real name, anyway." Tessa paused and regarded Jack. "I guess I could have met her and her mother while I was working as a social worker. I met so many women and children then that I most certainly wouldn't remember them all. Especially not after all this time."

"That's back when you worked in Atlanta, Georgia, right?" Jack asked, making a note in his notepad. "I'll check and see if there are any reports of a missing girl matching her age and description in that area when I get back to the office."

They continued to go over everything that Tessa had already told him this morning, with Jack taking more and more notes as they spoke.

Finally, Jack closed his notepad and stood up. "I think the best thing for me to do now is to meet and interview Susan myself. Who knows, maybe she'll be more inclined to open up now that she's been here for a while."

Tessa stood up as well and nodded at him. "I hope so, Jack. I certainly haven't gotten very far with her so far."

They walked to the kitchen, where Tessa suspected Angela had taken Susan to help with the chores. As they approached the door to the kitchen, they could see Susan was mopping the floor.

Tessa shook her head in wonder. *I really have to figure out Angela's secret*, she thought. "Susan," she called out. "Could you come here for a minute? I have someone that I'd like you to meet."

Susan glanced up from her work, looking over at Tessa and Jack. Before anyone said anything or reacted, she threw the mop in their direction, bolting through the hallway to the front door as if she had seen a monster.

CHAPTER 6

Susan's heart raced as she ran down the long hall, desperately trying to outrun the footsteps that were racing up fast behind her. She knew a cop when she saw one, and she knew for certain she wasn't up to facing the interrogation he would give her. She needed to get out of here fast before she blew everything.

She finally reached the door and yanked desperately at it, hoping to dodge out onto the lawn and hide until she could get away. Cursing, she looked for the bolt that was preventing her escape, but just as she found it, she was grabbed from behind and pulled back.

"Whoa now, Susan. Calm down. I just want to talk to you," Jack said, pulling her back gently but firmly, preventing her from getting out.

She spun around, glaring angrily at him. "I don't need to talk to you. I know my rights!" She spat out at him, full of defiance. Jack almost grinned at the angry face of the girl in front of him. *She sure is a little spitfire,* he thought, amused.

"I'm sure you do, Susan. But I'm not here to arrest you. I'm just trying to help figure out the best way that we can help you," Jack explained.

Still glaring at him, Susan squared her shoulders. "I don't need anybody's help. I can take care of myself," she insisted.

Tessa, who had run up behind them, raised an eyebrow at the girl. "Really? Then why did you come here last night asking for my help?"

Susan glanced down for a minute, trying to find an answer, before she mumbled, "I told you I just need a place to stay until I can get some money and figure out where to go next." She looked up at Jack in distaste. "What I don't need is any help from a cop, that's for sure."

Tessa sighed tiredly. After her late night and all the emotions that had been brought to the surface recently, she just wasn't up to dealing with an ornery teenager right now.

"Jack is not just a cop, Susan. He's here to help you, just like he's helped several women here. I'm sure that if we can find your parents and talk things through with them, we can figure everything out and get you back on track," Tessa explained.

Susan glared at Tessa. "Why would I want to talk to my parents? I've been on my own for a long time and I don't need them. They've already clarified that they want nothing more to do with me. Besides, I already told you, I'm eighteen. They can't tell me what to do anyway, and neither can you."

"Okay, Susan, that's fine," Jack intervened, keeping his voice low and calm. "But you still came here looking for help of some kind, and both Miss Graves and I want to give you that help. Why don't we head back to her office and sit down, and just talk things through." Jack was still gripping Susan's arm, so she decided that for now it was better to go along with them and cooperate as much as possible. Hopefully, if she could lie convincingly enough, she could find what she had come for and be out of here by tonight.

"Okay," Susan said, suddenly demure and giving Jack a smile.

Immediately the hair on Tessa's neck stood up, and she could hear the buzzing start. *Uh oh, she's up to something.*

Susan turned to walk toward Tessa's office, while Tessa threw Jack a warning look. He nodded silently back at her, understanding what she meant. He didn't need any special talents to see that this sudden burst of cooperation meant the girl was up to something.

Just down the street, in the same car that had followed Tessa the night before, Gabe was watching the tracker on his phone. "Well, she's still in there, but that was definitely a cop that went in that house. I can smell one of them a mile away. I wonder if she went and got herself arrested already. Probably did something stupid and got caught." He grunted in disgust and looked at the young man sitting next to him. "I knew we couldn't trust that girl to do the job right."

Ethan Turner sat quietly, staring out the window towards the big house, chewing on a fingernail. He was also worried about her ability to get the job done. She wasn't as street-savvy as him, and he hoped she could keep it together long enough to find what they needed. He hadn't really trusted her when she had volunteered for this assignment, but she insisted that she could do it, and she was his only choice.

"She'll be fine," he said, with more confidence than he truly felt. "Of course, that social worker was going to call the cops. We should've seen that coming. That's what social workers like her do. They preach about helping you out, and then they call the cops for help. It happens every time."

Gabe nodded in agreement. "Let's just hope she sticks to the story she was given. Personally, I think she's a loose cannon, and if she messes up, we'll all pay the price with the boss."

"She'll stick to her story. We practiced it over and over. She knows what's at stake if she messes up," Ethan replied, shuddering inwardly at the thought of what Snake would do if his own plan failed and he had to crawl back to Snake as a failure. Snake was ruthless when he felt cheated.

"Yeah, well, she better," Gabe remarked, "or she'll have me to deal with, as well as the boss." But despite his bravado, the look of worry etched on his face was hard to hide.

"What if the dame already spent all the money that Snake seems to think she has? A house like that can't be cheap, and those useless women she takes in sure can't pay," said Gabe suddenly, thinking aloud.

Ethan glanced over at him. He had been worried about the same thing. What if there wasn't money lying around in that big house like Snake thought? He would never admit he had been wrong and would blame the girl and the two of them for sure. None of them stood a chance against Snake if he got angry.

"His old lady was convinced that the social worker was super rich, and she said she saw all the money with her own eyes," he said.

Ethan was trying to convince himself, as well as Gabe, that if they didn't get that money, all the plans he had made for himself and the girl would blow up in his face. They knew they would never make their escape without it. *It just has to be there,* he thought desperately.

Gabe snorted derisively. "I always kind of doubted what that old broad told him. She was pretty desperate to get herself back in his good graces after he caught up with her and dragged her back. She would have told him anything to stop the beatings. Not that it did her any good," he sneered.

Ethan closed his eyes against the memory. Snake had been furious at the woman for trying to run away from him. He himself understood anger and the need to make someone suffer, but even he had thought Snake had gone too far with the woman. He understood why Snake needed to be tough and even cruel to the men around him. They were a tough bunch and always looking to take over, but women were just weak and stupid creatures. They didn't pose a threat to someone like Snake. A quick punch or slap would have been enough to get her back in line.

Ethan glanced sideways at Gabe. "I still wonder if he keeps her around somewhere. I never did see her again after she gave Snake the information about the money and the woman who helped her." He suspected Gabe knew a lot more about the goings-on within the gang than he did. Gabe just took another drag from his smoke and exhaled it angrily.

"Well, one thing's for sure. It's more than just money that Snake wants from that shelter lady. No one crosses Snake and gets away with it. And he was mighty pissed that she could hide his old lady for so long without him finding her."

Ethan almost felt a pang of compassion for the woman. She had made an enemy of a very ruthless man and didn't even know it yet. He sure wouldn't want to be the one at the receiving end when Snake was looking for revenge. He shook his head to clear his mind, opening the car window at the same time and trying to dispel some of the smoke emanating from Gabe's cigarette. He hated stinking like stale cigarettes, but Gabe smoked incessantly, and now it seemed to have permeated everything that Ethan owned. Sometimes he just wanted to shove that cigarette right down the older man's throat.

Ethan coughed and then took a deep breath to calm himself. He didn't have the luxury to feel anger or pity for anyone right now. He needed to stay on task and keep his end goal in mind. He had big plans for the girl and himself, and this time he didn't intend to fail. With any luck, he would be far away by the time Snake took his revenge on anyone.

Meanwhile, Susan squirmed uncomfortably in her seat, avoiding Jack's gaze and looking down at her lap. *Stop listening to them,* she scolded herself. *They're just saying the same things that grownups always say. They always promise to take care of you, and in the end, they leave you hanging all by yourself again.* But this time, she would not fall for it.

She looked up at them, insisting, "I know I look young, but I really am eighteen." She regretted not taking the time to put some makeup in her backpack, but she just hadn't thought about it. They'd been in a hurry to leave the hotel, and she had been nervous about what she had to do. Now she wished she had taken the time. Ethan always said that she looked really grown up whenever she fixed herself up and went out, and the other men she met certainly never asked her how old she was. She was sure if she had some, she could convince Jack she was older.

"Okay, Susan, then just give us your real name and let me confirm that. I just want to make sure your family isn't out there looking for you. If you are eighteen, then we just let them know you're okay. You don't even have to talk to them if you don't want to." Jack was trying to sound reassuring and as if he believed her, but he could see from Tessa's face that the girl was lying.

"Susan, please just listen to us," Tessa chimed in. "You don't need to go through whatever is going on in your life alone. If you're not happy at home, or if someone is hurting you, we can help change it. We just need you to tell us the truth so we can help."

It all sounded so easy and tempting when Tessa spoke like that. Susan longed for a safe and quiet place to hide. The events of her present life were overwhelming her, and she was fast discovering that she wasn't as tough as she always pretended to be.

She was also wondering if Ethan was being honest about all the promises he had made to her. Maybe, just maybe, if she did tell Tessa everything, she could finally have somewhere safe to go? She fidgeted around in her seat, trying to decide if she could trust these people and if she should confide in them when she accidentally bumped the tiny transmitter tucked tightly in her shoe against the corner of the desk.

I can't, she thought miserably. *He's counting on me to help him, and if I don't, he'll be coming after me as well as the others.* She turned and looked sweetly at Jack and Tessa. "I wish I could tell you what you want to hear, but like I said, I'm eighteen, no one is looking for me, and I just need a place to stay for a day or two until I can figure out where to go."

Tessa let out a heavy breath in exasperation. "Fine Susan, have it your way. But unfortunately, if that's the case, Hope's Haven is not the place for you. Sheriff Lewis will need to find a homeless shelter that has an opening to take you in." Tessa turned to Jack as she spoke, waiting to see if he would say anything more. She saw him studying the girl intently.

"We know you aren't eighteen, Susan. But lying about your age isn't a crime, and I have no reason to hold you on anything. You are, of course, free to leave if you want to, but Mrs. Graves is right. If all you're looking for is a place to stay, then a women's homeless shelter is the place that can best help you, not here." Jack glanced quickly at Tessa and then back to Susan. "I'll make a few calls right now and see if I can find anywhere that can take you in. Why don't you pack up your things now, and hopefully I'll be able to take you there when I leave."

Susan sat for a few more seconds, chewing on her lower lip, clearly undecided about something, and then stood up and exited the office, heading down the hall towards the room she had slept in last night.

"She didn't seem happy about leaving and going to the homeless shelter, that's for sure," remarked Jack after Susan had disappeared.

"No, she certainly didn't. But then, who can really blame her? After all, it's much nicer here than at a shelter. And if she really has spent a lot of time on the streets, she more than likely had been in a shelter before and knows how miserable they can be." Tessa watched as Susan disappeared into her room.

Jack watched her as well and said, "I think it's more than that though. I can even see that she's hiding more than just her age. I think she has ulterior motives for wanting to be here. My cop senses are smelling big trouble when it comes to her."

Tessa nodded in agreement. "I think you're right. She is here for more reasons than what she's admitting to. I just can't seem to figure out what. I'll have to question the other residents and see if anyone knows her, or if she said anything to any of them since she's arrived." She paused for a moment and asked, "Maybe she came here hoping to find someone who's staying here now?"

"Someone or something," said Jack thoughtfully. "I really think that the sooner I get her out of here, the safer it will be for you and the other women. There's something very wrong with that story she's telling us, and you may all be in danger."

Tessa looked at him quickly. "Jack, she's just a kid. I agree that she's up to something, but how could a young girl pose a danger to me or to the street-wizened women that are living here? Besides, Angela seems to have really taken to her, and she can usually smell trouble a mile off."

"Maybe so, but I still think the sooner I get her out of here, the better off you will all be," Jack said resolutely.

Susan sat on her bed and looked around in a panic. If that cop meant what he said, then she would have to leave in a matter of hours. That didn't leave her much time to find what she needed to find, and how was she supposed to search for anything with the two of them sitting right in the office? She stood up from the bed, frustrated.

Even though Ethan had told her she was most likely to find what she was looking for in that office, so far, she had struck out. True, she'd been caught pretty quickly every time she had tried to search, but even so, she had seen no sign of any money or safe boxes. What if Tessa was much more careful or cunning than any of them thought? What if it wasn't in her office? This building was enormous, and Tessa could have many hiding places here. *Or maybe it's not even here? Maybe she has it hidden away at her house, or even somewhere completely different?* Susan shuddered at the thought.

If she came up empty, she and Ethan would have missed their chance to get away. She would need to go back to Snake and tell him she had failed, and failure was never a good option with Snake. She wished desperately that there was some way she could get hold of Ethan and talk to him. He always seemed to know what to do, and right now she was at a total loss.

Tessa wiped her hands on the dish towel, smiling over at Angela. The older woman's three children were sitting at the table doing homework. For the time being, both Angela and Tessa agreed it was safer for the kids to be homeschooled.

Angela's husband might still be looking for her, and Jack had told them the easiest way for him to find Angela would be if she enrolled them in school. Tessa hoped that she could relocate Angela in a town further away, or even out of state when things cooled down a bit, so they could have a more normal life.

"Have time for a cup of coffee?" she asked, taking two mugs and heading over to the coffee pot she had just freshly brewed.

Angela nodded and walked over to the stools that were sitting at the counter of the large island. "I'd love some. I do believe that you're the only other person I have ever met that can keep up with me in coffee consumption, cup for cup," she joked.

Tessa sat down next to her and handed her the steaming mug. "Well, I guess we need to fuel ourselves with something, right?"

Angela nodded again and glanced through the open door to the laundry room, where Susan was dutifully folding the towels that had just come out of the dryer.

"What happened with that one this morning? Since she spoke with you and the sheriff, she seems really quiet and withdrawn?"

Tessa threw Susan a worried look. "Jack told her he was going to find a women's shelter for her if she wouldn't help us help her by being truthful. He's in my office trying to find somewhere for her right now. He's very concerned about her lack of transparency and is worried she might pose a risk to the rest of you. I imagine she's not happy about that."

Angela shook her head in disapproval. "Well, of course she's not! She's just a child, Miss Tessa. If she goes into a regular shelter, even one for women, those people will eat her alive. Those places are filled with drug addicts, prostitutes, and thieves. That's no place for a child, you know that."

"I do know that, Angela. But she keeps insisting that she is eighteen, and we have no proof otherwise. I can't take her to any kind of foster care or a safer place for young children if I don't have any proof that she is a minor. She insists that she's not running away from any kind of abuse or danger, so Hope's Haven is not an option for her. She's not leaving me many options." Tessa sighed, resigned.

"As much as I would like to, we can't just take in everyone who wants our help. Our funds are limited, and so is our bed capacity. We decided to dedicate ourselves to taking women from abusive situations and helping them get a clean start. There seemed to be the most need for that. There are other places for young women who only need a helping hand."

"I know that you and Miss Stephanie do the best that you can for all of us, and me and the rest of the women here truly do appreciate that, but that girl is no adult, and you'll be throwing her to the wolves if you take her to a shelter." Angela looked at Tessa, her tired eyes pleading with her. "Besides, I'm pretty sure she would be out of that shelter and on the streets again in less than an hour. I know her type, Miss Tessa. She's not as tough as she seems. Deep down, she is just screaming for someone to help her."

Tessa reached out and gently took Angela's hand. "I really wish that I could help her, but without her cooperation and honesty, there's not much else that I can do. It's in Jack's hands now."

Angela shook her head vehemently. "We have a chance to help that child right now. If we leave it to the cops and the system, she'll be a lost cause." She once again turned pleading eyes to Tessa. "Please, Miss Tessa, is there any way at all you could find it within you to let her stay? Even if it's only for a few more days, she may find it within herself to trust one of us. I think I'm getting close to gaining her confidence, but if she's forced back out on the street, I'm pretty sure she'll lose all trust in anyone again."

Tessa gave Angela a gentle squeeze. "She reminds you of yourself, doesn't she?"

Nodding, Angela looked over at the girl folding laundry. "I just wish that someone would have given me a chance when I was her age. She's still young enough to turn her life around. I'm afraid if we miss this opportunity, she'll end up making the same mistakes that I made out of desperation. She'll end up hooking up with the first guy that promises to take care of her, and chances are really good he's going to be another one of those abusive guys that take advantage of young women. It won't end well for her."

Sadly, Tessa knew Angela was probably right, but she also knew she couldn't help every lost soul out there. There were just too many of them, and as Steph told her all the time, if she didn't stick to the mission they had set for themselves, they would drown and be destroyed by the onslaught of people seeking their help.

"I feel as bad as you do, Angela, but I can't help her if she's not willing to tell me at least enough for me to know where she needs to go for the help she needs. If she's not willing to do at least that much to help herself, then there really is nothing more I can do for her."

Tessa drained her cup and picked up the two empty mugs, turning back to Angela. "If you can convince her to open up and tell you her age and her name before Jack finds a place to take her, then she can stay. Otherwise, as much as it pains me, there is really nothing more I can do for her." She set the cups carefully in the dishwasher and walked slowly down the hall towards her office, smiling sadly at her half-hearted attempt to buy Susan some more time. Even if she crawled to her office at a snail's pace, she doubted Angela would be able to gain the girl's trust before Jack took her away.

"How's it going?" she asked, as she walked into her office and watched Jack put down his phone.

"I think I might have a place for her," he answered, looking up. "It's not ideal, but it's all I could find on such short notice. I'll need to drive her a few counties over, but it's the best I could do.

Who knows, maybe the authorities there will have more luck finding out her identity?"

"What kind of place is it?" asked Stephanie, who had walked over from her office and was standing in the hall, looking at Jack dubiously.

He examined his phone uncomfortably and finally said, "It's a halfway house for both men and women." Holding up his hands in defense, he quickly added, "I know, I know that it's not ideal. I said that. But at least they can give her a room, so she won't be bunking with a bunch of people all crammed together into the same space."

"Jack! You know the kinds of people that end up in those houses!" Tessa countered. "They are ex-cons or recovering addicts mostly. Those men can be predators! We can't send a child to a place like that!"

Both Stephanie and Tessa looked at each other, aghast at the prospect of sending a young girl to a shelter like that. "She insists she's not a child, Tessa. She claims to be eighteen, remember? Until I can find out who she really is, I can't leave her here with you and the rest of these women. It wouldn't be safe. I have no choice."

Tessa glared at Jack. "We both know that she's lying about her age. She's not eighteen. I doubt she is even sixteen. There has to be something else that you can do?"

Jack gave both Tessa and Stephanie an apologetic look. He hated to disappoint them, especially Tessa, knowing what a good heart she had and how much she wanted to help others, but this time he really had no choice. When the two women had opened Hope's Haven in his district, he'd made an oath to himself that he would do everything to keep the women seeking refuge here safe, and his gut told him that allowing Susan to stay here wasn't safe.

Tessa was trying hard to wrack her brain for an argument to convince Jack, as well as herself and Stephanie, why it would be a good idea to keep Susan here, but even she was having a hard time.

Jack gathered his phone and his notepad, getting up to leave. "I'm sorry, ladies. I'd like to help her as much as both of you, but for now, this is the best solution I have."

"Miss Tessa, Sheriff Lewis, wait!" Angela came scurrying down the hall towards them with Susan firmly in tow behind her. Jack, Tessa, and Stephanie all turned, looking at Angela in alarm.

"What is it, Angela? Is something wrong?" Even as she posed the question to Angela, Tessa looked at Susan, wondering what the girl had been up to now and thinking that maybe Jack was right after all.

Angela pushed Susan forward. "All right now, honey. You tell them what you just told me." She gave the girl a little squeeze on the arm. "It's all right. They'll be able to help you."

Susan looked from Jack to Tessa and Stephanie, and back to Jack again, as if she were trying to decide. Finally, she cleared her throat and said in a quiet voice, "I'm pregnant."

CHAPTER 7

Speechless, Tessa stared at Susan for a full minute, trying to take in what the girl had just told them. Jack watched Tessa and waited for her reaction. She would know if the girl was telling the truth or if this was just another story that Susan had concocted.

Tessa's eyes were wide with shock, and she finally glanced at Jack with a light nod. *Okay, so it's true,* he thought. *The girl really is pregnant.* He cleared his throat and said, "Well then, I guess that changes things a little, doesn't it, Susan?"

Susan looked at him defiantly. "No, it doesn't. Not for me anyway. I told you I just need a little time to figure things out, and then I'll be on my way. That hasn't changed. Now you just know why I need some time."

Tessa looked at her kindly. "Do you know who the father is, Susan?"

"Of course I do!" Susan's eyes flashed angrily. "I may be down on my luck right now, but I'm not stupid enough to get pregnant and not know who the father of my child is!"

"I'm sorry, I didn't mean to insinuate that you were stupid. I just wanted to know if we should contact the father. Maybe he can help?" Tessa could see that Susan was sensitive to the subject, and she was trying to be as delicate as she could.

Susan sank down in her chair. "He already knows. He's trying to do the best that he can to help me out, but there are a few things we both need to take care of. When we have some stuff figured out, I'll find him, and we're both going to get away from here."

Angela gave the girl another gentle squeeze, urging her on.

"Okay, honey, tell them everything now. You need to come clean with how old you really are. No one expects you to do this alone, and Miss Tessa and Miss Stephanie can help guide you into the right hands," Angela said.

Susan looked at her hands, clasping them together and hunching her shoulders. "Does it really matter? I'm pregnant. What difference does it make how old I am?" she asked.

"It makes a lot of difference. It helps us know where to take you and who can best help you, Susan. It really is time for you to tell us everything," Jack said sternly.

Tessa walked around her desk and squatted down next to the girl, who was crouching miserably in her chair.

"It's going to be okay, Susan, I promise. I already know you aren't eighteen. I can imagine how scary this must all be for you. We all want to help both you and the baby you're carrying. You don't have to do this all on your own," Tessa reassured her.

Tessa could see tears welling up in the girl's eyes, and she prayed she had finally been able to break through the tough exterior and win the girl's trust.

"I'm fifteen, okay? I'll be sixteen in a few months, but I may as well be eighteen because I've been out on my own for over a year. It doesn't make any difference. I take care of myself," Susan admitted.

Now Tessa felt a lump in her own throat. She knew this time the girl was telling the truth, and her heart broke for her. No child deserved to be tossed out on the street at fourteen years old.

"Everything is going to be okay now, Susan. I'm proud of you. It must have been terrifying for you to be on your own so young. It's not easy for a grown woman to make it out in the world by herself. Now, if you just tell us your real name, we can figure out the best way we can help you," Tessa said, gently stroking Susan's arm.

But Susan pulled her arm back as if it had been burned.

"I already told you my name. It's Susan Smith," she said heatedly.

Tessa let out an exasperated breath. Apparently, the girl still wasn't ready to come clean with everything. Tessa wondered why and what she was still hiding.

"Do you have any idea how far along you are in the pregnancy?" Stephanie spoke up, hoping that if they could get Susan thinking about the child, they might find something out that way. Besides, right now it didn't really matter what Susan's real name was. The priority was to look after the well-being of the fifteen-year-old and her unborn baby.

Susan shook her head, glancing timidly over at Jack. "Uh no, not really. I've never been really regular if you know what I mean. Sort of, off and on anyway, so I thought nothing of it until I felt sick. That's when Eth... uh, my boyfriend, thought we had better buy a pregnancy test, just to see for sure."

Angela tsked from the doorway. "That's why children shouldn't be on their own. Way too young to be acting like adults and making grown-up decisions." Tessa gave her a warning look, saying, "Be that as it may, what's done is done, and now we need to figure out how to go forward." She stood up and leaned on her desk.

"How long ago did you take the test?" she was already scrolling through her contacts to find the number of the gynecologist she worked with for the women from the shelter.

"About two months ago." Angela gasped again. "Good lord child! And I suppose you haven't had any prenatal care since then?"

"What do you mean? Are you asking if I've been to a doctor?" Susan looked up at Angela confused. "If that's what you're asking, of course not. I can barely feed myself. I sure as heck don't have money to go to a doctor."

Tessa looked at Jack and noticed him staring at her. She knew he was thinking the same as her. How was Susan planning to feed a baby when she clearly couldn't even feed herself? Looking back at Susan, she said, "Go with Angela, Susan. I'm going to make some calls and see if I can get you an appointment at a local women's clinic that we work with. We need to find out how far along you are and make sure the baby is healthy. I'm sure they'll want to do a complete work-up on you, and I want to get you in to see them as soon as we can."

Tessa was already heading behind her desk as she spoke, ready to call the clinic and beg for an appointment if necessary.

Stephanie groaned inwardly at the thought of how expensive the work-up would be, already wondering how they were going to pay for it.

"Don't have Susan do any heavy lifting for now, Angela, at least until we know everything is all right with the baby," Stephanie cautioned, heading to her office to crunch some more numbers and come up with some money.

"Of course, I won't, Miss Stephanie." Angela looked at her, almost insulted. "This isn't my first time dealing with pregnancies, after all." Angela took Susan's arm, guiding her out of the office and back to her room. Jack and the women could hear her talking reassuringly to the girl as they walked.

"Well, that certainly does change things quite a bit," Jack finally spoke out from the corner of the small office where he had been standing, quietly taking it all in.

"Yes, it does." Tessa swept back the hair sticking to her forehead. "That certainly wasn't what I was expecting." She sunk down into her chair and was just about to make a call when Stephanie walked back in, gasping, "Wow, Tess, I sure never saw that one coming! I really wish you could have warned us!"

Tessa looked at her friend tiredly. "I've told you a million times, Steph, I don't read minds. If I could, believe me, we sure could save ourselves a lot of trouble."

"I know, I know, Tess. I was just teasing. It only seems like you sometimes can. So, you believe that she really is pregnant? Could you tell if she was telling us the truth?"

"Yes, unfortunately for her, she really is telling us the truth about her age and about her being pregnant. At least she really believes she's pregnant. I'm sure the clinic will be able to give us a definitive answer. Most of what she told us this time was the truth, for once."

"So what part of what she said wasn't true?" Stephanie looked at her friend curiously.

"She still isn't coming clean about her real name," Jack answered Tessa. "And that still makes my job that much harder. It's even more important for me to find her parents now."

Stephanie nodded. "Yeah, if she's a runaway, I'm sure the parents will want to know, and hopefully they'll be able to help with their grandchild."

"You would hope so anyway," Tessa remarked softly, thinking back to Hope's mother. Her family had wanted nothing to do with her or her unborn child. She could only hope things would be different for Susan.

"Well, like you said, Tess, the first step is getting her to a gynecologist to check her out and see how far along she is. Being pregnant and out on the streets really isn't an ideal situation. Hopefully, she doesn't have any hidden diseases to contend with as well," Stephanie continued.

Tessa frowned. "You think she might have been working the streets, don't you?"

Stephanie shrugged. "Well, it would make sense, wouldn't it? A young girl like her doesn't have all that many options to make money out there. There's a good chance that the boyfriend she's talking about could also be her pimp," she said.

"It's definitely an avenue I'll need to check into," Jack agreed. "Meanwhile, at least we have an age now. I'll recheck and see if there are any reports on missing girls around her age and description. I think I'll also check the juvenile records to see if there's anything in there matching her description. Maybe she already got herself in trouble with them."

Tessa started dialing the clinic number. "It looks like we all have our work cut out for us then. Hopefully, Angela can keep her contained and out of trouble until I can get her seen by the clinic. I just pray they can take her in soon."

Stephanie nodded in agreement. "Something tells me a girl like her will not sit around too long and wait for us. She's more than likely just waiting for that boyfriend of hers to show up again, and she'll scoot right back out of here."

A few minutes later, Jack pulled out of the driveway. The two men sitting in the car down the street reflexively shrunk down in their seats to stay undetected.

As soon as Jack's car was out of sight, Gabe glanced at the clock on the dash. "He sure was in there for a long time. Hopefully, that little girl of yours didn't sing like a canary."

"She didn't," Ethan said conclusively. "If she had, he would have taken her with him, and she's still in there, isn't she?"

"Well, I'm getting tired of waiting for her. It's been a long time since we set her loose in there, and we still haven't heard a peep from her. I'm wondering if she forgot what she's there for. For all we know, she's setting up a cozy little nest for herself."

"She'll come through, just quit worrying." Ethan tried to sound convincing, but he was worrying about that himself. Of course, neither Gabe nor Snake knew the girl was pregnant or about their plans to run away. Ethan was pretty certain that she'd been sincere when she told him that she loved him, but he had read that pregnant girls could do funny things sometimes, and that nesting comment had hit a bit too close to home.

What if she decides she would rather cooperate with the cops and assure herself a comfortable little nest to have her baby instead of following our plan? He was feeling way less confident about this whole situation than he was willing to admit to Gabe.

The more he thought about it, the more Ethan felt the familiar anger boiling up in his gut. *She had better stick to their plan. That was his kid too, and he had plenty of plans for both the kid and the girl. Snake wasn't the only one who knew how to make money off of people.* He cracked his knuckles violently. *If she did betray him, both she and that social worker would have more than just Snake to worry about!*

Later that evening, as Tessa rushed into her apartment, her arms were full of files, her purse, and the deli sandwich she had stopped for. Her cell was ringing incessantly, and she was struggling to fish it out of her purse without dropping everything on the floor.

"Hello," her voice was breathless as she balanced the phone against her shoulder and her ear, hurrying to the tiny kitchen to set her load down on the counter.

"Hey, there you are." Carter's cheerful voice rang out from the other end. "I've been trying to reach you all day. Don't you answer your texts anymore? I was just about to alert the National Guard to come and check on you."

"Nice thought, but they don't check on missing persons, Carter, you know that." She put the kettle on for tea and walked over to her sofa to wait for the water to boil.

"I'm sorry I didn't answer your text, really I am. I've been swamped all day. I just walked in the door, and I was going to call you back right now, honestly."

Carter chuckled. "Yeah, of course you were, Tess. But really, how did it go today? I was pretty worried about you. How did it go with that Susan girl? Did you find anything out about her?"

Tessa grimaced. "Yeah, sorry, I guess I should have called you sooner. I hoped maybe Steph had filled you in on some of the details. I've been super busy with setting the girl up in a clinic all day, and then I had a counseling session with two of the women at the shelter. Remember, just because we now have a runaway doesn't mean I can just ignore the women that are already there."

"Steph did fill me in on some of the details, or I really would have called the National Guard," Carter admitted. "She said that you were right, the kid really is only fifteen, and she's pregnant to boot."

"That's right." Tessa shoved off her shoes, pulling her feet up under her. "Just yet another troubled young teen who needs our help. There are so many of them around nowadays. It's so sad, really."

"And you always seem to find them, Tess. So, tell me, did you get her checked out at the clinic?"

"I just dropped her off. The gynecologist who we usually work with at the clinic couldn't see her any earlier and wanted to put her off a few days, but I begged, so she agreed to let me bring her in tonight. She'll do a work-up and run some tests. She said she may as well stay in the bed at the clinic tonight. She was a little concerned when she heard how young Susan was."

Carter sighed audibly. "And how much do you think that it's going to cost the shelter, Tess? Somehow, I don't think that will be a free stay, and like I said, you're running low on funds."

"You're sounding like Steph. The doctor assured me we can work out the cost later." Tessa got up to quiet the tea kettle that was whistling on the stove. "Don't worry so much, Carter. We always find a way. Right now, the girl needs help, and we need to know what we're dealing with. They've always been reasonable with us, and Steph and I were both worried that if we didn't get her in tonight, she would change her mind and run off on us."

"Yeah, I know you've always found a way to make things work, but if you don't start cutting costs or bringing funds in from somewhere, you're going to run out of money, Tess. You both have to at least try to be more reasonable with your resources."

"I thought you applied for that grant you were telling us about. Maybe that will come through. And then there is the state and the county. They agreed to help offset the costs of some of the women's care if we applied for help on their behalf. That should help pay some bills as well."

Carter grumbled into the phone. "Your women need to have a real name and confirmed identity to apply for that reimbursement, Tess. We've already been over this countless times. You can't keep taking in women who don't give you their exact information and then expect to cover their costs through a government agency."

Tessa settled back into her chair, setting her tea mug next to her and taking a hefty bite out of her sandwich. She was tired, hungry, and not in the mood for the same old chastising that she always seemed to get from Carter whenever they discussed money.

"I really do appreciate all the help you give Steph and me with the finances, Carter. Heaven knows that neither one of us knows much about how to balance the accounts, but we are a non-profit, and we are here to help people. Our priority has to be the women, not the money that we do or do not have."

Tessa could hear ice clinking over the phone, and she could imagine how Carter was probably leaning back in his expensive leather chair, high up in his luxury office overlooking the city, and taking a sip of his very expensive Jack Daniels on ice. He probably had his freshly polished shoes resting on his immaculately organized desk as he frowned into the phone, clearly exasperated with her.

The mental picture of him caused her to smile. How different he was now compared to the unkempt, carefree boy that she had grown up with.

"I understand that, Tess, and trust me, no one admires the work that you do more than I do, but the bills need to be paid if you want to keep the lights on and continue helping them."

"I do understand that, and you really are doing such a wonderful job of helping us keep it all together, Carter. I truly thank God every day for you and your help." She finished the last of her sandwich as she looked tiredly over at the files she had brought home.

"I'd love to chat some more, Carter, but I have about five applicants hoping we can take them in, and I need to look over their files tonight and figure out if they're a fit for us, or else find them somewhere else to go."

"Okay, Tess, I know you're busy saving the world, and I'll let you get back to it. Just please remember that I'm more than just your lawyer and stand-in accountant. I'm your friend, and I care about you….a lot. I'm worried that you're running yourself ragged even more than I'm worried about your finances."

Carter hesitated for a minute, and then continued, "You know, you wouldn't need to run yourself so ragged, Tessa. You could be at the penthouse right now, relaxing in the jacuzzi, instead of in a rundown apartment worrying about paying the rent. I'm not saying you need to give up Hope's Haven or your mission. I'm just saying that life with me could make things so much easier for you personally. Besides that, I can't think of a better way to end my day than coming home to you every day, Tess. I really believe we could be happy together."

Tessa sighed and rubbed her eyes, exhausted. "I know, Carter, and I care for you a great deal too. I just don't know if I'm ready for a relationship with anyone right now. Besides, I like my little apartment," she said, looking around. "Can we please not talk about this anymore for the time being?"

"Sorry, Tess. I know it's been a long day for you, and I don't want to pressure you. But just remember, whenever you are ready, I'll be here for you." She could hear his feet come off his desk and hit the ground through the speaker. "Save the world then, Tess, but don't forget, even you need to get some rest at one point." Carter hung up the phone, and she leaned her head back against the chair, emotionally drained as well as physically exhausted.

As annoying as he could sometimes be, she really did care for Carter. He had been a big part of her life for as long as she could remember. He and Stephanie had been the first friends she had ever had. Stephanie's dad had called them the three musketeers, and they had always done everything together, even confiding all of their secrets to one another. She also knew that, as close as he and Steph were, Carter had always had a special feeling for her. He had never made a secret of it to either her or to Stephanie, and as they got older, he had often gone to Stephanie for advice on how to win her over.

To Carter's credit, when Luke Graves had joined their little group and they had become a foursome in their junior year of high school, Carter had graciously stepped back and not interfered with Luke and her budding relationship. But she now suspected that his feelings for her never had waned.

Closing her eyes, Tessa allowed her mind to wander back to those carefree times when the four of them were so young, happy, and clueless of the tragedy that was to come.

"Eeeh!" Tessa squealed loudly. "Luke, stop that! You're getting me all wet!" But even as she scolded him, Tessa scooped up a big fistful of water and doused Luke until his t-shirt was soaked.

"You're going to regret that!" laughed Luke, scooping her up and dangling her over the water.

"You wouldn't dare Luke Graves!" Tessa shrieked, flailing her legs wildly. "If you get my hair wet, I swear I won't go to dinner with you all tonight! Steph and I worked all morning braiding it just right!"

"She's right. You put her down right Luke, and there had better not be a splash of water on that hair of hers! I did not spend the entire morning working

on her just to do it all again!" Stephanie waved her fist at him, but she couldn't stop herself from laughing at the sight of Tessa dangling helplessly in Luke's arms.

"Fine." Luke set Tessa gently down in the softly flowing river they had been walking in. "But I'll never understand why the two of you would spend an entire morning doing hair that you don't even need done until tomorrow."

"Because we only have today, Luke. I already told you that. It was dinner tonight with the four of us and being careful all day, or hours doing hair tonight and missing dinner. It needs to be done for the photoshoot by tomorrow at seven am, and Stephanie has an early morning class."

Tessa held onto Luke's broad shoulder for balance as she spoke and then gave him a quick kiss on the nose. "Besides, how often to you get a chance to go to dinner with an Indian Princess?"

"Oh brother," Carter shook his head in mock disgust. "Don't let that Princess thing go to your head, Tess. It's only a photoshoot. After tomorrow, you lose your crown and you're just plain old Tessa again."

"Hmmm, I kind of like the princess title thing, Carter. Can't you just arrange that too?" Tessa laughingly looked over at her friend.

"No Tessa, I can't arrange that too. You may do a photoshoot with a bunch of kids at the hospital tomorrow, some of whom might even believe that you are truly Pocahontas, but then it's over. No more Princess for you after that.

He wagged his finger at her, "And if I had known how much that title would go to your head, I would have never organized it!"

In spite of his words, Carter was laughing at Tessa along with the others. "For today, let's just enjoy the rare moment that we all have together again. It seems like the four of us haven't been creek walking together in forever," he said.

"It is really nice to have the group together again," Stephanie agreed. "But I have to admit, with that beautiful dark hair of yours and those stunning green eyes, all those kids really will think you're a real princess." Then she turned to Carter. "It was nice of you to arrange this photoshoot for those kids, Carter. They all have to go through so much pain every day, it will be really nice for them to have some fun for once. The nurse I talked to today said the kids are so excited

to have their pictures taken by a real live professional photographer, and of course with an actual princess."

She looked at Carter in admiration. "You always seem to know just the right people to make things happen."

"Ummm, she's a fake Princess, Steph, so let's not build up her ego any more than it already is," Carter joked. Then he said seriously, "I'm honestly just glad those kids can have some fun, even if it is just for a day. They have enough to worry about going through their cancer treatments."

They all smiled at him in agreement and Stephanie said, "You know, in spite of how much you try to hide your true self behind that calculating, businesslike veneer of yours, deep down you really are just a softy with a bleeding heart."

Carter shook his head in denial and looked over at Luke for help.

Luke was busy gazing down at Tessa, as he put his arms firmly around her waist and whispered in her ear, "Don't listen to him, Tess. You'll always be a real princess as far as I'm concerned." Then he grinned. "Just don't go running off into the sunset with that photographer dude. He's bound to fall for you if you look half as attractive tomorrow as you do right now in that wet t-shirt!"

His eyes danced mischievously as he glanced down at Tessa, who was still clinging to his arm.

Stephanie threw Tessa an amused look. "Maybe we should keep walking so the two of you can at least cool your feet a little. I swear you are going to start a forest fire the way you are looking at each other."

"Sorry." Tessa moved slightly away from Luke and started walking, still holding on to his hand. "It just seems like so long since we've had any time together. With Luke and I in different schools right now, we don't have a lot of time to see each other anymore."

"You could always transfer," Luke growled softly into her ear. "I miss you and I don't want to spend another three years apart."

"Oh Luke, I miss you so much too, but we agreed it was best to go to our separate schools and follow our own career paths. In the end, it will be worth it. Besides"—she glanced down at the glittering ring on her finger—"we have the rest of our lives to spend together."

As Stephanie and Carter looked discreetly away, Luke leaned down, taking Tessa's lips with his own in a passionate kiss. Tessa clung to him desperately, her heart was suddenly pounding in fear that if she let him go, she would lose him forever.

The shrill ringing of her phone broke into her uneasy slumber, waking her with a jolt. She looked down at the phone that had fallen from her hands, almost expecting to see Luke's name on the caller ID.

CHAPTER 8

"She's gone again," Stephanie's panicked voice came through the phone as Tessa shook her head, trying to clear away the last remnants of her dream. It had seemed so real, and she was taking a minute to realize what Stephanie was talking about.

"Wait, what? Who's gone?" Tessa stammered into the phone, comprehension slowly coming back to her muddled mind.

"Susan. She's gone. The clinic just called. The nurse went to check on her, and she's disappeared, clothes and all." Stephanie's voice was a mixture of confusion and anger.

"Why did they call you and not me?" Tessa looked down at her phone, realizing that she had missed numerous calls. She must have fallen into a really deep sleep. "Oh, wow, sorry. It looks like I missed their call. I guess I fell asleep pretty deep."

Never mind that, it doesn't matter. You deserve to sleep sometimes too. The real issue is what do we do now? After everything you've tried to do to help her, she just takes off! Should we try to find her? Tessa thought for a minute. "I guess she's technically not breaking any laws, and we can't force her to stay anywhere that she doesn't want to, but I will call Jack and see what he says."

"Okay, I guess," Stephanie let out an exasperated breath. "I'm fairly sure the clinic is going to charge us for the night. Carter is going to have a fit."

Tessa cringed, knowing Stephanie was right. "Well, there's nothing to be done about that now. I'll call the clinic in the morning and try to negotiate something." She looked at the time. "For now, I'll see how Jack thinks we should handle it, if he even answers my call anymore. It is pretty late after all."

Stephanie chuckled knowingly. "Oh, I'm fairly sure when he sees it's you, he'll answer. Just keep me posted and call me if there is anything he wants us to do."

As she hung up the phone, Tessa could hear Stephanie muttering, "Ungrateful kid," to herself. *She's not wrong,* Tessa thought sourly. A lot of the women they took in seemed to think the shelter had endless money just because it was a nonprofit and didn't charge them anything. She and Stephanie were constantly juggling and struggling with finances to help these women. It definitely stung when someone just disappeared and left them hanging with the bill.

She dialed Jack's number and was actually a little surprised when he picked up on the third ring. "Hey Tessa, what's up? Is everything okay?" His voice sounded more awake than it should have at this hour.

"Hi Jack, I'm sorry to bother you at this hour. I wasn't sure if you would still be up. Don't you ever sleep?" She could hear him chuckle on the other end.

"I could say the same to you. You're clearly still awake as well. So what's up?"

"Stephanie just got a call from the clinic we took Susan to. She's gone. Apparently, she left without saying anything to anyone. Her clothes are all gone, and she's nowhere to be found."

There was a silent pause at the other end, and she could picture how Jack's brows were probably furrowed as he was thinking.

She had come to know him well over the years, and it was her habit to study people and their mannerisms.

After a few seconds, he said, "They have cameras at the hospital. I could ask them if they'll let me look in the morning. I can see if someone came and picked her up, or if she left by herself. Something tells me that she didn't just leave the hospital on her own, but we should be able to see that with the cameras."

Tessa hadn't thought of that. Susan gave off such a tough and independent vibe; she hadn't even considered the possibility that someone else might tell her what to do.

"Do you think she's okay?" Tessa was worrying. "Maybe I should drive around the area and look for her? Maybe the boyfriend she was talking about found her. If Stephanie's hunch is right, and he's her pimp, then she and the baby could be in trouble."

"Relax, Tessa. If he did come and get her, she had to have called him. That's the only way he would know where she is. I'll look at the cameras in the morning, and we'll see what we can find out. For tonight, there's nothing you can do, and you had better get some sleep." Jack was silent for a minute, and then he gently added, "I'm just sorry that she didn't appreciate all the help you already gave her. I know how much you put into helping every one of these women, and I feel bad when they don't appreciate it."

Tessa could hear the heartfelt compassion in his voice, and it was nice to know that the hardened detective was human and had emotions. He rarely showed a softer side, but lately, he seemed to show her more and more kindness, and she suspected that some of that might be more than just friendly concern. It was hard for others to hide their true feelings from her, and she was certain that lately there was more going on in his head than he was telling her.

She knew she shouldn't be doing anything to lead him on. Like she had told Carter, she wasn't ready for a relationship right now. But it did feel good to have him show her the attention and compassion that she sometimes craved. And she couldn't deny that she felt an attraction to the rugged, but good-looking cop.

Sometimes, Tessa wished Carter would be a little less hard on her about the finances and show her a little more empathy and compassion. Of course, she knew he was right, and he was just looking out for her best interests. But sometimes it felt good to just be appreciated.

"Yes, it's tough when someone just takes off, that's for sure," she admitted. "I always worry about them until I know for sure that they're somewhere safe. And in Susan's case, she's so young and vulnerable, I'm even more worried."

"We may still find her, Tessa, so try not to worry too much. You should really get some sleep now. It looks like you're going to have another full day ahead of you tomorrow."

After they had said their goodnights and hung up, Tessa stood up, stretching deeply to work out the kinks in her body. She'd been exhausted when she got home, but now, the news of Susan's disappearance and her conversation with Jack had her wound up again.

She walked back into the kitchen to make some fresh tea and look at the files she had brought home. She looked them all over and quickly discarded all but one. She decided she would send this woman's profile to Jack tomorrow, for a proper vetting. As for the rest of the women, she would need to find alternate accommodations for them.

She, Stephanie, and Jack had agreed a few years ago, after they had some trouble, that anyone they wanted to admit into Hope's Haven would need to be run through a proper check with the local police department first. That way, they could ensure the safety of the women already living there and make sure no disgruntled husband or boyfriend was trying to sneak in a decoy and cause harm to anyone.

In return for the favor of vetting their potential residents, Tessa often helped Jack by listening in on his interrogations and letting him know if his suspects were lying or telling him the truth. The system was working well for everyone involved. The residents of Hope's Haven were safe, and she had become a somewhat regular fixture at the precinct. Some of the other cops had also discovered her hidden talent and asked for her help as well.

Even though Stephanie and Carter had both voiced their concern that the local cops were taking advantage of her, Tessa welcomed any chance she got to go into the station and look around. She secretly hoped that by staying close to where the action was, she might run into the men who had murdered her husband and child and attacked her, leaving her for dead as well.

As much as the detectives in Atlanta assured her they were still working on her case and hadn't stopped looking for suspects and motives, she suspected that after five years of dead ends, they had moved on to newer and more pressing cases, and she feared they had filed her case away.

Early in their friendship, Tessa had shared all the details that she knew about her case with Jack. He had promised he would keep his eyes open for anyone who could somehow be connected to the crime. She hoped that someday, someone would walk into his precinct with the knowledge that would finally give her the answers she so desperately craved.

The local detectives who knew about her case also looked into any connection that their suspects might have to Atlanta. Carter thought that the chances of finding anyone connected to the murders in Atlanta walking into a police station in Tennessee would be incredibly slim, and he had warned her she shouldn't get her hopes up too much.

Even though so far Carter was right, every time she walked into the station to help with an interrogation, she couldn't help hoping that she would finally hear something that would bring her closer to finding out who murdered her family.

Now, sipping the last of her lukewarm tea, she thought back on her dream from earlier that night. The memory of Luke's kisses was still fresh on her mind and left her tingling, but she realized it was one of the first times since the murder that she had dreamed about her husband without her daughter Hope being in her dream as well. The thought that she had not dreamt about her child tonight left her feeling discomfited.

Stephanie and Carter always advised her that it was time for her to move on with her life and that it wasn't healthy to live in the past. However, Tessa was terrified that moving on would sully the memories of her beloved little girl. Hope had been the light of her life, and Tessa wanted to spend every moment that remained of her own life keeping her memory fresh and vivid. She felt that as long as she could do that, Hope would somehow still go on living.

Her greatest fear was waking up one morning and not remembering the sound of her little girl's joyful laugh. Remembering her dream, she frowned, frightened that her fear was coming true. Was this the beginning of forgetting her precious daughter? Why was she dreaming of Luke and their relationship instead of Hope? So far, any thoughts or dreams of Luke had always been linked with Hope. She sometimes dreamed or thought of Hope without dreaming of Luke, but Hope was always there.

In her mind, Tessa replayed the passionate kiss that Luke had given her in her dream. *Had Luke ever kissed her that passionately in real life?* No, Luke had been the jokester of the group. He had always been happy and jovial, tickling her and Hope until they cried for mercy. Luke had been the one to keep things light when Carter took things too seriously. He had also been the only one who had ever made Carter laugh with abandon.

It had been Luke's cheery demeanor that had overridden any jealousy Carter may have felt after she and Luke had become a couple. His charm and humor had always won everyone over. It was almost impossible to not like Luke.

She missed his smile, his humor, and mostly the comfort he had provided her. Luke had been funny and loving, but never passionate. So, why was she dreaming about passionate kisses from him now?

Tessa looked out of the half-open curtains as the streetlight just outside of her window thoughtfully. After Luke's murder, the thought of finding romance again never crossed her mind. He had been her everything, her forever. When they had pledged their lives to one another, Tessa had never even considered that his death would negate that pledge.

But lately, she had wondered what it would be like to take another man into her life. She had started to consider the offer Carter was extending and even wondered what it would be like to spend time with Jack on less professional terms. As she thought about that kiss, she wondered if Luke was trying to tell her something. Was he releasing her, telling her it was okay to move on and find another man in her life? Was it even possible for her to find love again?

Her body shivered involuntarily at the thought of the kiss. Could she dare hope to find the passion that had been missing with Luke, or was that just something that she read about when she got the rare chance to delve into one of the cheesy romance novels that Steph was constantly handing down to her? Did she even want that kind of love?

Carter loved her, she knew that, and he had made it abundantly clear he wanted to spend his life with her. She cared for him as well, and she was certain that life with Carter would bring her security and maybe even happiness, but she wondered if it would give her passion.

Luke had been passionate about his job, almost to a fault, and the undercover work he had been involved in made her wonder if that had been the cause of the attacks. He had shared none of the details with her, choosing instead to be the happy-go-lucky husband

and father he had always been, but she had sometimes suspected that he had hidden many of his feelings from her.

Her mind then wandered back to Jack Lewis, and she tried to imagine what it would be like to kiss him. On the outside, he didn't seem to be any more passionate than Luke or Carter. In fact, with his drive and dedication to his job, he reminded her of both Luke and Carter. But unlike Luke, she could sometimes see a hidden sadness and compassion in his dark, steely eyes that she had never seen in either Luke or Carter.

Tonight, his voice had been soft and compassionate. Tessa hugged herself, pretending it was Jack's arms around her. Would he be soft and tender, or would his embrace and kisses be strong and demanding? Tessa wasn't sure if she would mind either way.

Abruptly, Tessa shook herself and stood up, angry with herself. She shouldn't be thinking about things like this. She was a widow, and these daydreams about other men felt like a betrayal to her dead husband. She had an important job to do, helping other victims, and she didn't have the time or the energy to waste fantasizing about things like this.

Even so, as she got ready for bed and pulled the soft comforter around herself, the faces of Carter and Jack danced in front of her eyes. Maybe Stephanie was right. She had gone way too long without some kind of male affection.

Outside, it was raining, and Susan sat huddled in the car, staring at the back of Ethan and Gabe's heads. The men had been arguing fiercely with one another, but now they were quiet, each stewing in their own heads, clearly furious with her and each other.

"I knew you would screw this up!" Gabe barked at her harshly before he turned his anger back on Ethan. "What were you thinking walking into that hospital? They have cameras in there, stupid, and I'm pretty sure they'll get a make on you now."

Ethan sat fuming silently, trying to contain his own growing anger. Gabe was right. He had messed up big time rushing into the hospital to get the girl after she had called him. He should have told her to sit tight and just stick to her story until she found what they were looking for. Instead, he had panicked like an inexperienced kid and charged in without thinking it through.

"Why did they take you to a hospital, anyway?" Gabe continued driving but glared at her through his rearview mirror. "You will not find that stash of money in the hospital now, are you? Did you tell them you were sick or something? Snake is going to skin you alive for this."

Ethan turned in his seat, giving her a warning glare. She knew he wanted to keep her pregnancy a secret. He had told her that if Snake found out, he would see that she got rid of the baby, and she was certain Gabe would run straight to tell Snake if he found out.

"I wasn't feeling well, so they took me to be checked out. They were just being nice," she whined pitifully.

"If they were being so nice, you could have just played along and gone back to the shelter tomorrow. Why did you call me to come and get you?" Ethan lashed out at her. "Now you've gone and messed up the entire plan."

Susan wanted to cry, but she did her best to hold it in. She hadn't told Ethan that she'd confessed to Tessa about the baby, knowing he would be furious. She told him she had been feeling sick, and that's why they had taken her to the clinic to get checked out.

Ever since she had found out that she was pregnant, she had been on an emotional roller coaster and in a panic. The kindness that Tessa and Angela had shown her had left her feeling drained and wishing she had a family to go to. She was thinking she had made a mistake trusting Ethan.

"I panicked, okay!" she lashed back at him. "It happens to everyone. I couldn't find any money, or any safety boxes or anything else anywhere in the house, and I just didn't know what to do anymore. I don't think that woman has any money. I felt sick, and when I told them, they insisted I go to the clinic. I got scared when they started asking me all kinds of questions, and I just wanted to talk to you. Is that so horrible?"

When they had dropped her off in front of the shelter, Ethan had been afraid she wouldn't be able to manage too well without him. She was very gullible and easily influenced by whoever was around her. He'd been worried about setting her loose on her own, where he couldn't keep an eye on her. She'd been even more clingy and dependent on him since they had found out she was pregnant, and it was becoming stifling and annoying.

"There is money there, you're just too stupid to find it," Gabe spat out, clutching at the wheel in his aggravation. It was still raining, and the lights of the oncoming cars were glaring through his windshield, making him even more irritable. He should be in a nice warm bed with a cold beer, watching TV, not carting two useless kids around town.

"I'm not so sure there's any money," the girl sniffled. "I looked everywhere and even talked to the other women. No one seems to know or talk about any money. Maybe Snake is wrong? Maybe he got the wrong information, and we're all just wasting our time?"

Ethan had been secretly worried about that possibility from the start. Snake had a way of making people confess to things and make up stories just to get him off their backs, but his entire plan hinged on getting at least some money from that social worker, and right now, it was not looking good.

"Are you trying to tell us that Snake made a mistake?" he sneered angrily, turning around and glaring at her again. He had to convince her to go back to that shelter and find some money, any money. This was his chance to break away from Snake, and he wasn't about to lose it. If he failed to get away and was forced to go back with no money, he knew he would have a heavy price to pay for his failure. Even if Snake went easy on the girl, Ethan knew he wouldn't go easy on him or Gabe, for that matter.

He still hadn't figured out what their connection was or why Snake treated this girl differently than the others he kept around, but he had noticed that lately Snake's patience with her had seemed to run out. Ethan had used the opportunity and dove in to take advantage of it. She had been more than eager to accept his affection, and now that he was so close to making his escape, he wasn't about to let her mess things up, especially knowing the consequences for him if Snake ever found out about her pregnancy.

"Snake never makes mistakes. If he says there's money there, then there's money there," Ethan spat out. He turned to watch Gabe's face as he spoke, hoping the older man believed that his loyalty to their boss was as strong as ever.

"That's right, little girl," Gabe agreed vehemently. "You'd better figure out a way to get back there and find some money. That place doesn't run itself on nothing, you know. That dame has to be paying her bills with something, and you'd better find it fast."

"She doesn't even live there!" Susan wailed desperately. "Maybe she has a great big house somewhere else, and that's where all of her money is stashed. She probably wouldn't keep it where just anyone from the shelter could find it."

Ethan hated how whiny she sounded, but he had to agree she could be right. He and Gabe already knew that the woman lived in a tiny garage apartment and not a great big house, but that didn't mean she couldn't still have stashed her money in there.

"We probably should check that apartment," he said to Gabe, glancing at the older man again. "Maybe she does have something valuable in there."

Gabe stared out the window. He didn't like the thought of breaking into anyone's place, especially right now. He'd been happy enough to send the girl in to do the stealing, staying in the background for this one. He'd just gotten released from serving a prison stint for stealing, and he wasn't keen on getting caught and sent back in. Apartments could have cameras in them, and his face was well known to the cops.

"Maybe we should check it out, but you're going in there alone this time. I don't want my mug on any cameras if there are any around. I've done my time, and I'm not ready to go back because of a hunch from a kid," he stated.

Ethan smiled. That actually suited him just fine. If there was any money in there, no one but him would know how much, and he could help himself to most of it. Then he would wait and see what the girl could find at the shelter, grab her, and they could make their getaway. He felt a prick of excitement in his belly. He only needed to play along with Gabe for a few more days, and he would be home free.

Ethan turned around and threw the girl in the back a stern look. "You're going back into the hospital."

"I can't," she wailed. "What am I supposed to say? They're going to ask where I went and why I left!"

"You can just say that you left to go for a walk. Those social workers will be thrilled that you're back and won't ask too many questions."

"And this time you'd better not mess up," warned Gabe, slamming on his brakes and pulling into an all-night market he had spotted. "I need to take a leak and get some beer. I'm done driving two whiny kids all around town. After we drop you off, it's time to relax."

After Gabe got out and headed into the store, Ethan turned around, looking at the girl slumped in the back seat angrily. "You're messing things up royally. What were you thinking, calling me and begging me to come get you!?"

She looked at him in shock. "I was scared, Ethan. That cop was going to take me to a different shelter, so I had to buy myself some time to look around. I had to tell them I was pregnant, and that's why they sent me to the clinic. I thought it would only be a few hours, but they kept me for the night, and then they started asking me all these questions about the baby and the father and how old I was. I didn't know what to tell them, and I didn't want to mess it up, so I wanted to talk to you. You said we were in this together, but I'm the one who's taking all the heat!"

Ethan was angry that she had told them about the baby, and he glared at her. This could complicate things even more.

"You should have never told them you were pregnant, that was your first mistake," he spat out. "But now that you did, you may as well play it up big. Make it seem like you're sick and need to stay in bed. Then, when the others leave you alone, you can look around and find us some money." He narrowed his eyes, looking at her menacingly.

"Snake and Gabe have been on my case about you already, and if you don't come through quick, I'm not planning on sticking around for the consequences. I'll be outta here without you, understand? And if you even try to rat me out to anyone, you're going to wish that you only had Snake to worry about."

He turned back around in his seat and glanced at the store casually. "Actually, a beer does sound pretty good right about now." He exited the car but then leaned back in, grabbing her by the shoulders.

"Just remember, you're mine now and you're carrying my kid. So, you do what I tell you to do. Find whatever money you can get your hands on; I don't care whose it is. In two days, you need to get back to that hospital. I'll be there to pick you up, and we'll be away from Snake for good."

After he let her go and slammed the door shut, she watched him saunter casually into the store. She was trembling and thinking she could really use a beer herself, but she was too scared of both the men to go in and ask.

If this was how Ethan planned to treat her, then she might have to make some plans on her own. She didn't intend to trade in one bully for another. She started rummaging around the front seat, hoping she could at least find a smoke, when she noticed Gabe's phone lying in the console.

Glancing around nervously, she quickly picked it up and dialed. "Hello, hello? Is anyone there?" said a voice on the other end. She felt a small sob of relief escaping her lips as she heard the familiar voice. "It's me!" she cried, her voice cracking with emotion as she spoke.

The voice on the other end gasped. "Oh my God, Patty! Is that you? Where are you?!"

CHAPTER 9

"What do you mean she's back?" Stephanie's voice sounded as confused as Tessa felt right now.

"I mean, she's back. She was found fast asleep in the very bed that was empty last night."

"Uhhhh, so you're saying that the nurse made a mistake, and that she's been there all along?"

"I'm not sure. She's sleeping, and the nurse who found her in bed this morning insists she wasn't there last night when she looked in on her and reported her missing. The nurse claims she checked the closet last night as well, and Susan's things were definitely all gone. When she went in this morning to change the bed and ready the room for a new patient, Susan was lying sound asleep in the bed."

Stephanie could feel herself getting annoyed. She had a full list of things to do today, and Susan was really getting on her nerves.

"Well, maybe it's time to wake sleeping beauty and find out what's going on. Frankly, I'm getting a little tired of her games, Tess. We have a list full of women begging for our help, and I'm feeling like this girl is just playing us."

"I know Steph, and I agree with you. Things are certainly never what they seem when it comes to Susan, but remember, it's not just about Susan. We have to consider that baby she's carrying as well. Jack met me here at the clinic this morning so he could check the security cameras. I figured I may as well wait here until he returns from watching them and see what he has to say."

Tessa looked around her. "I'm parked in front of her room right now. She's not just running off again if I can help it." As she spoke, she peered through the glass and into the room. Susan had not stirred since she had gotten here early this morning.

"Well, you can't babysit her all day, Tessa. You're needed at the shelter as well. Don't forget, there are still other residents here, and you're set up to do some counseling with some of the women later this afternoon." Stephanie knew she sounded petulant and that it wasn't Tessa's fault she was held up at the hospital, but she was finding it hard to hide her annoyance this morning. She'd been up all night with Charly. He'd been sick and whiny for most of it, and she'd hoped she could go home early today and make sure he was doing better. Normally, Tessa had no problem filling in for her, but with the Susan situation, it seemed she would need to stay and cover for Tessa instead of the other way around.

"What's up, Steph? It's not like you to be so short. Is something the matter?" Tessa asked, concerned.

Stephanie expelled a loud breath. Leave it to Tessa to make her feel guilty as well as annoyed by being so nice and perceptive. "No, I'm okay, really. Charly just had a rough night last night, and I'm tired. I think he either ate something bad, or he's fighting off the stomach bug. I was hoping to get home and check on him soon, that's all. Sorry. I didn't mean to sound so mad at you. It's not your fault, and of course, it's a good thing that the girl is back."

"Yes, it is a good thing, Steph. I'm really worried about her and her baby. But I'm sorry to hear about Charly. You do need to go home and check on him as soon as possible. Maybe you could just set the women up quickly for the day, and then you can leave Angela in charge? I'll get back there as soon as I can. Go take care of Charly and give him a hug from me." Tessa glanced up and saw Jack walking her way. "Here's Jack now, and it looks like he's carrying some tapes. I'm sure I can get back there soon. You run along and check on Charly. Angela can handle things until I get back."

Stephanie sighed and hung up the phone, knowing she wouldn't be going anywhere for a while. If Tessa could pull herself together and handle Susan, the least she could do was stay and do her job with the other women. She felt they were relying on Angela way too much.

Resolutely, she dialed her babysitter's number to let her know she probably would need her to stay for the afternoon. Tessa walked over, meeting Jack before he made it all the way to Susan's door.

"What did you find? I can see that you have some tapes in your hands?" He nodded grimly. "I do indeed, and they're very interesting. Sit down, I brought you some coffee. I want to let you know what I saw in them."

They walked to the lounge area across from Susan's room. There, they could speak privately and still watch her. Tessa took the steaming coffee, sipping carefully from the Styrofoam cup and trying not to grimace at the bitter taste. The coffee was awful, but she didn't want to hurt Jack's feelings by complaining about his thoughtful gesture. Settling back, she waited for him to start.

"She's still sleeping?" Jack nodded in the direction of Susan's room. "Like a log. I asked the nurses not to disturb her for now. I figured she needed her sleep, being pregnant and all, and I wanted to see what you found out before I questioned her."

Jack nodded his approval at her. "Good, I'd like to be there when she wakes up and hear what she has to say as well." Tessa looked down at her coffee, almost taking another sip, before changing her mind. She looked at Jack expectantly instead.

"So tell me, what did you see on the tapes? Did the nurse make a mistake?"

Jack shook his head. "No, she didn't make a mistake. Our little fugitive had quite the night. It's no wonder that she's still sleeping. She didn't get back here until a few hours ago. I'm surprised she was smart enough to sneak back in this morning with the cleaning crew. Your Susan may be more street smart than you give her credit for, Tessa."

"I see," Tessa frowned as she looked over at the sleeping girl's room.

"She snuck out of her room after the nurse checked in on her before the shift change. In the chaos of nurses handing off their notes and assignments, it looks like she could sneak to the station and make a call from a cell phone she saw lying there. We're not sure whose she used, unfortunately."

"Stephanie suspected that she might have called her boyfriend. I wonder if she was right," Tessa said.

"Probably. It would have been easier if she had used the landline, but we'll check all the cell phones later. Hopefully, we can trace the number she dialed to someone." He paused and sipped his coffee, seemingly oblivious to the bitter taste, and continued, "Anyway, about an hour after she made the call, the camera shows her sneaking out again, taking the staff elevator down to the ground level. She milled around for a while, walking in and out of the bathroom, until the tape shows a guy walk in from the parking lot. He talked to her for a minute, and then they both left. The cameras pick them up again getting into a car that was driven by another male, and he took off with both of them."

Tessa looked at him in confusion. "Wait, isn't there a night security guard at the doors, just to make sure that people can't just walk in and out?"

"Yeah, there's supposed to be, but I'm told it's not unusual for him to take frequent walks and coffee breaks. Frankly, the nurse I spoke with said they actually like it when he walks the floors. It makes them feel safer when they can see him."

Jack shook his head in consternation. "Of course, that leaves no one watching the entrances."

Tessa patted his hand reassuringly. "Well, at least it explains how she left with no one stopping her. I'm sure the guard was doing what he thought was the right thing."

"I'm going to talk to the head of security later this afternoon. They can't have just anyone walking in with none of the staff having a clue. They're lucky that this time it was just some young punk."

Jack furrowed his brows in disgust. "Anyway, I brought the tapes with me so we can study them closer. Maybe we can see if we try to enlarge them and make them clearer, so we can get a better picture of the men's faces."

"I take it that the resolution is pretty grainy, then?" Tessa asked.

"I'll never understand why places don't just update their camera systems, so they actually work. It's almost impossible to see anything on those old ones." Jack smiled at her. One of the first things that Tessa has asked him to do was to help them set up a security system with high-resolution cameras. She had told him she felt she owed it to the women to keep them as safe as possible.

"I agree with you completely. Unfortunately, not everyone will spend money on safety." He looked back at the room Susan was sleeping in.

"Anyway, grainy or not, it was pretty easy to see where Susan somehow made it back to the hospital and snuck in right after the cleaning crew. Once she was in, she made her way back up to her room, cool as a cucumber, and apparently went back to bed and to sleep."

"The boyfriend wasn't with her?" he asked.

"Not that I could see. They probably dropped her off a few blocks down, and she walked by herself. I figure they didn't want to get caught on camera again." Tessa thought for a minute. "Maybe someone else's camera caught them, and they might have better resolution. Do you think we could check around?"

Jack smiled at her again. "That's probably possible, Tessa, but I don't think I can justify sending my men around looking for cameras, seeing who dropped off a runaway. You remember that so far, no actual crime has been committed. I'm already pushing it by taking the time and resources to look into what I've got here."

"Sorry, of course you're right, Jack, and I really do appreciate what you've done so far. I guess I get too caught up in the drama happening at Hope's Haven. I forget you have a lot of more important things on your plate." Tessa looked down, ashamed of herself for taking so much of his time.

"It's nothing to be sorry about. It just shows how concerned you are for the women in your care. I think it's admirable how much you do for everyone." Jack stood up. "Anyway, I think that it's time to wake Susan up now and get her side of the story. Don't tell her about the tapes or what we know just yet. I'd like to keep our little ace in the hole quiet until we hear her side of the story and what she admits to on her own."

When they walked into the room, they saw Susan was already awake and gazing around the room, as if she were trying to get her bearings.

"Good morning, Susan," Tessa said, walking right over to the edge of the bed. "I hope you slept well."

Jack stood in the corner, deciding to just watch and wait to see what Susan had to say.

"Uh, good morning. Yes, I guess I slept okay. These beds aren't the most comfortable, but at least it's dry and warm here."

Tessa raised a questioning eyebrow at Susan, showing that she knew Susan had gotten wet last night.

"It seems you had a busy night last night, Susan. The night nurse called and informed us that you were missing. I was relieved to see that when I got here this morning, you were back."

"She said that, huh? I guess I do a lot of sleepwalking at night. I must have wandered around. I don't remember."

"With all of your clothes and your belongings? Most sleepwalkers don't usually take the time to get dressed, lace up their sneakers, and pack up their backpacks, Susan."

Tessa studied Susan's face and saw a myriad of emotions crossing it. Clearly, Susan knew she was caught, and no one was going to believe her sleepwalking story. Tessa could see she was scrambling to come up with something.

"Okay, fine! I got bored in here and took a walk, okay?" she finally admitted. "I know I have my rights, and I don't have to stay anywhere that I don't want to."

Jack noted the belligerent tone in her voice, amused that Susan had gone on the attack.

"No, you don't, but there are proper channels to check out of a hospital, Susan. Even you should know that. And as a minor, you can't take off without someone being here to sign you out. Did anyone come and sign you out or pick you up, Susan?"

Jack's ears perked up. Tessa was clearly giving her an opening, and he was curious about what Susan would admit to. "I've been taking care of myself for years," Susan scoffed. "I don't need anyone to sign me out just because suddenly a bunch of people think that I'm not eighteen. No one cared before, and nothing has changed for me. I'm grown up, and I go where I want to when I want to."

"So you went out alone?" Jack spoke up from his corner. He wanted Susan to either admit to her boyfriend coming or deny it. He was curious to know how much she would lie to cover her identity.

"Of course, I was alone. I wanted to take a walk, so I did. I walked around a bit, and then it rained, and I got cold and wet, so I came back." She looked up at Tessa. "I really am sorry if I worried you, but I needed some time to clear my head. You've made me think about a lot of things, you know. I just needed to clear my head, and I do that best by walking. All the talk about the baby and how I would have to take care of it, it's got me pretty confused."

Tessa watched Susan with sympathy. She knew she was lying about leaving alone, but she certainly wasn't lying about being afraid and confused to be giving birth to a child she wasn't ready for. Despite all her stories and lies, Susan was still only a child herself, and Tessa was determined to help her.

She leaned down towards her, patting her hand.

"All right, Susan. We'll discuss all this later. Get dressed now and wait here while I sign you out. The proper way this time. Then we'll meet with the doctor. I'm sure she'll have all the test results back by now, and she can let us know how far along you are and if everything is progressing normally. We'll need to start you on regular prenatal care, and I'm sure she will have a dietary program for you to follow."

Jack gave Susan one more glance before he followed Tessa out the door and over to the nurses' station. Tessa gave them Susan's name, asking for the discharge papers to be issued as soon as possible. She wanted to get her back to the safety of Hope's Haven as soon as possible, not particularly liking the idea that Susan's boyfriend could lurk close by, ready to snatch the girl up.

"That's it?" Jack asked, looking at her critically. "You will not call her out on her lies?"

Tessa looked up from signing the papers. "You said not to tell her we have the tapes."

"That's true, but even without the tapes, that story she told us is a bunch of nonsense. It's clear she was up to more than just taking a walk."

The nurse took the papers, looking at the two of them curiously, and then said, "The doctor asked me to let you know she wanted to speak to you in her office before you left, Miss Graves."

Tessa smiled and nodded at the nurse, then turned her attention back to Jack. "It's pretty obvious what happened last night, Jack. She's a young, pregnant girl. She tried to convince her boyfriend to come and take responsibility for what happened. Clearly, he didn't, and now she's back in the same boat she was in yesterday."

She took the papers the nurse handed her and started walking to Susan's room, turning back to Jack as she walked. "Hopefully now, at least she's ready to admit she needs help, and we're her best option."

Jack just shook his head and followed her in. *That woman is a hopeless optimist,* he thought.

Later that afternoon, Tessa looked up from her stack of paperwork, rubbing her eyes tiredly. The clock already showed 4:45, and she still had a mound of paperwork to be done. She'd been hoping to leave on time today and get some rest, maybe even work on some of her paintings. The last few nights had been late ones, and she was feeling the lack of sleep. Sighing, she looked back down at the work. *Maybe I can pick the most important stuff and take it with me.*

Stephanie had finally gone home to take care of Charly, and it looked like it would probably be a late night for her as well. DJ, her older son, and Dan were now also showing symptoms of a stomach bug. Tessa prayed that both she and Stephanie would be spared. They really couldn't afford to be sick just now with so much going on.

At the moment, Susan was resting peacefully in her room, but Tessa had an uneasy feeling that the drama involving Susan was far from over.

She looked back down at the files in front of her, deciding which ones to take and glancing over the ones that just couldn't wait. Two of her residents were being called into court on minor charges, and she was worried that their husbands would be there to cause an issue. She wanted to learn as much as she could beforehand so they would be as prepared as possible.

She jumped when she heard a slight cough and looked up quickly, letting out a little squeak at the looming figure standing at her door.

"Sorry, you looked so intent on what you were doing, I didn't want to startle you. I guess I scared you anyway." Beau Reeves, looking as handsome and rugged as ever, was standing there, holding two mugs of steaming coffee in his large hands. "I brought some coffee for you," he continued. "Angela said that it looked like you were putting in some overtime, and I thought maybe you could use a boost."

He walked into the office to hand her the mug, and she reached out, taking it gratefully. It might just be the ticket to get through the next hour or so.

"Thanks, but how did you get in? I thought that our property was secure enough that I would have caught you on the camera when you came in?"

Beau grinned. "I'm sure your property is plenty secure. I just went over the security with you last week, remember? I told you the other night that we had an adjoining pathway from the gardener's cabin at the end of my property. I used that to come over," he explained.

Tessa raised an eyebrow at him questioningly. She didn't think she had anything to worry about from Beau, but she didn't particularly like the thought of him coming and going at will through his secret path. He grinned again, as if he could read her thoughts.

"I was working on the old gardener's cabin, and Angela called me to unplug a sink in the kitchen she was struggling with. Since I was right there, I figured it was just faster to take the path. Don't worry, I'll make sure to announce myself in the future," Beau reassured her.

Tessa looked down at her coffee, embarrassed that he had read her so clearly. It was discomfiting enough for her that she couldn't discern his thoughts the way she could most people, and the thought that she was such an open book to him made it even worse. She was used to having the upper hand when it came to reading people.

"I'm sorry that Angela bothered you for that," she finally said. "It's not your job to fix the plumbing here. We have a plumber for that. I told her she should only use your number in emergencies. I will talk to her about it."

Beau perched on the side of her desk, his long, muscular legs reaching the floor easily. "Don't worry about it. I don't mind helping a neighbor at all," he said. He looked down at the paperwork scattered on her desk. "It looks like there are a lot of files for you to look through. I didn't know you had so many women here."

Tessa groaned. "We don't, but Hope's Haven tries to help women out even if they aren't direct residents. There are just so many women and children who need help, and so few agencies available to help them."

Beau nodded in sympathy and understanding. "That must cost this place a lot of money."

"It does, but it's not always just about money," she replied. She patted the two files in front of her. "These two women are due for a court date next week, and I need to figure out how to keep that date and keep them safe and hidden from their abusive partners at the same time."

Beau looked surprised. "I guess I never realized that these women get themselves into legal trouble as well. I kind of figured they were all just the victims."

Tessa frowned at him. "They are victims. Most of them have had really rough upbringings, which is why they end up with abusive men in the first place. Sometimes they get caught up in things by being dragged into it by their partners, and other times they just don't know any better. They're just doing the only thing they know how to do to survive. They haven't been taught to make the right choices in life." She leaned back and looked around her cluttered office.

"Unfortunately, the law doesn't care about all of that, and they have to face the court system the same as anyone else. It just makes it that much harder and more complicated to help them."

Beau sat silent for a few minutes. "Is that why you're so desperate to help that young girl who showed up here?" he finally asked.

Tessa nodded. "Yes, if I could just get through to her and guide her in the right direction before she gets herself too deeply into any more trouble, I might just stand a chance of saving her."

"That seems like a tall order. She pretty much gives off the impression she's already pretty streetwise."

"That's true, she does, but she would have to be fairly savvy to survive on her own as long as she has. Even so, somehow Angela could get through to her, and I'm hoping that, given the circumstances she's in, she's willing to trust me as well."

Beau was looking at her strangely, as if he didn't quite believe that was all there was to the story, and she looked away, uncomfortably, wondering if he could indeed read her mind.

"Years ago, when I was still a social worker, I met a young girl very much like Susan. No one was willing to help her either, and she had just as tough a shell as Susan. Maybe even more so," she explained. "I don't know why, but something told me there was more to her than the hard exterior she was showing us all. I decided she was worth the few minutes she was asking for, and it turned out to be a pivotal point for both of us."

Beau was perched on the corner of her desk, watching her intently as she spoke.

"It turns out that she was pregnant and had been cast out by her family and the family of the father. She truly had nowhere to turn, with no one to help her, and she was afraid and desperate. I convinced Luke, my husband, to let me bring her home, at least until we could find somewhere safe for her to go. She turned out to be a sweet, kind young girl. After she gave birth to her daughter, we could even help reunite her with her family." She looked at Beau, almost choking out her next words. "They still wouldn't accept the baby, though. And before she left, she begged Luke and me to adopt the baby. She told us she could never provide for her the way we could, and she wanted her daughter to get the love we had shown her. That's how we ended up with my precious daughter, Hope."

"Wow," he said. "I did not know. Do you still keep in touch with her?"

Tessa shook her head. "No. Sadly, only a few months later, her mother contacted us to let us know she had been killed in a car accident."

"I see." Beau sat sipping his coffee quietly for a few minutes. "I know it's none of my business, but I have to ask. Is Susan pregnant as well?"

Tessa looked at him, both surprised and irritated at his question. "Did Angela tell you? She really shouldn't tell anyone about the private affairs of our residents. I really am going to need to talk to her. Even though she doesn't officially work here, she does get paid to help, and she should know that discretion is of the utmost importance here at Hope's Haven."

"No, Angela didn't tell me, so you don't need to chew her out. She just told me that the girl was still here and that you were going to help her. Last I heard, you and that cop were taking her to a clinic. Since she's still here, and you didn't take her somewhere else, I figured there had to be a reason. That one seemed to be the most likely."

Tessa studied his face. She fervently wished that she could read him the way she could everyone else and know for sure if what he was telling her was the truth. If he was, he had an uncanny ability to read people.

Grinning at her, he took the last swallow of his coffee. "You're looking at me like you're trying to read my mind, Tessa. Don't worry, I'm not lying to you. Angela really didn't tell me anything. Over the years, I've just learned how to read situations really well. I kind of needed to learn that for my job."

"What exactly did you, or do you, do for work?" Tessa had been curious about that since she had met him. He had asked her and Stephanie all kinds of questions about the shelter and themselves, but somehow, he had always expertly avoided talking about himself.

Smiling, Beau stood up, reaching for her cup. "I'm retired, remember? Now I'd better make sure that the sink hasn't plugged up again for Angela. I promised I would check it before I left, and it looks like you still have a lot of work to do before you leave."

Is he avoiding the question again, Tessa wondered, watching as he turned to walk out. Before she said anything else, however, the phone on her desk rang. Beau paused for a moment before leaving, waiting for her to answer the phone, while she looked at the phone, puzzled. Most everyone knew the shelter closed at 5, and normally she and Steph could only be reached on their cell phones at this hour. She noticed Beau was still lingering in the doorway as she picked it up.

"Hello, can I help you?" she said, giving him a curious look.

A quiet voice at the other end said, "Uh, yes. Hello. Is this the women's shelter? I mean, can I talk to Tessa Graves, please?"

Tessa felt the hair on the back of her neck prickle. The voice sounded childlike, and it was again asking about the shelter and for her personally. The phone number for Hope's Haven wasn't that hard to find, but it wasn't advertised as a shelter for women, and how did the girl know her name? This was the second time this week this was happening, and it made her uneasy.

"What can I do to help you, honey?" she asked noncommittally. She wanted to know what this girl wanted before she gave her any information. She saw Beau was now leaning against the doorjamb, watching her face intently, and she realized the phone was still on speaker. *Darn,* she thought, but at this point, she did feel better he was still here.

"Umm, I really need to talk to Tessa Graves. It's super important. I think she can help my friend."

Tessa looked at Beau and then back at the phone, deciding. "This is Tessa Graves," she said to the girl on the phone. "Is this about Susan?"

"Susan? No, I don't know any Susan," the girl replied. "It's about my friend. She's been missing for a long time, and I think she might be staying with you. She finally called me last night, and she was crying and really upset. I begged her to come home, and I even told her my parents would help her, but she hung up on me before I could convince her. I think she's about to do something really stupid, and I'm afraid she's in danger." The girl's voice sounded desperate, and like she was holding back tears as she spoke. "I know she's not always the nicest person, but she's my friend, and she needs help." She hesitated a minute before quietly continuing, "She told me she's pregnant, and I'm afraid that she's going to do something bad to herself or the baby. Please, you've got to help her!" the voice at the other end sobbed.

Tessa looked at Beau, and they exchanged a knowing look. The girl had to be talking about their Susan. "Of course, I'll help her. I just need to know who you're talking about, honey. What's your friend's name?"

"I'm talking about the girl who's staying with you," said the girl, sounding frustrated. "You know, Patty, Patty Brinker."

CHAPTER 10

Tessa felt her adrenaline surge in excitement. Finally, she had a name!

"Yes, of course, Patty. You said she contacted you? Did she tell you where she had been staying before she came here?" Tessa prodded gently.

"Yeah, she called me out of the blue last night I haven't heard from her in almost a year. I tried to find out what happened to her when she left, but her mom wouldn't really tell me anything." The girl paused for a minute, continuing after taking a deep breath, "I mean, we've been besties since first grade. We talked every day. It was just so weird that she would just leave without telling me anything or saying goodbye, you know?" Tessa hoped the girl on the other end would at least give her some information. "Sandy Springs Junior High. We'd just started there when she left. Her mom said she went to live with her dad, but I knew that wasn't right. She never saw her real dad, she hardly even knew him, and besides, we both liked the new school. There was even a boy there that she was crushing on, you know? She wouldn't just go leave without confiding in me first. I mean, we talked about everything!"

"What did she say when she called? Did she tell you where she'd been for the year she was gone? Was she with her father?" Tessa was furiously making notes as she spoke. Who was this mysterious father? So far, Susan had only referred to her mother.

"No, I asked her where she'd been, but she just kept saying she had little time. That they would be back in a minute, and she wouldn't be able to talk then."

"Who was they? Did she tell you?"

"No, but she said she was scared, and she was worried that Ethan didn't really love her at all. She said she just wanted to come home, but she was sure her mom wouldn't let her. Then she told me she was pregnant and terrified of having a baby all on her own. She said she didn't want to end up like her mother, and she asked me what she should do."

"What did you tell her to do?"

"I told her to come to my house. I promised her I would convince my mom to help her, but she said she knew my mom didn't like her and would never help her now that she was pregnant. She said that she was desperate and just wanted to not be pregnant anymore and get away, but she felt so trapped. She told me she was staying with you at a shelter, but that they know where she is also, and she's convinced if she tries to run and they find her, they'll hurt her."

The girl swallowed a low sob. "Then, all of a sudden, the line just went dead, like she just hung up on me or something! I'm really afraid that she's going to do something terrible. I didn't know what to do or how to help her, so I looked up the name of the shelter she said she was staying at and called you."

"You did the right thing, honey. I'll help her and the baby, don't worry. Can you tell me your name and where you are? I'd like to be able to contact you again. I could let you know Patty is safe." Tessa held her breath, waiting for the girl to answer.

"No, Patty's right. My mom told me never to talk to her again, and if I did, she'd take away my phone. I can't tell you who I am, and I have to go now. Please help her!"

Before Tessa could say anything else, the line went dead. Tessa sighed, disappointed, and looked down at her notes. It wasn't much, but at least they had something to go on now.

A little later, Beau, Jack, and Tessa were all crowded into her little office. Her phone was on speaker, and Stephanie on the other end listening in.

"She wouldn't give you her name, huh?" Stephanie asked.

"No, but I think I heard someone calling her in the background right before she hung up. They might have used the name Sarah, but I'm not sure. She insisted she didn't want to get into trouble and she hung up the phone quickly."

"Well, at least we have Patty Brinker's name now. That should help, right Jack?" Stephanie asked. Her voice echoed like she also had the phone on speaker, and Tessa could hear one of the boys whining in the background.

"Listen, Steph, you had better get back to tending to those sick little boys of yours. I just wanted to fill you in on what we found out. If the kids are not better by tomorrow, you need to stay home with them and make sure you stay healthy as well." Tessa used her stern voice. She knew that her friend always felt guilty when she missed work for the kids.

After she hung up the phone, she looked at the two hulking men crammed into her office. They had shut the door for more privacy, in case Susan or Patty was skulking around.

"Well, what now?" she asked, thinking that it looked like it would be another long night. Her paintings would need to wait a little while longer.

"You will go home and get some sleep tonight! You look exhausted." Now it was Jack's turn to use his stern voice. After giving her a strict look, he continued, "In the morning, I'll start making some calls. I wish we could have traced the call, but at least we have a school name to check out now."

"We also have the girl's real name now. It should make finding her information easier, Beau said, staring at Jack. "She had to have been registered at the school wherever it is. Since Patty came here and recognized Tessa, we also know she had to have come from either around here or Atlanta. My bet is Atlanta, and that's where I'd start looking."

Jack threw Beau an annoyed look, and Tessa was expecting him to tell Beau not to lecture him about doing his job. Surprisingly, Jack didn't.

"Yes, I agree. That would be a good start. I'll look into school records first thing tomorrow morning," he said calmly, looking straight at Beau. He then turned to Tessa. "I'll also look into your phone records tomorrow, Tessa. Who knows, maybe we'll get lucky and someone can look into where the call came from quickly. It normally takes weeks, but it's worth a try."

"Okay, that sounds good. I guess there really isn't anything more I can do tonight then," Tessa agreed. Although she was eager to find out who Patty really was and where she came from, she was also relieved to get some rest before they started. The late nights really were exhausting her.

She stood up and said, "I should probably check in with Angela and ask her to watch Susan, but I imagine everyone is in bed by now, and I don't want to wake anyone."

Beau opened the door to the hallway, frowning as he watched the figure scurrying to get back into her room. "It looks like not all of your residents are in bed yet," he commented wryly.

"Uh oh, do you think she heard anything?" Tessa looked from one man to the other.

Jack shrugged his shoulders. "Maybe, who knows? She could have been standing there the whole time. How soundproof is your office?"

"I doubt that it's soundproof at all. This is an old building. They didn't use insulation the way we do now, and I haven't had the money to insulate it yet," she admitted.

Looking from one man to the other, Tessa sighed tiredly, resigned that her night would not be as restful as she had hoped. "I guess I'd better stay here tonight and watch her. I can't make her stay, of course, but I can at least be here if she tries to sneak out. Hopefully, if she does, I can try and talk her into staying."

Beau gave Tessa a sympathetic glance. She really did look exhausted, but he agreed that, given Patty's penchant to run, it was better if someone watched the girl for tonight.

"Do you have an extra room that you can crash in?" he asked. "I can sleep on the couch in the living room. It has a clear view of the door, and no one is going to leave without me noticing it," he said with certainty.

"No, we don't have any extra rooms. Besides, I could never ask you to do that! This isn't your problem, Beau, and I really don't mind sleeping on the couch for one night. Believe me, I've done it plenty of times," she reassured him.

Beau gave her a dubious look but followed Jack to the front door without further comment. "Oh good, I see that you have one of those little bells that tingles when someone uses the door. Let me just move it up a little higher. We don't want her to see it and avoid it."

As he spoke, Jack reached up and moved her little bell high up on the door, out of reach. Tessa would need a stool to move it back, but then again, Susan wouldn't be able to avoid it either.

"Lock up good, and check your backdoor as well," Beau cautioned, as he followed Jack out the door.

Tessa watched the men walking down the path for a minute, and then shut and locked the door securely. She wondered if Beau would take his secret path back, and if so, she hoped he would take a look around first. Somehow the thought of him checking her grounds wasn't as disturbing as it had been earlier. Tonight, she found it oddly comforting.

As she walked through the sweltering building, she checked all the doors and windows, making sure everything was locked tight. The old estate floors were loud and creaky. *At least Susan will not be able to leave without the floorboards giving her away,* she thought, satisfied.

Slowly wandering back to the couch in the living room, she picked up a light throw she had draped on the couch to wrap around herself. Positioning herself so she could see the front hall and door, Tessa cuddled in as best she could and started her long vigil.

Patty took a break from pacing around her room, sitting back down on her bed and trying to think. She hadn't heard everything that had been said as clearly as she wanted to. She'd been too nervous to put her ear too close to the door, wanting to make sure that she could make a clean getaway if she needed to. She was annoyed with herself for not hearing more, but as it had turned out, it was good she'd been prepared to run. She almost hadn't made it back to her room before the three of them headed out of Tessa's office. She'd opened her door a crack and watched the two men leaving, but instead of heading out herself, Tessa had locked herself and everyone else in, bedding down on the couch. That was strange, and it put a crimp in her plans yet again.

Patty had been watching and waiting all day for a chance to get into Tessa's office and look around, but Tessa hadn't left her office all day. At least Angela had left her alone for most of the day, thinking that she was asleep. It had given her a brief opportunity to move more freely, looking around the house for any other places that Tessa might have stashed a safe or some money.

Unfortunately, her search had yielded nothing yet again, and she was fairly certain that if there was any money, it was in the office or stashed at Tessa's house. She was restless and not sure what her next move should be. She thought she had heard the detective talking about tracing some calls tomorrow, and she wondered what calls he was talking about, and if it could have anything to do with her. Tessa was helping lots of other women, and they could have been talking about one of them. She was wondering if she was becoming paranoid.

Patty realized she had paced again and sat down, thinking about her call to Sarah. It had been a risky move, and she'd needed to hang up fast when she saw Gabe returning, but it had felt so good to hear her best friend's voice again, especially after the way Ethan had talked to her. For almost a year, he'd been her only friend and confidant. He'd always acted like he was concerned for her and her feelings and always seemed to watch out for her. That friendship had quickly turned into love, at least, and when he had told her about his plan for them, she had readily agreed. She'd believed he really did want to change his ways and better both of their lives.

Unfortunately, when they'd discovered that she was pregnant, he had become furious with her, blaming her for everything and telling her she had really messed up this time, and he wanted no part of her anymore. She had been terrified for herself and her baby and had told him she was going to go back to her mother. She had honestly actually considered it but had stayed, knowing her mother would not take her in any way, and she had nowhere else to go.

After a while, Ethan had seemed to settle down, telling her he was sorry and assuring her they could still continue with his plan. He had cautioned her against telling anyone else about the baby, convincing her that he was the only one who cared about her and their unborn child, and he would take care of everything.

Patty had believed him and faithfully kept her secret and stuck to their plan. She had happily volunteered to take part in stealing from Tessa Graves and Hopes Haven, telling Snake that she knew much more about the woman than she actually did. She had assured him that she would know how to get at the money when, in truth, she was just repeating what Ethan had told her to say.

When Gabe had joined them, and the two men actually told her what they planned, she had been horrified and afraid. She had only continued cooperating with them because she was terrified of what they would do if she didn't. If they ever told Snake she had lied to him, he would hurt both her and her unborn child.

Her only hope now was escaping with Ethan, and she prayed he was telling her the truth about his plans for them. For months, she had believed and trusted him, even forgiving his frequent outbursts of anger. But after the way he spoke to her last night, she was afraid she was only trading one tormentor for the other. She questioned if Ethan had really loved her or if it had been an act from the very beginning.

Patty had been desperate to talk to someone and had almost confided in Angela or Tessa a few times. So, when she had seen the phone last night, she had jumped at the opportunity and called the only person who had ever cared for her. She had quickly blurted out everything to Sarah, asking her for advice and guidance.

Sarah had agreed that Ethan didn't sound very nice and had advised her to get away from him as soon as possible. She had also urged her to come home. But right before Gabe came walking over to the car, Patty had finally mustered up the courage to ask Sarah if anyone was looking for her. The hesitation and silence on the other end told her everything she needed to know. She had hung up the phone hastily and settled back in the car, her heart pounding as much from disappointment and hurt as from fear of being caught.

All afternoon, Patty had laid in bed and thought through her options. She still wanted to believe that Ethan loved her and that somehow, once she got the money for him, they would make their escape and live happily ever after with their child. But she had been out on the street long enough to have developed a healthy dose of cynicism, and doubts had been nagging at her for a while now. She needed to protect herself with a Plan B.

She had watched and waited for her chance throughout the day. Even if she didn't find the large amount of money that Snake insisted was lying around, she would take whatever she did find and make her way to a new city on her own. She was sure a few hundred dollars was enough to get her a bus ticket to somewhere.

Patty had busied herself throughout the day, also locating the cash some of the other women had stashed away. *Women always hide money in their underwear drawers or the kids' toys,* she thought, amused at how easy it had been.

Now that she knew where to find it, she left it alone, not wanting to alert anyone just yet. She still hoped to find at least a little money in Tessa's office. While the women were sleeping, she could quietly raid their rooms and disappear with as much money as possible. If there was one thing she'd learned from her time with Snake and the gang, it was how to rob a place without making any noise. She wanted to implement her plan as soon as possible, figuring that the sooner she left here, the harder it would be for Snake or Ethan to find her. She hoped it would take them at least a day or two of not hearing from her before they came looking, and by then she would be far away.

Patty listened for a while, and when she heard nothing, she took her shoes off and slipped into a pair of socks. They were not the softest, but they would have to do. Instead of walking, she silently slid along the wooden floors, never lifting her feet or causing a creak. She slipped over to the living room and paused, watching the even breathing coming from the prone figure lying on the couch, telling her that Tessa was asleep.

Since her arrival at Hope's Haven, Patty's primary concern had been for herself and how she could use Tessa and Tessa's money to aid her escape from Snake and the gang life. She had learned to regard people as a means to get what she needed, not as actual human beings with feelings or vulnerabilities. Now, as Patty looked down at her, Tessa looked so vulnerable in her sleep that she wondered how old Tessa really was and what her story was. What made a woman like Tessa want to help so many people, and why was Snake so angry with her and bent on revenge?

Patty glanced back down the hall towards the office, no longer really believing that she would find a stash of money there. If Tessa Graves had any money, then it certainly wasn't lying around in her office, waiting for someone like her to help themselves.

She suddenly realized that there would not be enough money in the house for her to escape with. There was a small part of her wanting to wake the sleeping woman and warn her about what lay ahead. Maybe, if she told her everything, Tessa really could help her get away from Snake, as well as from Ethan. But then she shook her head sadly. No one was going to help her, not even Tessa Graves. She was on her own, and she needed to take the lessons she had learned from Snake and put them to use.

Tessa moaned in her sleep, and the girl slunk back slightly, hiding in the shadows in case she woke up. There was still a way that she could ingratiate herself to Snake and escape any retribution for getting pregnant and also get away from Ethan. He was not a kind man, but at least she had been safe under his protection. At the very least, he could protect her from Ethan.

Patty knew she would have to make a move soon, and she wished desperately that she could think clearly or talk to someone. Ethan had always been the one to tell her what to do, but that wasn't an option anymore. She needed to decide what to do and how to best protect herself, all on her own this time.

Still lurking in the shadows, she looked at the figure on the couch. Tessa had now settled down again and was snoring slightly. The woman was asleep and vulnerable, and Patty knew exactly what Snake would tell her to do.

"Get a knife," he would say. "Hold it to her throat and force her to give you the money. She knows where it is, and we deserve it as much as she does. Make me proud, Patty. Get the money and then get rid of her."

She shuddered at the thought, but she also knew that if she didn't act tonight, she might not have another chance.

Silently, Patty slipped and slid her way down the hallway towards the kitchen. Outside the window, Beau was watching the girl intently, studying her every move. As she quietly slid down the hallway in her socks, he crept along, window to window, never letting her out of his sight.

Silently sitting in the car outside of Tessa's garage apartment, Ethan looked over at Gabe, watching him survey the surrounding area with suspicion. "I'm telling you, I don't think that she's home. This is the perfect time. Let me go in and have a look around," he finally blurted out in frustration.

Gabe shook his head. "This just seems too good to be true. The chick comes home every night. It's too quiet around here as well. Why aren't any of the neighbors up and about? This smells like a setup to me."

Ethan looked at the older man, barely containing his disgust. Ever since Gabe had gotten out of prison, he was seeing boogeymen and setups everywhere, convinced the cops were following him, just waiting to pounce and put him back in jail. Before his arrest, Gabe had been one of the best and toughest men in Snake's gang. Now, all Ethan could see was a sniveling coward afraid of his own shadow.

"She probably just stayed at that shelter again. I'll bet she's got some elaborate bedroom set up there for herself to stay in when she doesn't feel like driving home. That place is enormous. I'm telling you, Gabe; this is our chance to get in and out fast and without being seen." Ethan was pulling the light cloth gloves he had bought earlier over his hands as he spoke.

"Where the hell is everybody tonight?" Gabe grumbled again. "Why don't I see anyone around?"

"Because it's late, and most people are asleep at this hour!" Ethan was running out of patience and tiring of having to reassure Gabe constantly. "This isn't a very populated place. Remember, we hardly saw anyone around last time we were here either. The woman doesn't have a lot of neighbors, and that's good for us."

Ethan tried to sound reassuring, but he was itching to get in that apartment and look around. He was tired of having to wait to put his plan into action, worried that the girl was second-guessing him. He wanted to act as soon as possible.

"Okay, fine. But I'm going to pull around that corner just out of sight. You'll need to walk back and forth on your own. I'm not going in. I need no more charges if you get caught."

As Gabe spoke, the car hummed to life, and he turned it towards the corner. Ethan smiled in the dark. *That suits me just fine,* he thought. This way, he would have plenty of opportunity to stash any of the loot he found, and Gabe would never see a thing.

He'd already been back here a few times on his own and had seen an abandoned shed just on the other side of the fence. He'd already cut a small hole in the fence, and it would be easy enough for him to slip through with whatever he found and hide it. That would leave him free to ditch Gabe and come back later to retrieve it.

"Don't you worry about a thing, Gabe. If there's money in there, I'll find it. This whole thing will be over in a matter of hours, and we can finally all move on with our lives."

Gabe looked at him strangely and snorted. "You better plan on coming back here whether or not you find that money. Snake has a lot more in store for that Social Worker. No one crosses Snake and gets away with it."

CHAPTER 11

Tessa awoke with a start, staring around for a minute and trying to remember where she was, and why she was sleeping on the couch at the shelter. Slowly, it all came back to her, and she stretched, working out the kinks as she stood up.

She walked to the kitchen, glancing out of the window as she passed it. It was still dark outside, but she could see the faint pink glow of the sun as it was rising. First, starting the coffee, she then crept towards Susan's room as quietly as she could and peeked inside. Relieved to see the sleeping figure of the young girl lying in her bed, she watched her for a few seconds, and then carefully closed the door, making her way back to the kitchen.

As she reached for a mug, she saw the shadow of the man lurking at the back door, and she nearly screamed until she recognized him. Beau held his finger up to his mouth and showed her to unlock the door and let him in. Opening the door for him, Tessa put her hands on her hips angrily, "You need to stop lurking around like that. You're going to give me a heart attack one of these days."

"Sorry, I didn't intend to be lurking. I just thought I would look around again, and then I saw you in the kitchen. By the way, I could really use a cup of that coffee myself." Although he sounded sincere in his apology, the grin on his face made Tessa doubt he was really sorry.

Sighing, she said, "Okay then, sit down, and I'll get it for you. I'm guessing you didn't sleep too well either?"

"I was a little restless. How did you sleep on the couch?" He took the mug of steaming black coffee gratefully.

"Okay, I guess. I woke up a few times, but I heard nothing, so I guess I must have fallen back asleep."

"Nothing from our little runaway?" He raised his eyebrow at her questioningly.

"Nope, she was fast asleep the whole night. Not a peep out of her. I guess she's finally settling down. I just checked on her, and she is still snug in her bed."

Beau gave her a sardonic look. "Are you sure that she didn't get up at all last night?"

"I'm sure. I'm a fairly light sleeper, so I'm pretty certain that I would have heard her. She slept in her room all night." Beau hid his humor in his cup as he took a careful sip, deciding that for now, he would keep Patty's nocturnal activity to himself.

"That's good then. Hopefully, Jack will find something today about her true identity. I'd like to find out what her real story is and what she's really doing here."

"What do you mean by that? She's here for help because she's pregnant. Why else would she be here?"

"I can't help but get the impression that she wants more than just help with her pregnancy. There are several shelters that help young teenage girls, and they would have been way easier for her to get to. Why did she come to Hope's Haven specifically?"

Tessa thought for a minute. "Because she remembered me from when she was a child and didn't know where else to go. At least that's what she said. I just accepted that without really questioning her too much. As soon as I found out she was pregnant, I didn't want to put any more pressure on her by asking too many questions. I figured she was going through enough already."

Looking at him quizzically, she said, "I guess you're right, though. Even if she did remember me, there would have been plenty of more accessible places for her to go for help. Do you think we should question her more directly about why she came to Hope's Haven?"

"I don't think it would hurt to ask. Maybe if you asked directly, you could get a better read on it. You seem to have a knack for knowing when people are being honest or not." Beau had watched Tessa around some of the other women, and she did seem to have an uncanny sense for ferreting out the truth. Somehow, she always knew if they were hiding anything.

Tessa gave Beau a curious look. She had never told him about her enhanced senses, but he seemed to know something about it. Even though she could tell if someone was being deceptive when they were responding to a direct question, unless they did a lot of talking, she could not read their true intentions. In Patty's case, as long as she kept silent, Tessa could only tell she was hiding something, but not exactly what she was lying about.

"Well, I guess it wouldn't hurt to ask her and see what she has to say. I'll try to question her when she comes for breakfast. Maybe you're right, and she is hiding a lot more than her identity."

Beau nodded, satisfied for now that she would pursue it and be on alert. Patty's actions last night worried him, but he decided he would talk to Jack before telling Tessa anything. It wouldn't do any good to alarm her just yet.

"That's a good idea, but I hope Jack comes up with something more concrete on her identity soon. That could answer a lot of the questions we have about her." He gave Tessa a concerned look. "Until we do know more about her, I think it's best to keep our eyes open."

Tessa gave him an indulgent smile. "I'm sure that she doesn't mean any of us any harm, but I'll ask Angela to watch her as well."

Tessa's phone pinged, and she glanced down at the screen. "Well, it looks like Jack might have something on Patty already. He wants me to come into the station as soon as possible. Apparently, he has something he wants to tell me."

"That's great," Beau said, getting up from his perch on the stool. "I'll get out of your hair then and let you go. But keep me posted. I might even help."

"Of course, I will. Any extra help with this poor girl is appreciated, and for some reason I don't understand, she seems to have taken to you," Tessa remarked, taking their mugs and rinsing them before she placed them in the oversized dishwasher. Ignoring his grin, she added, "I think I'll run home first and take a shower before I go to see Jack. It's been a long night, and I feel like I need a pick-me-up. I'll text you later, after I've met with him." As Beau headed for the back door, she gave him a smile. "I wanted to thank you for all of your help. I really do feel better knowing that help is just around the corner." Beau smiled back, nodded, and left.

After he was gone, Tessa carefully wrote out instructions for Angela, texted Stephanie an update on what was going on, and then headed out to her car, sinking gratefully back into her bucket seats. She turned the radio on, and the soothing tones of the guitar medley she'd been listening to last time she was in her car filled the interior, soothing her scrambled mind.

Taking a deep breath, Tessa tried to ground herself by focusing on the here and now and letting go of her jumbled thoughts. Since Patty had first shown up, Tessa's mind had been in turmoil, with dreams and thoughts of Hope being an ever-present reminder of what she had lost. Even after five years, the wounds were just as raw and painful as when she had lost her precious daughter.

Slowly, she pulled down the long, majestic driveway towards the closed gate, imagining how Hope would have loved playing among the mature trees, and how she would have begged Luke to build her a treehouse in the oak in front of the house, with its big wide branches. Luke would have happily done it too. Hope had had her Daddy wrapped around her little finger, and he had rarely denied her anything.

Tessa heard the clink of the gate as she pressed the remote to open it, and as she pulled through, she listened as it closed solidly behind her again. She imagined she could almost hear the giggles of a small girl playing in the yard as she drove off.

Humming along to the familiar melody on the radio and remembering how Hope had loved this song, a sudden thought caused her to slam on her brakes. She pulled over to the side of the street and blinked, wondering if this was truly a sign from Hope and a second chance for her.

Before she could reflect any further, her phone rang with its familiar ring for Carter. She picked it up immediately. "Carter, is everything okay? It's awful early for you to be up?"

"I hope that you're on speaker phone, Tessa. I happen to know that you're driving, and you can't possibly be home yet," Carter's voice sounded reproachful.

"Relax, Carter. I'm pulled over on the side of the road. I wouldn't dream of talking on the phone while I'm driving. How did you know I was in the car?"

"You sound a little sarcastic, Tess, but I'm glad to hear you've pulled over. I just called the shelter, and Angela said you just left. Why are you pulled over? Did you break down?"

"No, I just had a sudden thought, and I needed to take a minute to think." Tessa took a deep breath, trying to collect her racing thoughts before she spoke. "You know that I've been having a lot of thoughts and dreams about Hope lately, right?" she asked.

"Yes, I do know, and I'm sorry that you're struggling so much. It can't be easy for you to show up at the boys' birthdays and not think about Hope," Carter sounded sympathetic but also curious.

"No, it's not easy. It's never easy, but I wouldn't miss watching them grow up for the world, you know that. Steph is my best friend, and I feel the boys are partly mine as well." Tessa paused before continuing, "I think this time it's more, though. Carter, I really think that Hope is trying to tell me something."

Carter frowned into the phone. This was dangerous ground for Tessa. She had had a breakdown shortly after the murders, convincing herself that Hope was still talking to her. It had taken almost a year of therapy for Tessa to come to grips with the fact that Hope was gone and no longer able to communicate with her.

"Tess, I know you miss Hope, but she can't talk to you anymore, no matter how much you wish she could," he said.

"I know that, Carter. I really do," Tessa replied. "This isn't like before. I don't mean that she's actually talking to me in words, but she's still out there in spirit. She's still a little angel, a little force of nature that's looking out for all of us. You do believe that much, don't you?"

Carter sighed audibly. "Yes, I do believe that she's still out there watching out for all of us. Steph and the boys often say that Hope has been looking out for them."

Tessa gave a satisfied nod at the phone. "Well, I think that she's trying to make me aware of something. That's why she's been so prevalent in all of my thoughts lately."

"Okay, so what do you think she wants you to be aware of?" Carter sounded doubtful, but he was curious despite his concern.

"Patty is carrying a child. A child that she's not ready or prepared to take care of. She doesn't seem to have any family around that's able or willing to take her in and help her either. I think that's what Hope is telling me. I think she wants me to adopt Patty's baby!"

Carter groaned. "Oh no, Tessa! You can't get your hopes up about that. We don't even know anything about Patty yet! She may have parents that care a great deal for her and will want her and the baby. You haven't talked to Jack yet, and we don't know what he found out. You're setting yourself up for heartbreak by thinking like that, Tess!"

Tessa took a deep breath, willing him to understand. "I know, Carter. I know that could happen, but deep down, I really feel like this is a possibility. If Patty's baby needs a home, why not me? I got Hope under similar circumstances. This could be my second chance, Carter!"

Now Carter was really worried. He had suspected that Tessa wanted another child someday and had even hoped that if she agreed to marry him, they might adopt, but this was ridiculous.

"Tessa, please, stop. This is completely different from Hope's situation. We know nothing about Patty or the father of her baby. Her situation might be completely different than what she is even telling us." He paused, hoping to get through to her. "Remember, even Hope's situation turned out to be much more complicated than you originally thought. Her mother wasn't entirely truthful with you either, and you almost lost her. I don't want you to have to face any more heartache."

"But I didn't lose her!" Tessa stopped, realizing what she'd just said, and continued solemnly, "At least not then. Carter, you know that even Hope's biological father and her grandmother realized that the best option Hope had was Luke and me." Tessa remembered her shock at finding out who Hope's true father was, but she needed Carter to understand. "I think Patty was sent to us by Hope, so she could bring her child into the world safely and give me a second chance at being a mother."

Carter heard the conviction in Tessa's voice, and he knew it was useless to argue with her any further right now.

"Okay Tess. Let's just wait and see what Jack has to say about what he discovered about Patty and her family. We can talk about this further then. Just promise me not to get your hopes up too much until we do."

"I promise I'll try not to, Carter. I'll call you later and let you know what Jack found out."

Tessa put her car into drive and started driving to her apartment again. But in spite of her promise to Carter, she couldn't squelch the feeling of joy and excitement that had overcome her since she had the thought of a new baby. *I just know that I'm right. This is meant to be.* Her heart was soaring, and the dark cloud of oppression that had been hanging over her was suddenly lifted. She was looking forward to a nice hot shower, finding out what Jack had to say, and then later this afternoon, she would work on her paintings. The day that had started out with her being exhausted suddenly seemed bright with adventure and promise.

When she pulled off the ramp at her exit, she saw the streets were busy with emergency vehicles. Tessa frowned, hoping that her road wasn't blocked off. She was eager to get home and wasn't very keen on having to take a long detour to get there. To her relief, the firetrucks and other emergency vehicles seemed to leave. Maneuvering her way around them, she drove until she saw her apartment just up ahead. Once she saw her building, she hit her brakes, staring in shock.

The smoldering remains of what used to be her upper garage apartment sat charred and damaged in front of her. After what seemed to be an eternity, she heard a knocking on her window.

"Tessa, is that you? Thank heaven you weren't inside." The concerned face of Bill Wyler, her landlord, was looking at her through the window.

"No, I wasn't here. I spent the night at the shelter. What happened?" Tessa could barely stammer out her question as she stared at the ruins of what had been her home for almost five years.

"We don't know yet," Bill admitted. "But the fire chief said it looks like it started in your apartment. Thank goodness most of the damage was contained to that area. The rest of the building should be salvageable."

"My apartment?" The dread Tessa felt hit her hard. "Is there anything left?"

"I doubt there's too much left, but we won't know until things cool down and the fire chief lets us in to survey the damage. More than likely, there's a lot of smoke damage to anything that didn't burn." Bill looked at Tessa quizzically. "Any idea what might have caused the fire? Did you have a space heater or something? Leave anything on the stove?"

"Of course not! It's sweltering out, and I haven't even been home in almost two days!" Tessa exclaimed hotly.

She knew he had to ask, but she was angry nonetheless. True, it was his building and his property, and he had undoubtedly suffered a loss, but her entire life had been up in that apartment. All of her pictures and memories of Hope and Luke had been stored in there.

"My pictures!" she wailed, slamming the door to her car and rushing over to the building, only to find it taped all around with yellow caution tape.

"You can't go in there, Tessa." Bill came up behind her and laid a cautioning hand on her arm. "They'll let us know when it's safe to go in and rummage around, but right now they need to send an inspector to check the structure. The chief said it'll be at least a few days before we can enter."

"But I need to get my pictures!" Tessa cried. Right now, that's all that she could think about. She couldn't bear the thought that she wouldn't be able to look at the smiling faces of her family every morning.

"I promise I'll let you know as soon as they give us the all-clear," Bill assured her. "In the meantime, I hope you got that renters insurance I told you to get. You should probably contact them as soon as possible and let them know what happened."

Tessa just nodded numbly. At the moment, she couldn't remember if she had or hadn't, and if she had, she was certain the policy had been in the apartment anyhow, along with all of her other important papers. No matter what, it wouldn't replace her cherished memories.

Bill stood at her side for a few more moments, noting that the emergency crews had all cleared out for now, and the two of them were alone. "Look Tessa, I need to get going. I have my own insurance I need to contact. Are you going to be all right? Do you want me to contact anyone for you? I can cover a hotel for you until we get this figured out if you need."

Tessa shook her head. "No, I'm okay. I just need some time to process this." She swallowed a sob. "Everything I had was in that apartment!"

"I'm really sorry, Tessa. I'll keep in touch with you and let you know when you can go up and look around." He gave Tessa one more sympathetic glance, and then headed to his car. As badly as he felt for her, he was eager to get his own claims underway.

Tessa heard the crunch of tires on the gravel as the car pulled out, and then there was silence. It was still early, and her part of the street was more industrial than residential. It would be a while before anyone started arriving. She could hear a few birds chirping again, but instead of the fresh smell of the trees she was accustomed to, the rank stench of the smoldering wreckage assaulted her senses. She could almost taste the chemical smell of burned wires and insulation, while putrid smoke tendrils permeated the air. The sound of the water from the firehoses dripping off what was left of the roof filled the stillness.

This can't be happening, she thought. Moments ago, her heart had been full of hope and happiness that she hadn't felt in years. Now it was once again shattered.

Tessa strolled around the back of the building, trying to assess the damage better. As she walked, she tried to remember what papers had been out on her desk, which ones were in her file cabinet, and which ones she had locked up in that funky safe that had come with the apartment.

The big, heavy safe had been a major selling point for her landlord when he had first shown it to her. Apparently, it had been in the apartment for as many years as the building had stood, being too heavy and bulky for anyone to move. He had boasted that it was fireproof as well as theft-proof. For Tessa, it had always been more of an annoyance, but over the years, she had used the bulky thing to store some of her valuables, just to get them out of the way.

My pictures, she thought. *Did I put any of my pictures in the safe, or did I leave them all in my desk? I know I intended to store them, but I don't remember if I did or didn't.*

She walked around, glancing up and praying that she had when she heard a rustling sound behind her. She spun around quickly but was met with only a branch creaking as its water-laden leaves bent it down awkwardly.

Poor tree, she thought. *I hope it makes it.* She had enjoyed its shade many times when she had gone outside to do her painting.

Dread filled her heart even more as she thought about her paintings. There had been at least ten or so of them sitting in various stages of completion and spread around her apartment. Some had been drying, while others had been waiting for finishing touches. Still, others had been neatly packaged and were awaiting delivery to their respective consignees. Each one of them had a piece of her heart, and now they were just as lost to her as her pictures of Hope and Luke were.

Tessa knew she needed to call Stephanie and Jack. They needed to know what had happened, and Jack was probably waiting for her at the station to tell her about what he had found out about Patty. What would she even tell them? *Hey, sorry I'm late Jack, but my place just burned down.* The whole situation just seemed so surreal.

She kept walking around, looking up at the smoldering walls, wondering what was left of her precious memoirs. Having lost so much already, was it possible that now she had even lost whatever mementos she had left from her former life? *I should have brought extra clothes to the shelter,* she thought. *I don't even have anything to wear now.* Despair flooded into her heart, and the surge of happiness she had felt less than an hour ago seemed like a distant memory.

I need to call Steph and see if I can stay with her. But even as the thought crossed her mind, she knew it wasn't possible. Stephanie and her family were dealing with a nasty stomach flu right now, and they couldn't take her in. She definitely didn't need to get sick right now. There were just so many other problems she needed to take care of.

Mechanically, she dialed Stephanie's number, staring up at what used to be her kitchen window and seeing only a black hole with smoke still coming out of it.

"Morning Tessa. What's up?" Stephanie's voice sounded weak and hoarse over the phone. "Steph, I'm sorry to bother you. I know the kids are sick, and you really don't sound too hot yourself, but I have to tell you something."

Stephanie's voice now sounded alarmed. "What's wrong, Tessa? You sound like you're crying. What happened? Where are you?"

Hearing Stephanie's heartfelt concern was too much for Tessa, and she couldn't contain herself anymore. She sobbed uncontrollably. "Steph, I'm at my apartment. It burned down! It's a complete wreck, and everything is gone! All of my pictures, all of Hope's things. There's nothing left, Steph! What do I do?"

Stephanie could barely make out the words through Tessa's sobs. "Oh no, Tessa! That's just not possible! You poor thing. I'm on my way!"

The thought of Stephanie flying down the highway in her ratty pink robe, fuzzy slippers, and red runny nose brought Tessa back to her senses. "No, absolutely not. There's nothing you can do here, anyway. You need to stay home and take care of yourself and those boys."

"Then you need to come here. You can borrow some of my stuff, and we can figure out what to do." Even as she suggested it,

Stephanie looked around her shambles of a house and sick family, knowing that was not a good idea.

"I can't come to you right now, Steph. You sound like you're all pretty sick, and you already have enough on your plate. Besides, I can't afford to get sick now too. One of us still needs to run the shelter." Tessa dabbed at her eyes and tried to get her crying back under control.

"But what will you do then? Where are you going to go? Oh Tessa, all of your beautiful paintings!" Stephanie's voice was croaking as she spoke, and she was coughing hard by the time she stopped talking. It was clear she was really ill, and Tessa felt awful for causing her even more concern.

"Don't worry, Steph. Bill, my landlord, says that he'll pay for a hotel for me if I need one, but for now, I think I'll just head back to the shelter. Go back to bed, Steph. I'll figure this out. I've been through worse and survived. You just need to rest and take care of your family right now."

Stephanie made her promise to come by and at least pick up the clothes and toiletries she would leave for her by the front door. Then, Tessa hung up and once more surveyed the surrounding damage, leaning heavily on the wall behind her. Sighing, her heart filled with despair, she walked back towards the front of the building.

Maybe she would just pick up the clothes from Stephanie and find a hotel to stay at. She didn't think she could face the women at the shelter right now. She would need a chance to process her own grief first.

Tessa dialed Jack's number to update him on what had happened when she was grabbed from behind and almost slammed to the ground. Struggling desperately against the man holding her tightly, she tried to turn her head around to see her assailant. However, the arms holding her were too strong and rough, and a cloth of some kind was being jammed into her mouth, almost making her gag. Her world suddenly went dark, and she realized a bag had been shoved over her head tightly, making it hard to breathe.

Still clutching her cell phone, she desperately started punching numbers blindly, hoping to call for help. However, her phone was roughly slapped away from her. Someone was trying to grab her arms to tie her hands behind her back, and Tessa started to kick and struggle as hard as she could, determined to keep her hands free. She could feel herself being dragged. She remembered an episode she had seen on a crime show, warning potential victims to never allow themselves to be taken away from the original scene, and she struggled even harder.

Tessa was desperately trying to keep herself from being dragged into a car. The gag in her mouth was choking her. She was finding it harder and harder to breathe, but at least, so far, she had avoided having her hands tied.

Someone was trying to push her head down, shoving her from behind, and she felt the hard edge of a car door digging into her ribs.

"Just jam her in for God's sake! Tie her hands when you get her in the car. We've got to get out of here before someone sees us!" The voice was harsh and angry, and Tessa could tell it came from an older man.

"That's easier said than done. She's like a hellcat! I could use a bit of help here, you know!" This voice sounded younger, out of breath, and it was close to her ear.

Tessa kicked out to where she assumed the man was standing and heard a satisfying yelp, letting her know that her kick had connected. She doubled her efforts to get loose, and the man holding her lost one of her arms. She immediately wailed it at him and then braced it against the car, leveraging it along with her feet, to keep herself from being dragged in.

"Quit struggling, lady. You're just making this harder on yourself," a voice hissed in her ear. "This is all your own fault! If you wouldn't guard your money so much, I would have found it, and none of this would have happened. The girl and I would be long gone by now."

Money, what money? In the split second it took for the question to cross her mind, she felt a hard punch to her stomach, causing her to double over, retching in pain. The man shoved her in the car, immediately jumping on top of her, holding her immobile.

CHAPTER 12

"Get in the car and let's get out of here! What's the holdup?!"

Through the convulsions of pain and nausea, Tessa heard the younger man, who was sitting on her, yelling out at someone and cursing under his breath. By now, he had gotten her hands together and was busy tying something around them. As hard as she tried, she found it impossible to muster enough strength to fight him off. Her stomach convulsed in agony, and she struggled hard to get any air with the gag shoved into her mouth and the man sitting heavily on her, crushing her lungs.

"What the…?" She heard the man muttering and cursing, and then suddenly the heavy weight was off. She fought to get air and some strength back. As she struggled to breathe, she could hear sounds of shouting, and what sounded like a skirmish outside the car. She wondered if the two men were fighting with each other or if, maybe, by some miracle, a neighbor had seen what was happening and called the police.

After what seemed like an eternity, she finally heard someone approaching the car door, and she tensed up in fear. However, this time the arms that held her were strong but gentle, and she could feel the hood that was still jammed over her head being lifted.

Tessa blinked at the sudden assault of brightness to her eyes, looking around to see who was holding her. When she saw him, her eyes welled up with tears of relief.

"Shhhh, it's okay. You're safe now. I've got you," Beau's voice was gentle and soothing, and he was taking the gag out of her mouth as he spoke. "Are you all right? Did they hurt you?" he asked, now cutting away at the ties holding her hands behind her back.

Tessa gratefully sucked in as much air as she could, and then said, "No, I think I'm okay. Thank God you got here in time." She then looked at him in shock and confusion. "What did they want with me? I heard them talking about money. I don't have any money. Do you think they were trying to rob me?"

Beau looked her over for a minute, trying to assess the extent of her injuries, before answering her. "I'm not sure what they wanted, but my guess is this all has something to do with Patty Brinker."

"Patty? What would she have to do with any of this?" Beau backed himself out of the car they were still in, pulling her gently out after him. She looked around and saw that they were in the alley behind her burned-out building. She looked around the deserted street, realizing that no one would have been able to see her being abducted back here. She finally saw a man lying motionless on his back, eyes closed and blood pooling from a swollen face.

"Who's that? Is he one of the men who was trying to kidnap me? It looks like he's hurt. We have to help him, Beau."

Beau shook his head in disbelief. "I've already called the police, and they're on their way. They can get him an ambulance if he needs one. Right now, he got what he had coming to him, and he can lie there all day for all I care."

He then carefully put his arms around her waist. "Come on, let me get you to my car. You need to sit down and rest for a minute until the police show up. I want to make sure they take this loser to jail and lock him up. As soon as they've taken your statement, I'll take you to the hospital so they can look after you."

Tessa shook her head. "I don't need a hospital. If I sit down for a minute, I'll be all right." She looked around the alley, shuddering at the memory of the rough arms that had grabbed her, and instinctively leaned in closer to Beau. "There were at least two of them. I know I heard two men talking. What happened to the other one?"

Beau grimaced in apparent aggravation. "The little coward ran off as soon as he saw me fighting with his partner. I tried to chase him down, but I didn't dare go too far and leave you alone, tied up in the car. We don't know if there are more of them around."

By now, they had reached Beau's SUV, and Tessa could see the flashing lights of police cars coming down the street. The lead car squealed to a stop right in front of them, and Jack jumped out of the driver's seat, running towards them as soon as his feet hit the ground. Beau smirked when he saw Jack running. "Well, look, there's the cavalry now, coming in full force and late to the party as usual."

Jack ignored him, heading right over to Tessa and taking her hands in his. "Are you injured anywhere? Do you need to go to the hospital? Did they hurt you?" he asked, looking at her in concern.

"No, no, I'm okay, Jack. I just need a minute to collect myself." Tessa looked at Beau, gratefully. "I'm just so happy that Beau showed up when he did. I don't think it would have gone well for me if those men had succeeded in their kidnapping attempt." She looked over towards the alley just in time to see the EMTs emerge from behind her still smoldering building. They were wheeling the unconscious man towards a waiting ambulance. "Jack, do you think that man could have anything to do with Luke and Hope's murder? The one holding me kept accusing me of hiding money." She looked from Beau to Jack. "Luke was working undercover when he was killed, but no one would ever tell me what case he was working on. Maybe his killers believed Luke took something from them and came to the house that day to find it. If they believed that I still have whatever it was they killed Luke over, they might have finally come to find it and finish me off as well?"

Jack shook his head. "I doubt that man had anything to do with the murder of your family, Tessa, but we'll question him as soon as he gets checked out at the hospital. Right now, unfortunately, he doesn't look all that good."

As he spoke, Jack looked at Beau accusingly. Beau just shrugged nonchalantly, ignoring him and handing Tessa a bottle of water. She took it gratefully, relishing the feel of cold liquid running down her throat as she leaned back on the seat, watching Jack walk over to the officers waiting by the ambulance.

Tessa could see him saying something to them, and then the officers got in the ambulance, and it drove off, carrying them and the man who had attacked her. Jack continued doling out instructions to the other officers standing around, and she watched as they all dispersed around her normally quiet neighborhood, putting up crime tape and combing through the area.

"What happened here, Tessa? When did the place burn down? Everything is still hot and smoldering," Jack asked her when he finally returned to the SUV. He surveyed her burned-down apartment critically.

"Why didn't you call me and let me know?"

"I didn't get a chance. I called Steph and told her, but while I was dialing your number, one of the men grabbed me and slammed my phone away." She hugged her arms around herself defensively. "I don't know how the apartment burned. My landlord said it must have been last night sometime, while I was at the shelter keeping an eye on Patty. When I got here early this morning, the fire department had already put the fire out. Bill, my landlord, was here and told me they knew little yet, but it looks like it started up in my apartment."

Beau and Jack exchanged a glance. The fire and Tessa's attempted abduction were most likely related.

"At least you got one of them," Jack said, looking at Beau. "If he comes to soon, we should be able to get some answers from him at least. Although from the looks of it, it might take a while for him to wake up."

Beau nodded morosely. "I'm just sorry that the other one got away from me."

Squatting down by the SUV, Jack looked at Tessa kindly. "I hate to even ask you right now, but do you feel well enough to tell me what happened? The sooner we can get your story, the faster we can find the other guy and find out what they wanted."

She nodded at him, trying to ignore the pounding in her head. She desperately wanted a hot shower and to just lie down somewhere, but she also wanted to catch the man who had tried to kidnap her. She took another drink of water and tried her best to recount what had happened.

"After I called Stephanie and told her what happened, I walked around the back of the building to see if there was anything that I could salvage, but everything was just a smoldering mess. I was just dialing your number to let you know as well when someone grabbed me from behind, stuffed a gag in my mouth, and then covered my head with something. After that, I couldn't see anything, but I could hear at least two men talking."

Tessa paused a minute, determined to give Jack as complete a report of what happened as she could remember and tried to collect her thoughts. "I felt myself being dragged toward the street, and then the man holding me started talking. He said something about how it was my fault he had to do this and how he and the girl would have been long gone if I had just not tried to hide the money from him."

She looked at Jack and at Beau. "Do you think he was talking about Patty?" She shook her head in confusion. "He couldn't have been talking about her. She would never be involved with something like this. And why did he keep insisting I was hiding money? I don't have any money to hide."

Again, she thought about the night of Luke and Hope's murder. The police still didn't have a definitive motive for why her family had been targeted. Could someone have thought she and Luke were hiding large amounts of money?

Jack looked at Beau and then back at Tessa. "Hopefully, when we have time to question the guy we do have in custody, we'll get some answers to those questions. They'll fingerprint him at the hospital, and it's possible we'll know his identity in just a few hours. When we find out who he is, we may have some answers as well." He then stood up and stepped back from the car, saying, "I did find some information about Patty, but I think you need to get some rest before we get into that, Tessa."

Tessa nodded, her pounding head in agreement. After the fitful night she had spent on the couch and the events of the morning, she was worn out, and her head felt heavy and groggy. Any information about Patty would need to wait until she had a few hours to lay her head down and process what had just happened.

Turning to Beau, she said, "I left my car parked just down the street. If you could drop me off at it, I think I'll just head back to the shelter and lay down for a bit."

Jack looked at Beau, for once in silent agreement, as Beau said, "I don't think that you should drive anywhere right now, Tessa. I'll take you home in my car, and I'm sure Jack can spare an officer to drive your car back to the shelter for you."

"No, no. That's unnecessary. The police have enough to do with this mess. I can drive myself just fine." Tessa shook her head vehemently and tried to ignore the throbbing.

"Nonsense, you've been through a lot this morning. I'll be over to talk to you and Stephanie later," Jack urged. "Just let Beau drive you to the shelter for now, and I'll take your car back later in the afternoon. We can talk about what I found out about Patty Brinker after you've rested." He then gave Beau a stern look. "I'll want to talk to you as well. I'm curious to know how you just happened to be here when all of this was happening. It's a good thing you were, of course, but it is a little coincidental."

Tessa wanted to argue, but at this point, she was just too tired. Everything was so overwhelming; she was doubting she really could drive herself safely. Beau gave Jack a nod and bent down to buckle Tessa firmly into his SUV.

Leaning back into the soft leather seats, she closed her eyes, trying to block out the events of the morning. After what seemed like only minutes, she felt the SUV slowing down and heard the gate opening. The tires crunched on the gravel as she felt the SUV drive forward.

I must have dozed off, she thought groggily, painfully trying to force her eyes open.

When she finally did get them to open, she looked around in surprise. Instead of driving down her driveway towards the shelter, as she had expected, they were driving on Beau's driveway towards his house.

The house was only partially visible from the street, so she straightened up, looking around curiously. "Why are we going to your house instead of the shelter?" As she asked, she realized she was really just surprised and not the least bit alarmed by the change of events. *Why do I trust a man that I hardly know?* she wondered.

Turning his head to look at her, Beau said, "I see you're awake. We're actually not going to my house, although I'd be more than happy to give you a private tour anytime you want. For now, though, I think it's best you should get some rest."

True to his words, Beau drove past the house and around the back, following a slightly narrower gravel path that wound up higher and higher until they stopped in front of a partially hidden little cottage that was sitting up high on a hill. Tessa gasped. "Wow, this place is beautiful. I never even knew this was here. Did you build this place?"

Beau grinned, clearly delighted at her reaction. "No, I didn't. This is the gardener's house that I was telling you about. It was built shortly after the original owners finished building the main house. It was pretty dilapidated by the time I bought the house, but I've been working hard trying to bring it back to its original beauty."

Tessa carefully stepped out of the SUV, gazing in wonder at the cottage and walking around the little gem, mesmerized. She completely forgot to ask Beau why he had brought her here. When she reached the back of the cottage, she stopped in amazement.

"Wow, the view from here is absolutely stunning! I think I can see the entire valley below us." Looking over at Beau, she said, "I'll bet you can see the most amazing sunsets from this very spot."

He nodded, following her gaze to the mountains just on the horizon. "You can actually see both the sunrise and sunset, depending on which direction you look. I think it was built on the highest point of the properties around here to take advantage of the views." He took her arm, carefully guiding her back to the front door and took a key out of his pocket as they walked. "Come with me. I can't wait to show you what I've done inside. I promise you it's every bit as amazing."

Tessa followed him into a wide-open room. The sun was streaming through the large glass doors on the other side of the space, bathing the entire room with sunlight. Off to one side of the area was a spacious little kitchen, and Tessa noticed two other doors leading to what she assumed were a bedroom and a bathroom.

"Oh Beau, this place is absolutely gorgeous! I can see that you've spent a great deal of time and expense updating it."

Turning to Beau curiously, she asked him, "I noticed that you always call this the gardener's cottage, but I find it hard to believe anyone would pick the best spot on their property to build a residence for their gardener." She walked to the doors in the back of the house, leading out to a veranda, again admiring the amazing view.

"He must have been one heck of a gardener to deserve this," Beau grinned mischievously. "Who said the gardener was a man?" Tessa looked at him shocked, and he chuckled. "Rumor has it the owner built this place to keep his mistress and his wife separate, but close enough so that he didn't need to leave the grounds when he wanted to see the mistress. When I bought the place, I found the plans for it, and they simply stated, 'Gardner's House,'" he informed her. "I figured that was as good a way to refer to the cottage, so I kept it."

"That's just horrible! The poor woman," Tessa gasped, shocked at the revelation, and not sure if she felt worse for the wife or the mistress.

Beau just shrugged his shoulders, clearly not as appalled as she was. "If it worked for them, who are we to judge? Anyway, I'm glad he built it. It's given me a project to work on over the last few months, and I don't mind saying this hidden little gem has increased my property value by quite a bit as well."

Tessa turned to look at him. For some reason, it was strange to hear a man like Beau talking about property values. He always seemed so mysterious and above the everyday concerns of normal people like her, and he certainly never gave the impression that he worried about money.

"Well, you've done an amazing job on the renovation," she said. "I appreciate you showing it to me, but I'd really like to get back to the shelter now." The fatigue from the events of the last few hours was catching up to her, and she wanted nothing more than to lay her head down somewhere. "I should see what Angela and the other women have been up to as well."

Beau gave her a strange look. "I didn't bring you here just for a tour, Tessa. I thought that you could stay here at the cottage for a while. Your apartment is uninhabitable right now, and staying at the shelter is not a good long-term solution for you." He waved his arm around. "This place is finally done. You'll be able to take the path right over to your property without needing to go out on the street, and now that it's finished, the cottage will be sitting empty."

Tessa looked around the beautiful little cottage, her head shaking in disbelief. She had never lived in such a high-end, updated place in her life, and it was much too posh for someone like herself to even imagine living here, even if it was only for a little while.

"No, Beau, I could never do that. This place is gorgeous. I could never afford the rent here. My apartment will probably be repaired in a few weeks, and until then, it's no problem for me to stay at the shelter. Besides, once Stephanie and the family feel better, I can stay with her."

Beau shot her an annoyed look. "I didn't ask you to pay rent. I said you could stay here, not rent it. You need a place to rest and decompress for a while, and this place is available. It makes the most sense for you to stay here." He looked around the little cottage. "You'll have complete privacy, and you can even park over at the shelter if you prefer and walk over, so you never need to pass the house. After all the work I did, it would be nice to see the place occupied and not just wasting away. It's a win for both of us."

Tessa gazed out at the view from the glass doors and then back to Beau, undecided. She wanted to argue, but waves of exhaustion were once again washing over her, and she couldn't think of a single argument to counter what he was saying. Besides, the thought of putting her head down onto what she was certain would be an amazing bed was very tempting.

Walking over to the bedroom door, Beau opened it wide and let her see inside. Just as she had suspected, the room was bright with streaming sunshine, and the bed did look incredibly inviting.

"Just go into the bedroom and lay down. If, once you've rested, you don't want to stay here, you don't have to," he told her. "You can decide what you want to do after you've slept and have a clear head." He walked in, closing the shades, and the room was suddenly dark and soothing. "Lie down, Tessa, get some rest. The bathroom connects from this room as well, so if you want to take a shower first, go ahead. I called and had my housekeeper bring over towels and a bathrobe. You should have everything that you need. Just make yourself at home and call me when you wake up. I'll see that Jack doesn't disturb you until then either."

While Tessa was still trying to figure out how to argue with Beau, he quickly exited the cottage and closed the door behind him. She heard the rumble of the SUV's motor, and then the crunch of the tires on the gravel. Suddenly, everything was silent, and Tessa was alone in the darkened room.

Well, as long as I'm here, I may as well take that shower I've been wanting and get some rest, she thought, still exhausted but somewhat giddy about the prospect of staying in such luxury.

Later that afternoon, Jack was giving Beau a troubled look as he asked, "Are you sure?"

"I watched her through the window the whole time, ready to jump in if I needed to. Thankfully, something changed her mind before she acted, but it was pretty clear to me what she had been thinking."

"This really does surprise me. I figured she wasn't the innocent little girl next door, but I also didn't take her for a hardened criminal. It scares me to think that she could have actually hurt Tessa, or anyone else in the house for that matter. I should have kept a better watch on her." Jack was staring down at his notes as he spoke, but the frown on his face was visible. "Tessa is usually so good at picking up on people's intentions. I'm surprised that she let her guard down like that."

Stephanie's hoarse voice came over the speakerphone. The two men had called her before their meeting and added her to the conversation.

"I know why she is ignoring any warning signs," she croaked, almost immediately breaking into a coughing spell. Once she recovered, she continued, "I think that she's hoping she'll be able to adopt Patty's baby, just like she could adopt Hope. And I'm guessing her dreams of getting a second chance at motherhood again are probably clouding her judgment with the girl."

"Well, I don't think we should completely condemn the girl yet," Beau interjected. "Remember, I said that it was clear she thought about something, but she also changed her mind and didn't act on it. She ended up going off to bed and left Tessa undisturbed."

"That's true, and that's the only reason she still deserves our help, but that was too close for comfort," Stephanie said. "I hate to think Tessa could be in danger." Stephanie couldn't see him through the phone, but Jack was nodding his head in agreement.

"In spite of all the vetting we try to do, you two never really know who you're admitting at the shelter. I honestly don't think it's safe for either of you to spend the night there alone," Jack said, looking over at Beau. "I appreciate you letting her stay at your guest house. I just hope she stays there until she finds somewhere besides the shelter to stay."

Stephanie coughed again. "Well, as soon as we're all healthy again, she can stay with me. I agree with you, Jack, that the shelter is not the best place for her to stay long term. Even aside from the safety issue, Tessa really needs a place to unwind. She is way too vested in everyone else's problems for her own good. The poor woman needs a place where she can shut off."

"Well, until we know where our little friend Patty went now, I would certainly feel better if Tessa just stays where she is," Jack announced. His next question was directed to Beau. "You said you saw her sneak out right after Tessa left this morning?"

Beau nodded. "That's what prompted me to go to Tessa's apartment. I was just about to head home to take a shower when I saw her sneaking out the back door. She was clearly trying not to be seen. I'm assuming she found the crack in the fencing at some point earlier in her stay because she went right to it and snuck through it without having to leave through the gate. Before I could follow her, she was out on the street and disappeared. I didn't see where she went, but after her actions last night, I decided that I'd better head to Tessa's apartment and make sure she was safe. Thank God I could get there in time."

"I can't even imagine what could have happened if you hadn't made it." Stephanie croaked.

"I don't think Patty would have had the time to make it to the apartment before those goons went after Tessa," Jack mused. "We now believe they were probably the ones who set the fire, and they were most likely waiting for her to come home so they could grab her. What I really need to find out is what they were looking for in that apartment and why they tried to kidnap her."

"Has the big guy said anything yet?" Beau asked.

"No, apparently he's still in bad shape and hasn't woken up yet," Jack responded. "I won't be allowed to question him until he gets the all-clear from the emergency doctor, but we do have him under guard around the clock. The results from the fingerprints we could take from him should be back soon, though." Throwing Beau a sour look, he said, "You didn't need to break his nose, did you? If he wasn't in such rough shape and if you'd have gone a little easier on him, we wouldn't have to wait to question him."

Clearly not feeling bad at all, Beau just said, "He got what he deserved, and frankly he's lucky that I thought about questioning him at all. If I hadn't, he wouldn't even be close to talking yet."

Jack's phone rang shrilly. He picked it up, frowning as he listened to the person on the other end. He thanked the caller curtly and looking at Beau announced, "We have some news."

CHAPTER 13

Tessa awoke with a start, her eyes slowly adjusting to the dark, unfamiliar room. Slowly, as she drifted back into consciousness, the events of the past few hours came flooding back.

Stretching her sore body carefully, she savored the comfort of the soft duvet that was still covering her half-clothed body, wondering if she dared take a shower in the overly luxurious bathroom she had bathed in earlier, before sinking exhausted between the expensive sheets. The oversized tub had been a luxury she hadn't been able to deny her stressed and exhausted body, and now she wondered what it would be like to refresh herself in the spacious, modern shower.

Throwing off the covers, she covered herself with the robe she had found earlier in the bathroom and padded over to the shades that were darkening the room. As she slowly drew them open, she realized that the bright sunshine she had fallen asleep to had been replaced with a dusky haze. What time is it and just how long did I sleep? she wondered, opening up the bedroom door, her bare feet padding softly on the hardwood floors of the newly renovated living room.

Looking at the clock she had seen hanging in the kitchen earlier, she gasped. *It's 7 o'clock!* Was it really possible that she had slept through the entire day? She looked out the glass doors and saw that the glow from the moon was lighting up the sky just enough for her to see a few clouds illuminated in the dark.

Still padding carefully around the room in bare feet, she was grateful for the moonlight, until she finally located a light switch. The soft glow instantly illuminated the room, and she gazed around in appreciation, until she remembered she had been looking for her cell phone.

Searching around her, she finally spotted it lying neatly on the coffee table in front of a modern little fireplace, surrounded by small but comfortable-looking chairs that were facing a soft, inviting couch.

On the couch, she saw some neatly folded clothes, recognizing them as belonging to Stephanie. *So, someone was clearly in the cottage while I slept,* she thought, not sure if she should be disturbed at the thought of someone poking around while she had slumbered unaware.

Sliding down onto the comfortable little couch, she looked at the phone she was holding and saw she had several texts waiting for her attention. The first one was from Stephanie, instructing her to sleep as long as she could and assuring her that everything was under control at the shelter. Steph also informed her she had sent some clothes for her to borrow until she could replace some of what she had lost in the fire.

There was also a text from Beau stating that he had brought her some provisions for her dinner tonight, and he hoped he hadn't disturbed her while he dropped them off. He said he had also left some clothes he had picked up from Stephanie, and they both agreed it was best she rest until tomorrow. He asked her to call him if she needed anything, and he informed her he would stop by in the morning to take her to Jack's office.

The last text was from Carter, requesting she call him as soon as she could, and she could see that she had missed several calls from him as well. Sighing, she decided the shower would have to wait until she found out what was so urgent.

Carter picked up his phone on the second ring. "Tess, where are you? Are you all right?"

"Yes, Carter, I'm fine, and I'm actually right next door to the shelter in a posh little cottage. Judging from your voice, I'm guessing that Stephanie already filled you in on what happened earlier today."

"Yeah, she did finally fill me in. But not until I tried to call you several times. I finally tracked her down. I would have thought I'd be one of the first people that either of you would call when your place burns down and someone tries to kidnap you." His voice sounded hurt, as well as angry.

"I'm sorry, Carter. I know I should have called you, but everything just happened so fast. Honestly, thinking back on earlier today, I think I was in a bit of shock. It's not every day that my apartment burns down, and someone tries to abduct me all on the same day."

"Sorry, Tess." Carter sounded contrite. "I didn't mean to sound accusatory. It's just that when Stephanie told me what happened, I nearly lost my mind with worry. I just needed to hear your voice and find out that you were really okay."

"I really am fine, Carter." Tessa tried to sound reassuring. "I think I need a little while to process what happened, but things could have been so much worse if Beau hadn't shown up when he did."

"What was he doing at your apartment anyway at that time of the morning?" Carter sounded angry again. "I mean, I'm glad he was there and all, but am I the only one who finds it odd that he was around right then?"

Tessa furrowed her brow. The same thought had been ruminating in the back of her own mind, but with so much going on, she hadn't had the chance to ask him yet.

"I'm not sure why he was there, Carter. I haven't had the chance to talk to him about that yet. I kind of just zonked out after he brought me here. I still feel a little groggy and overwhelmed, to tell you the truth, and I honestly just want to lie down again. I'm sure I'll get a chance to ask him in the morning."

"I don't like the idea of you staying on his property, Tess. I already told Steph that I think it would be better for me to come and pick you up tonight. I know that, for some reason I can't fathom, you and she trust this guy completely, but frankly, I don't. Until we find out why he was at your apartment today, I think it's just safer for you to stay with me."

Tessa was shaking her head at the phone, looking around the peaceful cottage as she listened to him. She was absolutely certain there was nothing sinister here, and she hadn't felt so at peace and comfortable in a long while.

"No, Carter, I can't stay at your place, you know that. It's just way too far from the shelter for me to commute every day. Besides, I really do just need my space until I can get all of this sorted out in my head. At least until Steph and the kids feel better, this does seem like the perfect solution. Then I can stay with her."

Carter was silent for a minute, and then said, "Why are you avoiding being alone with me lately, Tess? You know I would never pressure you into anything you aren't ready for. There's a spare bedroom you can stay in for as long as you like, and I can redecorate my study into an art studio if you want me to."

Carter's apartment was a high-rise in the middle of the city, with him living close to the top floor. In order to gain access, she needed to brave the claustrophobic elevator that opened directly into his apartment. She knew he considered it modern and comfortable, but Tessa had always thought of it as sterile and uninviting.

"I know you mean well, Carter," Tessa said, "but I just don't think that would work for me. We've discussed this before. I can't live in the middle of the city, and even if I could, I'm not ready to move in with you."

"If you had been staying here in my apartment, you would have been safe today, Tess. There are no alleys where someone can hide, and nobody can just sneak in. I have a doorman and a security guard." Carter paused, then continued, "I don't like the idea of you being by yourself all the time. It's just not safe, especially right now. At least stay here until we find out what those goons wanted and why you're being targeted."

"You're thinking that it could be connected to Luke and Hope's murder too, aren't you, Carter?" Tessa trembled, partly from fear, and partly from excitement. If the men who had attacked her family were really after her after all of these years, she could finally be on the verge of finding out why they killed Luke and Hope.

"I honestly don't know, Tess. Maybe," Carter admitted. "Today was a close call, and I don't want you to be in a position where someone can attack you again. I want to make sure that you're safe and protected. I can do that if you stay here."

"I'm safe here," Tessa assured him. "The entire grounds are just as secure, if not more so, than your apartment is. Trust me, it's much riskier for me to drive back and forth from the city than just head next door to go to work. You have nothing to worry about, Carter. I promise."

Hearing Carter grumbling faintly into the phone, she suspected it was more about her not staying with him than about her staying safe. However, he finally conceded.

"Have it your way then, Tess, but I want you and Stephanie to call me tomorrow as soon as you find out anything. At least promise me that."

"I promise I'll call you right after the meeting with Jack tomorrow morning. Now you get some sleep yourself and stop worrying about me. I'm fine." She hung up and then texted Stephanie to let her know she was up and okay. She also filled her in on her conversation with Carter. Afterward, she stretched and wandered over to the kitchen.

Scouring through the refrigerator, she saw Beau must have brought over some Chinese food. She smiled. In one of their conversations, she had mentioned she was partial to Chinese food, and she was touched that he had remembered.

She warmed the food, made herself some tea, and then headed out to the back veranda to enjoy her meal in the warm night air. After she had eaten her fill, she leaned her head back in the soft cushions of the chair, allowing her daydreams free rein. She let herself imagine how Patty would come to her and ask her to take in her baby once it was born, much in the same way that Hope's mother had asked her. Her arms could almost feel the soft skin of the newborn, and she could practically smell its clean, precious baby smell.

Tessa was picturing how she would set up a nursery in one of the bedrooms at the shelter and how she would need a new apartment to accommodate both her and a baby when a cold nose suddenly touched the hand that she had left dangling over the seat cushion.

Shrieking, Tessa jumped up and frantically looked to see what it was. However, she only heard the rustling of bushes as something quickly ran away. Shuddering, she gathered up her empty dishes and hustled into the kitchen, shaky and eager to crawl under the covers again where she felt safe.

Tessa woke the next morning to her cell phone pinging next to the bed. She had been in such a hurry to hide under the blankets last night that she had forgotten to close the shades. The sky was already glowing red with the promise of another bright and sunny day. Looking down at her phone, she saw it was from Beau. He was informing her that he would come by in an hour to collect her and take her into town to meet with Jack.

She watched the sunrise before she showered and wandered into the kitchen. There, she found a coffee machine all set up and ready to brew some coffee, so she pressed the button. Before long, the aroma of freshly brewing coffee quickly engulfed the tiny cottage. Breathing it in gratefully, she noticed that someone had left freshly baked muffins, fruit, and pastries on the counter. Surprised at Beau's thoughtfulness, but also somewhat annoyed that he had once again snuck in while she slept, Tessa took a muffin and walked to the sliding glass doors, nibbling hungrily at the delicious baked treat.

As soon as she slid open the door, she could feel the warm breeze coming off the mountains in the distance. She watched as the sun started to make its way over the horizon. Just as Beau had promised, the sunrise was promising to be spectacular.

As she looked over the clear, glass railing encircling the veranda, she saw that below her was a steep slope. It stopped and leveled out at the woods that surrounded the cottage, as well as the shelter next door. Although the dense trees protected both properties from prying eyes, Tessa couldn't help but think it was not a great place for a child to play.

You don't have a child, she reminded herself harshly, and walked back into the kitchen where she poured the strong coffee into a large mug, placed her muffin on a plate, and then headed back to the veranda, hoping to find some peace from her restless thoughts by watching the dawn of a new day.

As she slowly sipped her coffee and nibbled on her muffin, she watched, mesmerized, while the sun rose, making its way lazily over the mountains in the distance. She had hiked those mountains often, and she wondered if there was anyone on them right now, also welcoming the morning light.

Leaning back with her eyes closed, she tried to picture what the woman who had lived here at one time would have been like. She had spent her mornings sitting back and enjoying the warmth of the morning sun on her face, just like she was doing at this very moment.

She opened her eyes and looked around, wondering what it would be like to wake up every morning to such luxury and beauty. How could anyone help but face the day with joy, waking up to such a beautiful scene?

Is that why the woman had been content to be the man's mistress? Tessa wondered if she could trade her pride and her independence, settling on being just the mistress. She couldn't help but wonder if that was why Beau had remodeled this cottage so carefully. Was there a woman waiting for him somewhere?

Cradling her mug carefully in her hands, she reflected on the path her life had taken. It had all turned out so differently than she had hoped or expected. After losing the family she had devoted her entire life to, she now had an eternity ahead of her, to face all by herself.

After the attack on her family, she had suffered a great deal of what the doctors had called survivor's guilt. She still couldn't understand why she had been the only one to survive, while her poor, precious daughter had been robbed of the chance to ever grow up. And she also still believed that Luke, who had been so kind and strong, and even funny, had so much more to give to the world than she ever could. Why had he died and not her?

Stephanie and Carter had both spent countless hours trying to convince her that she was just as valuable as they had been, and that she deserved to be alive and happy. The grief counselors she had seen had told her that what she was feeling was normal, and she really was deserving and significant, but it hadn't been until she had come up with the idea of Hope's Haven that she'd truly felt any desire to live again.

Having finally found a purpose for her life, she was eternally grateful for the secret donor who had enabled her to buy and open Hope's Haven. If it hadn't been for them, she may never move on from her grief. But in the years that had passed since she had opened it, she sometimes wondered if Hope's Haven was still all she really needed from life.Sometimes, Tessa longed for the love that she and Luke had shared, especially in the beginning. They had been so giddy around one another, barely able to keep their hands to themselves. True, after being married for a few years, the giddiness had ebbed into a kind of tender caring, but that was normal for a married couple, wasn't it?

Recently, Carter had made his feelings for her clear. She wondered what it would be like to marry again. All she needed to do was say the word, and he would be all too happy to come in and sweep her off her feet. She imagined that married life with him would differ greatly from her life with Luke. Luke's work as an undercover officer had sometimes taken him away for longer periods of time, causing a lot of anxiety and even straining the relationship at times.

Life with Carter would be peaceful and safe. He earned more than enough money, so she would never need to scrimp and scrounge again to make payments, and she was certain that he would build her the home of her dreams if she requested it. He told her countless times how much he loved her, and she knew she would never find the special bond they shared with anyone else. He knew most of her deep dark secrets, even accepting that she couldn't ever give him a child of his own. That had been a bitter pill for Luke to swallow, and she shuddered at the thought of ever having to tell another man that she was incapable of having his children. Carter had even hinted at the possibility of adopting another child someday, and the idea of coming home every night to the familiarity and easiness of Carter and his companionship sounded nice. But she also knew he wanted her to give up Hope's Haven, and she wasn't ready to do that. At least not yet.

Shaking off her daydreams and walking back into the now sunlit living room, she studied her surroundings. Everywhere she looked, there was an understated opulence, and standing in here now, with the sun streaming in, she felt a sense of happiness and wonder that she had never felt in Carter's overly luxurious penthouse apartment. If Carter had asked her yesterday what type of house she wanted him to build for her, she would probably have described the same modest ranch that Stephanie lived in, and truly believed that was all she wanted. But now, after seeing this, she felt a certain amount of envy for the person who would get to live here permanently. She once again wondered who Beau had really remodeled this little cottage for.

Chiding herself for her thoughts, she hurried towards the bathroom. It was Beau's cottage, and it was his business who he had remodeled it for, not hers. In the meantime, she planned to enjoy her short stay here as fully as possible.

A little while later, she stepped out of the steamy shower, fully refreshed, and grabbed one of the fluffy, oversized towels that had been hung on the warming rack. *Of course he has a towel warming rack,* she thought, amused. Wrapping herself up in it, she took a minute to just luxuriate in its infinite softness before walking out into the bedroom to find some clothes for the day.

By now, the bedroom was fully engulfed in the sunshine streaming in from the glass doors, and she let the towel drop to the floor, taking a moment to feel the sun fully warming and drying her still-damp body before searching for the pile of clothes Stephanie had lent her. *Shoot,* she thought, looking around, annoyed. *I left them on the couch in the living room.*

Tessa picked up the towel she had dropped, loosely wrapping it around her body again, before opening the door and padding out into the living room to retrieve the clothes she had spotted laying on the couch the night before. *I thought the view from the deck was nice, but I have to admit that the view I have now is so much better.*

Tessa whirled around in panic, pulling the towel closer to her body, searching for where the voice was coming from.

"What are you sneaking around here for?!" she asked, more alarmed and embarrassed than angry.

"I'm not sneaking around. I made all the noise that I possibly could. I knocked and rang the doorbell and even banged my cup on the counter while I fixed my coffee. It's not my fault you can't seem to hear anything," Beau replied, still looking at her appreciatively, grinning and sipping at the coffee he was holding.

As usual, Tessa could not get any insight into his mind and did not know if he was telling the truth or if he had intended to surprise her and find her in a compromised position.

"Well, you caught me off guard regardless, so now the least you can do is turn around and give me a chance to grab some clothes and go back into the bedroom and get dressed," Tessa said, her cheeks burning and her heart hammering loudly in her chest. However, she wasn't certain if her heightened emotions were due to anger or annoyance. She had seen the admiration in his eyes, and that was when her heart had really started racing.

By the time she had dressed and combed her hair, Tessa had gathered herself enough to walk out of the bedroom with some semblance of dignity. She was determined to chastise him for walking in on her with no warning.

"Do you always walk in on your guests when they're trying to get dressed?" she asked him coolly, joining him on the veranda where he sat lounging in a chair, watching a hawk circle by.

"No, like I said, I have had no guests until now," he answered, turning to look at her with a cocky grin. "But if I was guaranteed a glimpse of what I saw this morning, I would certainly consider it."

"I thought you were a gentleman, but I guess I was mistaken about you," Tessa countered, shocked at his lack of remorse.

Beau shrugged indifferently. "I have no idea where you would have gotten that idea from. No one's ever accused me of being a gentleman before." He got up and walked past her to the kitchen.

"Did you eat anything yet?" he asked, changing the subject. "I'd like to grab another cup of coffee and a muffin before we go.

I'm starving, and it sounds like Jack has lots of information to share with us. It could take a while."

Still not sure what to make of his answer, and not knowing what else to do, Tessa followed him into the kitchen, watching while he poured them both more coffee.

"Thanks," she said, taking the mug from him. "But I'll skip the muffin. I already had mine earlier, and by the way, they were absolutely delicious."

As Beau perched at the counter and took a big bite of his, a satisfied smile ran over his face. "Mmmm, I have to agree. Ellie really outdid herself this time. I swear that every time she bakes something, it just gets better and better."

"Ellie?" Tessa looked at him questioningly. "Is that your girlfriend?" she asked, feeling a slight twinge of jealousy in her gut.

This time Beau actually laughed out loud. "Hardly. I think her husband would skin me alive if I even suggested such a thing. Ellie is my housekeeper, and she has just recently begun cooking for me. She wasn't so sure about her new assignment at first. She couldn't even boil an egg when she started, but she has certainly shown some major improvement."

Tessa was a little ashamed at the relief she felt hearing that Ellie was only his housekeeper, and a married one at that. She hoped Ellie was a matronly, older woman. Somehow the thought of Beau being around a young woman every day bothered her more than she cared to admit.

Trying to dispel her thoughts, she drained her cup and announced, "We should probably get going soon and see what Jack has to say about Patty. I was supposed to have met with him yesterday morning already, and I feel horrible about sleeping through the entire day yesterday."

Beau looked at her compassionately. "You needed the rest, Tessa. We all agreed on that. Even that pompous friend of yours named Carter said to let you sleep. You went through a lot, and honestly, it was already almost afternoon when we got here anyway, so you didn't sleep all that long."

Tessa had worn a sleeveless shift from the clothes Stephanie had provided her, and Beau eyed the dark bruises that were appearing on her arms angrily. "Are you sure that you're okay? Those men were pretty rough with you, and those bruises look painful. Maybe we should stop and get you checked out at the hospital on the way?"

Tessa looked down at her arms. Truthfully, she hadn't even noticed the marks until now. She'd known she was sore, but she had been too busy taking in the views from the cottage and processing her own thoughts to spend any real time examining herself.

"I'm fine. Trust me, these bruises are nothing compared to what I've seen on some of the women that come to us from their abusive husbands." She eyed the door. "I was thinking maybe you could show me the path you take to get to my property before we go. I would have gone to check on the shelter earlier if I had known where it is. I really should check in with Angela before we leave."

As Beau nodded and drained his cup, she continued, "I can take my own car to the police station, and then you have your freedom to do what you need to after the meeting with Jack. I'm sure that you have a hundred things to take care of as well."

Beau stood up, placing his plate and mug into the sink. "Nope, the only thing I have planned for the day is escorting you around. That's the beauty of being retired." He walked to the front door, jingling the keys he was holding. "I'd be happy to show you the path before we go, that way you can go back and forth as you please." He held out his hand with the keys. "Here's a set of keys for you so you don't need to leave the door unlocked when you do leave."

"Oh no, I won't need those, Beau. I'll be staying at the shelter tonight, and I'm sure that Steph and the kids will be well enough by tomorrow so I can stay with her. I really just wanted to know where the path was and see if it was visible from the house."

"I'm afraid Stephanie and her kids won't be better soon," Beau informed her. "She called me this morning asking me to let you know she was in the emergency room with one of them." He scrunched his face for a minute, trying to think. "I think she said the kid's name was Charly."

"Oh no, he's that sick?" Tessa asked dismayed. "Poor little Charly!"

"Yeah, I guess he is. Apparently both of the kids, Stephanie and her husband have RSV, but it seems to have hit the one kid especially hard. She said that he is getting some relief with a nebulizer right now, but she said the doctors are telling her it will be at least two weeks before they're well enough to get around."

He looked at her pointedly, still holding out the keys. "So you can't stay with them, or you will get it as well." He waited patiently for the news to sink in.

"I need to see how Charly is doing," Tessa said, shocked that what they had thought was just a stomach flu had taken such a bad turn.

"No, you can't do that either," Beau said. "Stephanie says he's in the quarantine section of the hospital. No one can see him right now but her. Apparently, this stuff is super contagious. They're not allowing anyone else in, and the rest of the family is supposed to stay at home and away from everyone as well."

"Poor Steph, she must be worried sick." Tessa chewed on her lip, wracking her brain for how she could help her friend and feeling completely helpless. She finally announced, "I guess all I can do is order some meals for Dan and the kids until it's safe for me to go over and help them. In the meantime, I'll just have to stay at the shelter."

"I thought you said all the rooms were full?" Beau decided not to mention just yet that Patty had run off again and that her room would be empty. He really did still hope they would find her soon.

Tessa frowned. "Yes, they are full. I'll just sleep on the sofa then."

"That's crazy. You can't sleep on a sofa in a living room where women are coming and going all day long. You'd be completely exhausted after just one night, and then you won't be helping anyone."

Beau crossed his arms. "The best plan, for now at least, is that you stay here. You're close to the shelter, but you can still have some time for yourself," he said, narrowing his eyes. "Unless, of course, you want to go to the city and stay with your buddy Carter Williams? Even he agrees that it's not a good idea for you to stay at the shelter at night by yourself." The look on Beau's face clearly said he would not listen to any more arguments. "We all agreed that staying at the cottage is the best, and the safest, solution for you."

Tessa did not like the idea of everyone deciding what was best for her, and she also didn't like the idea of intruding on Beau either. He seemed very nice right now, but he had always seemed a bit intimidating to her.

"I can't take advantage of you like that, Beau," Tessa said. "It doesn't feel right. My apartment burning down is not your problem, and it's not fair for me to inconvenience you. I guess maybe I could stay with Carter if I need to." But even as she tried to argue her point, the thought of spending the next few weeks either at Carter's penthouse or on the shelter's couch filled her with dread.

"Just take the keys, Tessa, and let's get going. Jack is waiting, and you still want to check in with Angela. I already told you it's no inconvenience for you to stay here. As far as I'm concerned, the matter is settled."

Shoving the keys into her hands, he held the door while Tessa grabbed her purse, reluctantly dropping the keys inside of it. Even she had to admit that, at least for now, it really did seem like the best solution.

But as soon as Stephanie was better, Tessa was determined to move out of the cottage and in with her friend. Carefully, she followed Beau down the steep hill until they reached the edge of the woods. Once there, Tessa could see that someone had cleared a path that was barely visible from the yard. If Beau hadn't shown her where it was, she would never have seen it.

"Wow, I would never have found this," she remarked, looking around.

"I only found it by chance myself. It blends in with the rest of the woods, and it was pretty overgrown when I stumbled on it. I've only cleared it a little so far, but I'm guessing years ago it must have been a pretty beaten-down path," Tessa looked at him curiously.

"Do you think the same man who built the gardener's cottage made the path?" Beau couldn't help but grin mischievously.

"I guess it's possible. Although I can't imagine why he would put in a path leading to the neighbor's house," Tessa gasped, grasping at a thought, "You don't think he had a mistress over at my house too, do you?"

Beau laughed loudly. "I have to admit I never even thought of that." Then he gave her a wink. "I was thinking more like maybe the 'gardener' was secretly visiting someone over at your house."

Tessa shook her head in disbelief. "Oh my goodness, it certainly seems like all of these wealthy people were quite busy cheating on each other back then, doesn't it?"

Beau laughed again. "Maybe when you're that rich, you need to amuse yourself and keep your mind occupied."

While they were talking, they had been walking the path. Before she knew it, they were heading out into a clearing just below her kitchen door. They needed to push aside a few vines to get out in the open. Tessa assumed that the vines that had covered the entrance to the path were why she hadn't seen it until now.

Stepping out into the clearing, Beau looked at his watch. "Well, now that you know where it is and how to get here, I suggest we go back to my house and get my car. I'll drive us back over, and we can leave right away when you're done talking to Angela. I think it would be quicker, and it might be better if no one else knows about the path. At least for now."

Tessa glanced up at the big house that had sheltered so many women over the years, nodding her agreement. There were at least two newcomers who hadn't been here long enough for her to decide if they could be completely trusted yet, and she had to agree that the fewer people who knew there was a hidden path, the safer it was.

"Yes, you're right. Let's head back. I don't want to keep Jack waiting any longer than we need to."

Beau stepped back out of the way. "You go first, and I'll follow you. That way, I can make sure you don't get lost and can find your way back alone. It's still a little overgrown in parts."

Tessa smirked to herself, thinking, *I know how to follow a path, Beau. I grew up in the woods.* But as she moved along, she could see that indeed, the path was curvy and hard to follow at times. She was busily scouring the ground for the beaten-down areas when she heard a low, menacing growl coming from just up the path in the direction she was heading. She froze instantly. That growl sounded like it was coming from something big, ferocious, and most alarming of all, it sounded close.

As she stared at the path in front of her, Beau came up behind her, almost running into her.

"What's wrong, Tessa? Are you lost?" he asked.

Before she could answer him, a huge black snout emerged from the bushes, effectively blocking the path. Attached to the snout were two huge dripping fangs.

Tessa watched in terror as the ferocious creature slowly stalked towards them.

CHAPTER 14

"Cash, back off and cut it out!" Beau's stern voice cut through the silence. The huge black dog responded immediately, lowering his head and tail and slinking off in the other direction.

"What was that?!" Tessa asked, still shaken at the thought of her throat almost being ripped out.

"Sorry about that. That was Cash. He's the resident guard dog. He came with the property for free when I bought it. I was told that the previous owners had trained him to guard the place from the time he was a puppy, and sometimes I think he takes his job a little too seriously. I was going to introduce you to him properly later today, but it seems he got out of his kennel somehow and found us."

"He lives here too?" Tessa looked at him dubiously. As inviting as the cottage was, the idea of sharing her home with a ferocious wolf dog was not exactly appealing to her.

"Don't worry. As soon as he realizes you belong here, he'll leave you alone. It took me a while to figure him out, but we have a pretty good understanding now. I feed him, and he leaves me, my staff, and most of my guests alone."

As Tessa and Beau emerged from the path, she said, "I'm not so sure I trust your halfhearted reassurances, Beau. That doesn't sound like much of an understanding."

Beau smiled at her. "I'll introduce you later on when we get back. You'll see, he's pretty harmless once he gets to know you, and it's actually kind of reassuring to know he's patrolling the grounds at night."

Wondering if that was the same wet snout that had touched her hand last night, Tessa didn't think she liked that idea at all. She wasn't so sure she liked the idea of running into the ferocious animal again but decided not to argue the point right now. She still had the sanctity of her shelter if she needed to escape.

After Tessa had checked on Angela and the other residents at Hope's Haven, she sent Jack a text, letting him know that she and Beau were on their way.

"I'm actually kind of surprised Jack agreed to have you come along on this briefing. He's usually much more secretive with his investigations. You sure you're not a cop?" Tessa asked, looking over at Beau as he drove.

"No, I'm not a cop. But I do have a bit of experience and knowledge of the law," Beau sounded vague and non-committal, as he usually did when she asked him about his background. "I think he just decided when it came to your safety, it would be better to include me and have my help." Beau gave Tessa a sideways glance. "You really do seem to have a knack for getting yourself in trouble."

"I do not," Tessa tried to sound indignant, but even she had to admit that trouble did seem to find her often. "Well, maybe a little," she admitted. "But when you're helping the women I help, trouble is bound to happen."

"I imagine that's true. Jack probably decided having an extra set of eyes and helping hands around to keep you safe was a good idea," Beau commented, cautiously steering around a truck that was blocking the road.

Tessa looked at him curiously. "That's an odd thing to say. He's in charge of an entire county, why should he worry about keeping me safe? I know he asks for my help occasionally, but other than that, I'm just another citizen in his district."

"Yeah, right," Beau chortled. "You'd need to be blind not to see that the sheriff's interest in you goes a little beyond that of just a normal everyday citizen, Tessa. I doubt he makes house calls to any of the other citizens he helps."

Tessa remained quiet. *Jack is interested in me?* She had suspected there was some interest in her, but it seemed it was apparent to others as well.

She had met Jack shortly after opening Hope's Haven. One of her residents' irate husbands had shown up, threatening them, and when she had called the police, Jack had been the one to respond. At the time, his demeanor had been cool and professional, even detached. However, as she needed the police's help more often, their relationship had evolved into a mutual respect. It also hadn't taken long for Jack to realize that Tessa's heightened senses were a tremendous help with vetting her residents and questioning any abusive spouses they rounded up. Soon, he had called on her, asking for her help in questioning other suspects, and their relationship had evolved into an easy friendship.

She liked Jack but hadn't given the possibility that there might be more interest from Jack's part much credence. As they pulled into the parking lot of the police station, she shook her head dismissively, certain that Beau was wrong about Jack. When they walked into his office, Jack held out a chair for Tessa and nodded at Beau curtly.

"Tessa, Beau, come on in. I've been waiting for you. I have a lot I need to talk to you about." Jack sat down across from them and looked at Tessa with concern. "How are you feeling, Tessa? I'm glad you had time to rest, but I still think that you should have gone to the hospital and gotten checked out." He eyed the bruises on her arms critically. "It looks like those goons were pretty rough on you."

Tessa regretted that she had not chosen a long-sleeved dress this morning. "I'm fine, really, Jack. I can barely feel the bruises. They look worse than they are, honestly. Now, tell us what you found out about Patty. Angela told me she disappeared again yesterday morning. That's a long time for a young, pregnant girl to be wandering the streets alone."

"We're all out looking for her, Tessa. I've got an APB out with all the patrol cars, and they're all watching for any young girl matching her description. If she's still around the area, we'll find her."

Beau leaned forward in his chair, impatient to find out what else Jack had to say. "So, what is it you found out? You said yesterday you might have some more news about her true identity."

"We followed up on the leads from the call that Tessa got from the young girl. We checked for schools with the name Sandy Springs Junior High." Jack looked from one to the other. "It turns out there are quite a few schools by that name. Anyway, we asked them all for lists of the names of girls in Patty's age group, hoping to find her Patty's name, and we finally had a hit. Turns out that the school is in a small suburb just outside of Atlanta."

Tessa also leaned forward in her seat, watching Jack with anticipation, while Beau's face never changed his intent expression.

"We called the principal and asked about Patty Brinker. It turns out that the girl you spoke with was right, Patty has been gone for about a year."

"And no one bothered to look for her?" Tessa asked, aghast.

Jack held up his hand to quell her anger. "Take it easy, Tessa. Patty was signed out legally by her mother, and they were told that she was transferring to a school in Tennessee. He did find it strange that no other school ever contacted them requesting a transfer of her transcripts, but he never followed up on her."

"So it would appear that she never was enrolled in another school in Tennessee?" Beau said, his brow furrowed.

"It does appear that way," Jack agreed. "Anyway, I asked him if Patty had had any close friends at the school and was told that she was always hanging out with another girl by the name of Sarah Jacobs. They had both been in the same class together, but shortly before Patty left, Sarah's mother had requested that Sarah be moved to a different class, away from Patty."

"I wonder why?" Tessa mused, "Did they give you the name and address of Patty's mother?"

"Yes, I did get that as well. But there's more before I get to that." Jack looked through his notes. "Sorry, go on."

Tessa sat back, trying to still her racing thoughts. Why would Sarah's mother suddenly try to separate them, and why had Patty's mother taken her out of school? What had the girl been up to?

"I could get the address and phone number of Sarah's mother as well, and as soon as I got off the phone with the school, I called Mrs. Jacobs."

Both Tessa and Beau watched Jack with anticipation.

"She was surprised and angry when I told her we believed that her daughter had recently spoken with Patty, and then contacted you for help, but I could convince her to calm down enough to tell me what happened," Jack paused, again shuffling through his notes.

"Just like Sarah told you, she and Patty have been best friends since grade school. Mrs. Jacobs hadn't been too fond of the family, but she said that Patty had always been well-behaved and polite, so she hadn't objected to the friendship."

"Why didn't she like the family?" Tessa asked.

"According to Sarah's mother, Patty's family was a little, shall we say, rough around the edges. She actually called them white trash. They lived on the other side of town, and Mrs. Jacobs was convinced that the family was connected to the gang activity going on over on that side of town."

"Let me guess." Beau drawled wryly. "The Jacobs are fairly well off and Patty came from the wrong side of the tracks?"

Jack nodded. "Yeah, something like that. But to her defense, the woman said that she treated Patty like a daughter, even taking her on vacation with them when she could. Her only rule was that Sarah wasn't allowed to go to Patty's house."

"So what happened? Why did she suddenly change her mind about Patty?" Tessa couldn't understand a woman turning her back on a girl she had regarded as family.

"According to Mrs. Jacobs, right around the time the girls started Junior High, Patty started really acting out. She was dating boys, drinking, and trying to influence Sarah to do the same. Mrs. Jacobs decided it was in her daughter's best interest to keep Sarah away from Patty, and that's why she requested that Sarah be moved to a different class and demanded that Sarah stay away from Patty."

"I wish she would have at least tried to find out why Patty was acting out," Tessa said, reflectively.

"Apparently, she did call Patty's mom to let her know what Patty was up to, but she said Patty's mother just got mad and told her that Patty was just fine and to mind her own business." Jack was reading his notes as he was talking and shaking his head. "The interesting thing is that Patty and her mother don't share the same name. The mother's name listed on the school papers is Victoria Bannan, not Brinker," Jack remarked, looking up at the two of them.

"Hmmm, sounds like the mom must have divorced and remarried at one point," Beau said.

"Divorce and remarriage are pretty common nowadays. That's not a reason for Patty to be acting out." Tessa looked at Jack. "Do we know anything else about the mother? Bannan does sound vaguely familiar, but I'll have to check my files and see if she really was someone I helped in the past."

Jack continued, "I did a background check on her. She is listed as married to a man named Wyatt Brinker right now. He works at a Machine Shop in the same suburb that Patty went to school.

They've been married for about 5 years. But that's not the most interesting part." He paused for dramatic effect.

"Okay, so what is the interesting part?" Beau asked, now watching Jack closely.

"Wyatt Brinker has a criminal record. He was associated with a Biker Gang known as the War Kings for about 15 years or more. They're pretty well known for dealing in drugs, robberies, and extortion. Wyatt was convicted of an attempted kidnapping, for which he served time. According to his records, he has been on the straight and narrow for about 5 or 6 years now, ever since his release."

Beau looked over at Tessa. "Now that's interesting."

"There's more…" Jack continued. "The gang he was with is headed up by a man named Harley Brinker, better known as Snake, among his peers."

Tessa let out an audible gasp. "You don't think that he is related to Patty, do you?"

Jack nodded. "According to the court documents granting Mrs. Bannan's divorce, she was married to Harley Brinker before she remarried Wyatt Bannan. The divorce papers she filed said that she was seeking a divorce from Harley because of spousal abuse."

"So she really could have come to me for help. It looks like Patty was telling the truth," Tessa whispered.

"It's definitely possible," Jack conceded.

"Her divorce was granted about 7 years ago. That would have meant Patty was only about 8 years old," Tessa said. *That's old enough for her to remember the circumstances and my name, but it was before I opened up Hope's Haven,* she thought silently.

"So we still need to figure out how she knew where to find you," Beau reflected.

Agreeing with Beau, Jack said, "It's definitely time that we pay Mrs. Bannan a visit. From what I could find out, she works as a waitress at night, so we should be able to find her at home tomorrow afternoon." He looked at Tessa. "I'd like for you to come with me. I'm curious if you recognize her or if she would recognize you. Also, you could let me know if she is answering my questions truthfully or not."

Tessa ignored the questioning look Beau threw at her and said, "Of course I'll come with you, Jack. In the meantime, I'll look up my records and see what, if anything, I can find on a Victoria Brinker or a Victoria Bannan."

"You said Patty was looking in your files under the B's the very first time that you caught her snooping, right?" Beau asked.

Tessa nodded. "She might have been trying to look up information on her mother."

"Or on her father," Beau said. "I'm definitely curious to see what you find in your records."

"I hope that I still have them," Tessa frowned. "I wasn't able to take all of my clients' files with me when I left Atlanta. Only the ones that had been deemed a closed case. I took them in case I needed them at Hope's Haven, but if Victoria was still an open case, I would have left it with the agency."

Jack nodded. "Let me know if you do find anything. I can also try to call the social services center you worked for in Atlanta and request the file if you have nothing. Unfortunately, that could take some time and probably a judge's court order."

"Then hopefully I find something," Tessa remarked. "Have you found out anything about Sleeping Beauty yet?" Beau inquired, looking at Jack while trying to repress a smirk.

Jack looked at him sternly. "Thanks to your rough handling, I haven't been able to question him yet, but the doctors say they hope that tomorrow he may be more coherent. I'm hoping I can go in first thing, before we head to Atlanta, and see if I can talk to him."

Beau nodded. "What about his prints? Anything there?"

Jack looked at them curiously. "Actually, yes, and this is where the plot thickens. The man's name is Gabriel Rogers, with a rap sheet as long as my arm. He was just released from prison a few months ago."

"Why would he want to kidnap me?" Tessa was trying to think if any of the women from the shelter had a last name of Rogers, but she was drawing a blank. "Do you think he was after one of the women staying at Hope's Haven?"

"That's still a possibility, but the interesting part about Mr. Rogers is his associates," Jack replied.

Beau looked at Jack curiously. "What do you mean?"

"Gabriel Rogers has been a member of the War Kings pretty much since he was in diapers. The same War Kings that Harley Brinker is leading," Jack said. Tessa looked at him, her eyes wide with disbelief.

"So Tessa's attempted abduction does somehow involve Patty," Beau said matter-of-factly.

"It certainly seems that way," Jack agreed. "There are just too many coincidences for it not to be related." He turned his attention to Tessa. "When you check your files for a Victoria Bannan, I think you should see if the name Harley Brinker pops up as well. My gut tells me he may have the reason you were targeted. He may even be the one that sent Patty to you. We just need to find out why. Hopefully, you can find something in those files of yours."

Tessa nodded at him numbly, but she continued to sit silently, staring out the small window in the cramped little cubby that Jack called his office. She finally looked at Jack. "The time frame you're talking about is right before my family was attacked," she stated dazedly. "Do you think Harley Brinker had something to do with Luke and Hope's murder?"

"I don't know yet, Tessa. I will, of course, check into that, but don't get your hopes up just yet. This could all still be unrelated. We don't know if Brinker was even the mastermind behind your abduction. That could have been the last-minute brainchild of the two goons we picked up. I'm hoping I'll get some answers from

Rogers soon. He doesn't seem to be the brightest bulb, and I'm guessing he won't want to go back to prison, so hopefully, I can convince him to cooperate with us." Jack's next question was to Beau. "Is Tessa still staying at your property?"

Beau glanced over at Tessa first and then answered, "Yes, for the time being, Tessa has agreed it's the best option."

Giving Tessa a stern look, Jack said, "I know you won't like this, but I don't think you should leave the shelter or Beau's place without someone escorting you. If you need to be somewhere and Beau can't go with you, then I'll have a police escort come and get you. Until we know how this all ties together, I don't want you to take any chances."

Tessa shook her head vehemently, protesting, "That's ridiculous. I have a shelter to run and court dates for some of the women that are coming up. I can't just sit around and hide for the rest of my life."

Laying his hand on her arm, Beau tried to calm her, "I doubt Jack is talking about the rest of your life, Tessa. We're thinking more like a few days, maybe a few weeks. You won't do anyone any good if you're hurt. Your friend Stephanie needs you at the shelter right now, healthy and sound. She has enough on her plate dealing with her family. I don't think you want her to worry about you as well."

Tessa clamped her lips shut, knowing Beau was right. Stephanie was still in the hospital with poor little Charly, and she certainly needed nothing more to worry about right now.

"Fine," she agreed. "But only for a few days, until Stephanie is back on her feet and her family is healthy."

Jack rose, holding out his hand to shake Beau's. "Thanks. I know that it's a lot to ask of you, and I do appreciate your help." He held the door for Tessa as she rose to leave, saying, "I'll be by to pick you up around eleven tomorrow. Hopefully, I'll have been able to talk to Rogers by then."

A few minutes later, Tessa and Beau were sitting in the SUV. He looked over at her as he started the car. "Do you need anything before we head back? You might want to shop for some clothes or other things that you need while we're out?" he asked. Tessa nodded silently, but she continued staring blankly at nothing. "Come on, Tessa, it won't be that bad. Some people actually think I'm pretty good company. Besides, you'll have your freedom back in no time at all."

Tessa's eyes welled up with tears, and she looked at Beau. "It's not that. I really do appreciate your company, as well as your offer to stay at the cottage. It's lovely."

"So then what's wrong? Why the sad face?"

Her lip trembled. "What if this Harley Brinker really does have something against me? If it was him that murdered my family, it would be all my fault that Luke and Hope are dead." Tessa put her hands over her eyes to shut out the horrible thought that she was the cause of her family's destruction.

Beau drove on in silence, knowing that if it was true, and if Brinker had murdered her family, there was nothing he could say to convince Tessa it wasn't her fault. He was so deep in his own thoughts, trying to think of something comforting to say, that for once he didn't watch his mirrors and failed to see the beat-up sedan that was following them just a few cars back.

Ethan maneuvered carefully behind the car just ahead of him, trying to stay far enough back so as not to be seen. "We'll follow them for now. Hopefully, he takes her to that other dame's house. That place should be really easy to break into. If we end up back at the shelter, you'll need to show me where you snuck out yesterday, and we'll just have to get to her there later tonight when everyone's asleep."

Patty was slunk down in the seat, staring at the disheveled young man next to her. "Why can't we just get out of town now and leave her alone? I already told you I don't think she has any money. I just want to get away from here as fast as we can before Snake comes after us. Come on, Ethan! Now that we have the car, let's just get away!"

Ethan turned, sneering at the girl next to him. "And what exactly do you think we are going to buy food or gas with, huh? 'Come on' yourself, stupid," he said, mocking her. "We have a plan, and we're sticking to it. That woman's money is our ticket to freedom. She might not have as much as Snake thinks she does, but she's got to have something. That place doesn't run without cash, and she's got to have stashed it somewhere."

Ethan fell back even further, trying hard to remain undetected. He already knew the way to both the shelter and the other woman's house. As long as he knew which general direction they were taking, he would catch up to that social worker soon enough. One thing was for certain. He had no desire to run into the man that was with her any time soon. He'd witnessed how poorly Gabe had come out of that encounter.

Sitting next to him, Patty was sobbing silently. She had no desire to help Ethan with his plan anymore. Now that she had come to know Tessa and the other women at the shelter, she wanted nothing to do with hurting any of them.

Wiping her eyes with the back of her hand, Patty gave Ethan a sorrowful look. "What's happened to you, Ethan? You've changed so much in the last few days. Maybe it's because you've been around Gabe too long, and he's changed you? I loved you because you were different from the other gang members. When did you turn into a cold-hearted criminal?"

Without ever taking his eyes off the road, Ethan swiftly reached out and slapped her hard in the face. The force of the blow sent her head slamming into the window beside her. "Don't you ever call me a criminal again, you hear?" he snarled. "You just need to shut up and do as you're told. From now on, you're mine, and you'll do what I say. As long as you do that, you don't have to worry about a thing. I have everything under control."

Using the same hand he had just slapped her with, he took her hand and started kneading it between his fingers. "I have no intention of letting Snake find us. I'm done with that washed-up old man telling me what to do. I'm ready to start my own gang, and I'm making my own connections. We don't need him anymore."

Dropping her hand abruptly, he looked at Patty, who was cowering next to him with her hands over her face, and scoffed. "Just think, Patty darling, you can be the first girl in my little enterprise, just like your mommy was the first girl in Snake's little harem. It's so nice for you to follow along so nicely in your mother's footsteps, isn't it?"

Laughing at his own little joke, Ethan slapped the wheel of the car. "And that brat you're carrying should bring me a hefty sum as well."

He reached over again and gave the back of her head a little swat. "Oh yes, things are certainly looking up again."

CHAPTER 15

W*ell, there it is*, Tessa thought to herself. *It's been here the whole time, right in front of my nose.*

"Here it is." Tessa pulled the file out and laid it in front of Beau. "Victoria Brinker. She came to me at my office in Georgia about 8 years ago."

They had arrived back at the shelter a few minutes ago, after making a few stops. Tessa replenished some toiletries that she needed, and Beau had insisted on buying her a few clothes as well. She had tried to resist, but he had convinced her it was just a loan until her insurance came through.

After dropping her purchases at the cottage, Tessa had been eager to look through her files. Now she sat at her desk leafing through the file she had just pulled out, while Beau peered curiously over her shoulder. She read the overview of the case when Beau leaned down further, his chest accidentally brushing against her back. Tessa instantly felt a tingle in her stomach at the contact and did her best to ignore it, trying to focus on the file in front of her.

"It states here she was attempting to get away from an abusive relationship. She had a seven-year-old girl in tow, along with a three-year-old boy." She looked up at Beau. "Even at seven, Patty would have certainly been old enough to remember that her mother came to me for help, and even my name."

Beau nodded. "True, but it still doesn't explain how she knew where to find you now. You helped her while you were still back in Atlanta." He gave her a slight nudge, impatient to see what else was in the file. "Keep reading. Let's see what else it says. We may get some of the answers we need."

Tessa read on. "It does say that her husband was a part of a motorcycle gang."

"Okay, there it is," Beau sounded excited. "Does it say the name of the gang?"

Tessa leafed through the file, frowning. "No, the woman who interviewed her didn't make a note of that. I guess we didn't think it applied to helping the woman get out of the relationship."

Beau swore softly. "Read on. What else do we know about her?"

"Apparently her husband had accused her of cheating with another gang member. She told us the little girl was his child, but she wasn't sure about the little boy, and he was doubting he was the father." Tessa turned to the next page, frowning. "Actually, I can see why I don't remember any of this. I didn't handle the case myself after she was admitted. Apparently, the woman had told the social worker who was working with her that her husband had been okay until he suspected she cheated on him, and that's when he went ballistic. The worker had suggested that they go to counseling, and she apparently made the arrangements for them."

"That's it?" Beau sounded disappointed.

"No, I remember it now! She came back a few weeks later!" Tessa sounded excited as the memory of the thin, bedraggled woman walking into her office with two children in tow came back to her vividly now. "She first called herself Vicki Smith, but when I recognized she'd already been there, she admitted Smith was her maiden name. I finally convinced her to tell me her married name and her husband's name if she wanted us to help her." Tessa leafed through her file excitedly, "Let me see, what did she say it was again?"

Finally, she pointed at the papers in front of her. "Here it is. Brinker. Harley Brinker was her husband's name."

"That's it then. Jack is right. Victoria Bannan was married to Harley Brinker, and Patty is probably his child." Beau peered over her shoulder, brushing her again and causing another electric jolt to go through her.

"What did she come back for? Looks like the counseling session didn't go too well." *Focus,* Tessa chided herself, annoyed by her body's reaction to his nearness. *This is important!* Reciting more from memory than from her notes, she said, "Vicky asked me to get her out of the city. She told me she'd agreed to go to counseling only because the woman had contacted Harley, and he had threatened her and her children. As soon as she got the chance, she ran again and came to us with only the clothes on her back. She looked pretty beat-up and seemed terrified."

Beau let out a low whistle. "I guess cheating on the gang leader isn't too smart, is it?"

Tessa gave him a scathing look. "She told me she didn't cheat on him. Apparently, Snake had various enterprises, one of them being a prostitution ring." She sat back, shuffling through the notes, but knowing most of what she knew would need to come from her memory. "I didn't write down everything she told me. I was afraid that some of what she said could be used against her, and I didn't want her to end up in jail or losing her children," she admitted.

Beau gave her a skeptical look. "Isn't that against company policy?"

"Of course it is, but my priority has always been the women, not company policy. Anyway, she told me that she and Snake had been together since she was sixteen when he was just making a name for himself on the streets."

Shivering slightly, she gave Beau a sad look. "I'll never understand why women sell themselves so short, but she was one of the first girls that he sent out on the streets to work for him."

"He sent his wife out on the streets?" Beau's eyes were narrowed, the disgust clearly apparent on his face.

"She wasn't his wife at the time," Tessa reminded him. "She was just a naive teenager who was looking for love and acceptance, and she thought she found it with him. Anyway, as his enterprises grew, so did the money. He provided her with nice things, and she equated that with love."

Tessa now ignored her notes completely, closing her eyes as she tried to remember what Vicky had told her. "She said that after she got pregnant and had their daughter, Snake stopped sending her out on the streets, and she mainly oversaw the care of the rest of the women."

"So she became a pimp of sorts herself?" Beau's sympathy for the woman was quickly diminishing.

"It's not all her fault," Tessa felt the need to defend her. "These women are brought into the lifestyle so young, many of them don't know any better. Remember, she was out on the streets too, and she probably considered it a legitimate way to make money."

Beau just looked at her doubtfully. "If you say so. What else did she tell you?"

"Snake must have gotten himself arrested at one point, and they wanted her to testify against him. While they were waiting for his trial, he proposed to her. She was thrilled, of course, and said yes, but later found out his lawyer had advised him she couldn't be forced to testify if they were married."

"The guy is slick, that's for sure," Beau commented, scowling. "She was hurt, but since her newfound status gave her some clout with the other members of the gang, she said things went okay for a while."

Looking very unsympathetic, Beau asked, "So why was she so terrified? It sounds like she knew what she was involved with."

"She did know, but then Snake got arrested again, and this time he apparently spent some time in jail. While he was gone, some other gang member tried to take over. Snake could get most of his members back when he was released, but he had lost a few of his girls and a lot of his empire. The dissenting gang member was found dead, but no one could prove that Snake was involved." Tessa glanced at her notes. "However, when he decided it was time for her to go back out on the streets, she stated that he told her if she didn't go out and work again, she would end up like the dead gang member, so she did as she was told. She ended up pregnant a little while after starting work, and of course, she had no way of knowing if it was her husband's child or someone else's."

Beau was shaking his head, trying to fathom what must have been going on in the woman's head. "That doesn't sound like cheating to me."

"Not yet, but during the time that she was being forced out on the streets again, she lost the clout she had with the other gang members, and some of them began abusing her as well. Apparently, Harley was busy wooing another young girl, and he wasn't doing anything to stop them. One of the older members of the gang took pity on her and attempted to keep her safe."

"Aahhh, and so the affair begins," Beau said.

"She denied they had anything going on, but I suspect she may have been lying about that. When Harley got wind of the rumors, she said he turned into a raging monster. Her Prince Charming apparently hit the road, and she was left to deal with the aftermath."

"I guess there is no code of honor among criminals." Tessa just shook her head at his words.

"No, somehow these women always end up taking the brunt of the abuse. Anyway, she said she finally couldn't take it anymore.

The beatings were happening daily, and she was afraid for her children, especially the little boy. That's when she came to us for help."

"So you helped her get away?" It was a question, but Beau stated it as a fact.

"Yes, of course. I found a shelter for abused women in Atlanta and had her picked up directly from the office. I remember sitting there all night with her and the children until we could finally find someone to pick her up." Tessa rubbed her eyes wearily at the memory.

"To be honest, I almost didn't agree to help her. I knew she was also guilty of a number of crimes, but she seemed so terrified and desperate that I didn't know what else to do." Beau gave her a puzzled look.

"So you weren't sure that you should help her? Why not? That doesn't sound like you at all."

Tessa tried to remember the woman and the circumstances of that night. "Because I suspected she was on drugs, and I was worried about her taking the children. She seemed very strung out, and the little girl seemed unusually quiet. The time before, when I had met the little girl, she had been super active and vivacious, almost hyper, you could say." Tessa shook her head at the memory. "This time when I tried to talk to the child, she barely acknowledged me and never said a word. When I confronted Vicky about it, she explained that she and the children had been on the streets since the night before, and they were all just exhausted. But my gut was telling me that there was more to the story and the girl might also be drugged."

Beau looked at her strangely. "I've heard you have a knack for knowing if people are being truthful or not. Is that what your gut was saying?" Tessa looked down. So Beau did know something about her newfound gift.

"No, I didn't have any special senses then. It was just a normal gut reaction. My gift didn't appear until after the blow I received to my head the night my family was murdered. I suspect that blow was meant to kill me as well."

Beau touched her shoulder and said, "I'm sorry. I shouldn't have brought it up. I didn't know."

"Anyway," Tessa continued, trying hard to ignore the heat from the hand still caressing her and radiating up her body, "I made a note of it in the file and asked the social worker who picked her up to keep an eye on Vicky and make sure that the children were all right."

"Did you ever hear any more about this Vicky Brinker?" Beau asked.

"No, I tried to follow up. Somehow, the little girl and the blank look she had that night stayed with me for a long time. I wanted to find out if she was all right, but the shelter told me they had sealed her records for the safety of the woman and her children. I only have the notes that I already had. I never could find anything more about what happened to her or the children, and I just assumed we had been successful in relocating her and getting her away from her husband."

"I think you should call Jack and give him all the information you have in your file on this Vicky Brinker," Beau suggested. Rising from the corner of her desk, he added, "I'm going to head back to my place and make some calls of my own. I still know a few people in places that can get some information not always available to the police. Let me see if I can find anything."

Tessa looked at him curiously and said, "Maybe someday you'll fill me in on what it is you did before you retired so comfortably?" She was curious about the kind of people he was talking about.

Beau just grinned at her. "Sure, someday you and I can have ourselves a little kumbaya and spill all the secrets of our lives, but for now let's just see if we can uncover the secrets of Patty Brinker."

"Sounds good," Tessa agreed, suspecting that Beau was not about to tell her anything any time soon, and she would need to discover it on her own.

Before he got to the door, Beau turned around. "You still have your key, right, and you'll find the path? I don't want you to get lost on the way home later."

Tessa looked at him doubtfully. "I do, and I'm sure I'll find my way, but what if I run into Cujo again? He might not decide to back off when he doesn't see you with me."

"I'll keep Cash in his kennel for the evening, I promise. It'll be perfectly safe for you to use the path. Text me when you get back, and I'll come over. I want to make sure that you have everything you need, and if you're up to it, I'll even introduce you to Cujo officially."

Tessa grimaced. "Okay, I will text you, but I'm not so sure I really need to meet a vicious wolfdog tonight."

Beau laughed at her while he walked out, and Tessa took one last look at her files before dialing Jack's number. Jack answered her call on the second ring, and Tessa told him what she and Beau had learned from her files.

"It sounds like Patricia Brinker really is our mystery girl," he agreed. "The time period works for sure. I wonder if she knows who her father really is and if she was in contact with him before she showed up at your place."

"It sounds like that's certainly likely. She kept talking about a boyfriend, and it probably is the guy that got away from Beau. If it is, then it's pretty clear they all worked together. I just can't imagine that Patty would have known they wanted to kidnap me, and I still can't figure out why. I hope you can find something out from the Gabriel guy in the hospital tomorrow."

"So do I, Tessa. If you don't mind, can you fax over the file on Vicky Brinker, and I'll see if I can track down the social worker who picked them up back then? Maybe we can find out where she took them, especially if we tell her that the girl needs help. People are a lot more talkative after some years have passed." Jack sounded hopeful, and Tessa prayed he was right. The thought of Patty and her unborn child on the streets alone made her uneasy.

"Okay," she said, "give me a few minutes, and I'll have it on your machine. Be sure to let me know as soon as you find out anything, no matter what time it is. My gut is telling me that Patty's in trouble, and we need to find her fast."

Jack agreed to call her regardless of the time. He had learned over the last few years to follow Tessa's gut feelings. They were rarely wrong.

As soon as they hung up, Tessa gathered the file, faxing it to Jack's office and listening to the loud chattering of her old fax machine. She wondered where Patty was right now and prayed for her safety. When she was done, she stuck the file in her bag instead of filing it again, determined to spend some more time looking at it carefully later. She might have missed something, and she needed to find Patty fast before the girl did something drastic.

Walking into the kitchen, she found Angela and some of the other women busily preparing dinner, while their children were gathered around the table doing some schoolwork.

"Hi Angela, how are things going?" Tessa said.

Hope's Haven had strict rules that every child of school age had to spend a minimum of two hours a day working on schoolwork, and Tessa and Stephanie had meticulously built up quite a stock of books and worksheets for every age group.

"Things are good, Miss Tessa," Angela responded. "How are poor Miss Stephanie and those little boys of hers feeling today?" She turned and looked at Tessa with a concerned face.

Tessa felt a surge of guilt, realizing she hadn't called Stephanie all day. She'd been so caught up trying to find out the mystery behind Patty and why she'd been attacked, she hadn't even thought to take a minute and check on her best friend.

"I'm afraid I haven't even checked on her yet, Angela. I've been so caught up trying to find Patty. I'll call her as soon as I get a chance."

Angela frowned at the mention of Patty. "I sure hope that we can find that girl soon. I swear I haven't seen a little soul that lost in years. I can see she's just wavering between a helpless, innocent little child and a hardened street woman. I just know we need to find her fast, or the innocent part of her may lose that battle with herself."

Sighing silently, Tessa thought that was exactly the same feeling she'd had all day, and it didn't help her sense of unease to hear that Angela felt it too.

"I'm trying, Angela. Trust me, I'm trying," Tessa assured her. "Just promise to call me right away if she comes back, or if you hear anything from her."

Angela nodded, and Tessa gave her instructions on how to place an order with their usual grocery store. She knew she'd be busy with Jack tomorrow, and with the house full of women and children, Tessa was sure they were more than likely low on supplies. This store was one of the few in the area that delivered and also allowed the shelter a grace period to pay.

As they went over the list, she cringed, realizing how high the bill would likely be. Noticing her discomfort, Angela assured her, "Don't you worry about a thing, Miss Tessa. I've got this. And I'll try to be as economical as I can too."

Tessa gave the older woman a grateful smile. She tried her best to keep the money worries away from the residents, but somehow Angela always seemed to sense when things were tight.

"Thanks, Angela, but make sure you order what we need to keep all the little ones fed. You order plenty of milk, fresh fruit, and vegetables. Some of these kids haven't had a healthy meal in quite a while. I'll figure out how to pay for it later; that's not for you to worry about."

Tessa spent a few more minutes walking around and checking on the schoolwork that the children were working on. She even stopped to help some of the older ones with the more advanced lessons. Many of their mothers barely had a middle school education.

Finally, she glanced at her watch, realizing it was already getting late. She took Angela aside again and said, "I'd better get going now. I'll be staying at a cottage next door, so I won't be far if you need anything. Please call me if Patty shows up, or if anyone else comes by and wants to get in."

Angela raised an eyebrow, curious. "Next door at that place that Mr. Beau's been working on?"

Feeling herself blush, Tessa spun away before Angela could see. "Yes, that one. Just call if you need anything." As she scurried away, she missed seeing the delighted smile on Angela's face.

Sitting just outside of the Shelter, down the street, Ethan was furious and screaming at the crying girl sitting next to him.

"Stop your stupid blubbering and just show me where that hole in the fence is. I'm going in there tonight and getting what I came here for. We've been watching the place all night, and I know she's still in there. It's time for her, the dame, to face the music. I'm sick of waiting, and I need to get that file on your crappy mother out of her office before the cops find it and tie it to you and Snake, and then to me," he growled. "I can't believe you were too stupid to get it while you had the chance. What good are you anyway?"

Patty had just confessed that Harley Brinker was her father, and she had been trying to find the file on him and her mother in Tessa's office.

"I tried," she sobbed. "But she walked in on me before I had the chance. Please, it doesn't even matter if she finds out who I am. Let's just get out of here. We can still start a new life with our baby, just like you promised me. I don't want to be involved in anyone getting hurt. Everyone at the shelter was so nice to me."

Ethan grabbed at her face roughly with one hand, squeezing tightly and bringing it close to his sneering face. "That's just wonderful for you, isn't it? I'm so glad to hear that while I was out here planning and working for our future, you were in a nice, cozy house living the grand life, huh?" He pushed her back in the seat, fuming. "Well, guess what? It's my turn to live the grand life now, baby. Gabe is in jail and out of the way, and for once, Snake does not know where we are. Finally, it's my turn to call the shots, and I'm not letting this opportunity get away."

Turning his body to her, he shoved her again. "And you're going to help me, you hear? I'm sick of your petty sniveling and your constant whining. That might have worked on Snake, but it will not work on me. From here on out, you'll do what I tell you and shut up about it."

Patty looked at him with red-rimmed eyes, shock and terror clearly etched on her face. This was so much worse than anything she had ever experienced with Snake.

"What about our baby, Ethan? You said that you loved me and wanted to raise it, just like a proper family. I would have never gone against Snake if I hadn't thought that you meant it."

Ethan looked at the girl next to him in disdain. "Have you even looked at yourself lately?" he asked. "You're trash, and that's all you ever were. Don't fool yourself, you and your mother were just a way for Snake to make money, and now you'll be a way for me to make money." Leaning back on his seat, he closed his eyes, speaking patiently, "See, that's what girls like you do. They make money for the men that they belong to. And as for that brat that you're carrying"—he smiled slyly—"I already have some people lined up who are more than willing to pay for a cute little baby."

When Tessa finally let herself into the little cottage, she let out a sigh of relief. True to his word, Beau must have locked the wolf dog into his kennel for the night, and she had navigated the little path without incident. She set her bag down on the counter, noticing that someone must have come in and washed the breakfast mugs from this morning.

When she opened the refrigerator, wondering what to eat, she found a casserole with a note telling her how to warm it up. As uncomfortable as it was to think of someone cleaning up and cooking for her, she was tired and hungry and had to admit that it was nice having a hot meal tonight without having to make it herself.

She put the casserole in the oven and headed to the bedroom, deciding that a nice warm shower would be just the thing before dinner. Once there, she saw that the few clothes she had purchased today had been hung neatly in the closet. Rummaging through the items, she found a t-shirt and comfortable pants but vowed to talk to Beau about the maid service. She was perfectly capable of cleaning up after herself and didn't need anyone to do it for her.

After her shower, she dressed quickly and walked back out into the kitchen, marveling again at the luxury that surrounded her and how spoiled it made her feel. Since the casserole still had another few minutes, and she could see that the sun was just setting on the other side of the mountain, she poured a glass of wine from the bottle she had seen earlier and sat on the deck to watch Mother Nature's display. *I can't imagine it ever getting old watching the sun rise and set every day from here,* she thought wistfully. *I may as well enjoy it for the little time that I have here. Soon enough, it'll be time for me to move on.*

While she sat watching the sun turn into a fiery red ball, she could hear someone knocking at the door and reluctantly left her chair to answer it.

"So, you did make it home okay." Beau stood at the door with a loaf of bread and a sheepish grin on his face. "Ellie told me she dropped a casserole off for you, so I brought the bread in hopes that you would invite me to join you."

Tessa couldn't help but laugh at the silly way he held out the bread to her. "I can hardly say no to a request like that, now can I? Especially since you own the cottage and paid for the food."

Beau walked in, stating, "That's not how I want you to look at it. The cottage is yours for as long as you need it, and I don't intend to intrude." Sniffing the air hungrily, he continued, "Except for when I invite myself for casserole. That sure does smell good, and I'm starved. I don't think I ate all day."

Tessa's stomach growled as well, and she realized she hadn't eaten anything since this morning's muffin either. "Well, let me set the table while you cut the bread then. We'd better eat before we both wither away."

They sat in silence for a few minutes, each savoring their food, until finally Beau had satisfied himself enough to talk.

"I see you found the way on the path okay tonight."

Nodding, Tessa replied, "Yeah, no problem, but I think I'll need to walk it a few more times before I try to navigate it in the dark." Taking a sip of her wine, she added, "Thanks for locking Cujo up tonight. I'm glad I didn't run into him."

"His name is Cash, not Cujo, and as soon as you get to know him, you'll see that he's not that bad. You might even like it when he accompanies you on the path at night. At least you'll know that no other creature will dare come near when he's around."

"Ummm, no thank you. I think that I'd rather risk it with the squirrels and raccoons. They seem tamer to me than that wolf."

Looking at her in amusement, Beau said, "Actually, one reason I came over tonight was to introduce you to him properly. I can't have you walking around at night until he knows that you're now a part of the household. Ellie, or someone else, might forget and let him out. The sooner we get the introductions done, the better."

Tessa felt her stomach tightening into knots at the thought. It had been a rough few days, and she didn't feel ready for a formal meeting with the vicious predator. "I think I read somewhere that wild animals can sense when you're at your weakest, and they will take advantage of that. I'm feeling extremely tired, so I really don't think it's a good idea for me to meet him tonight." She looked at Beau pleadingly.

He just sighed, shaking his head. "He's not a wild animal, Tessa. Cash is a well-trained guard dog, that's all, and the sooner he officially learns to ignore you, the better."

Chugging down the last of her wine, she stood up and declared, "Fine, then let's just get this over with. If he's going to rip my throat out, it may as well be now."

"You're impossible." Beau laughed as he walked to the back slider. "Take a seat on the deck, and I'll bring him here to meet you. No sense in you walking all the way to the kennel."

"Here? To the cottage?" Tessa squeaked in alarm. "Do you think that's a good idea? I don't want him to know where to find me!"

Beau grinned. "I'll be right back, and you'll see there's nothing to worry about."

It was extremely dark, and Tessa heard, rather than saw, Beau walking down the path toward the big house. She poured herself some more wine, hoping to numb her fear, and then hastily set the glass down again. Hadn't she read somewhere that dogs hated the smell of alcohol?

She perched nervously on the edge of her seat for a few minutes, waiting for Beau. But after he didn't return, she relaxed a bit. *Maybe he can't find him,* she thought. *Maybe Cujo even ran away.*

Her arm was resting on the edge of the seat, and she leaned her head on her hand, watching as the moon struggled to come out from behind the clouds. It was completely dark now, and all she could hear was the sound of crickets in the distance. She hoped the moon would come out and light up the sky before Beau came back.

She was lost in thought and dozing when she felt the cold nose touching her arm. She leapt up with a startled shriek, nearly jumping out of her skin. Darting back instantly at her sudden movement, the big black dog bared his fangs at her, growling ferociously.

"Cash! Down!" Beau's stern voice rang out in the dark, and once again, the dog lowered his fangs and backed away obediently. "Well, I guess that wasn't a good start," he said apologetically, appearing from the dark path.

"I'm sorry, I shouldn't have screamed. I didn't hear him and got startled when I felt his nose on my arm." Tessa's voice was still trembling.

"No, it's my fault. He ran out ahead of me. I think I need to touch up on our commands a bit. He clearly forgot what heel means."

"He doesn't seem to know what 'down' means either," Tessa said while apprehensively watching the dog, who was still standing. "So now what?" she asked, her eyes never leaving the gigantic beast, who was also gazing at her.

"You sit down, and I'll bring him over for the introductions," Beau instructed.

Tessa was not so sure she wanted to sit and make her throat even more available to the beast, but she trusted Beau knew what he was doing and sat on the edge of a chair.

"Cash, come." Beau sat next to her and patted his thigh, inviting the dog to join them.

Cash looked from Beau to Tessa and never moved a muscle.

"It doesn't seem like he knows what 'come' means either," Tessa said, anxiously waiting for the dog to make a move.

"Come on boy, come here." Beau continued to pat his thigh. "Come and meet Tessa."

Cash continued to stand motionless, looking from one to the other.

"At least he's not growling or snarling," Tessa remarked, waiting, and watching Beau futilely try to get the large dog to come over.

Finally, she said, "You've never done this with him before, have you?"

Sitting back in the chair, Beau finally stopped patting his thigh. "Nope, never, but I thought I'd try it. It looks to me like that mutt is enjoying making me look bad in front of you."

Looking over at the dog, Tessa had to agree that he did look slightly amused.

"Well," she said, rising slowly and not taking her eyes off the creature. "This is clearly not working, and he knows where I live now, so we'll try this my way."

She eased her way back through sliding doors and into the kitchen, taking the leftover casserole and bringing it out to the deck. Slowly and carefully, she took a few steps towards the dog, setting the dish down and hoping the beast didn't decide to lunge at her before she had time to back off.

Cash watched her suspiciously before he finally took a few steps toward the dish, sniffing it cautiously. He lapped at the casserole while his big shaggy tail wagged in pleasure at the unexpected treat. After he had licked the dish clean, he sat down and eyed Tessa expectantly.

"Sorry boy, that's all there is," she whispered, hoping he didn't intend to see if she tasted like dessert.

The dog wagged his tail at her voice and slowly approached her, sitting politely directly in front of her.

"What does he want?" Tessa asked nervously, her eyes never leaving the animal now sitting almost on her feet.

"I have no idea," Beau admitted. "I told you I only inherited him with the house. I've never had a dog before."

Throwing Beau a sour look, Tessa said, "So, you decided it was a good idea to introduce us when you did not know what he would do?"

Looking unperturbed, he replied, "It seemed to work out okay with everyone else."

Slowly, Tessa reached out her hand, allowing the dog to sniff it, before slowly moving it to the top of its head and stroking his soft and silky fur. "Wow, he feels so soft, and he seems to like it," she commented, watching the dog's eyes soften as he let out a contented sigh.

"Well, that went well then." Beau sank back into the cushions, thoroughly satisfied with himself. "Now you can fill me in on what Jack had to say and what else you found out about Patty?"

Tessa sent Beau a scathing look, which he ignored, and filled him in on what she and Jack had talked about, still stroking the dog's warm fur while she talked.

A few hours later, Ethan stealthily slunk in through the hole in the fence, staying as close to the shadows as he could. His foot got caught on the root from a large willow and he tripped, almost falling to the ground. He cursed violently but silently. He was in a foul mood, and as he rubbed his scraped knee, he vowed that when he finally caught up with Tessa, she was going to pay.

But not tonight, he thought angrily. How had she been able to leave without him noticing? He'd been watching the house since he followed her earlier that day, and he was sure he had seen no one coming or going. Even so, when he'd called and asked for her an hour ago, the woman who answered the phone had told him Tessa Graves had left for the night and he would need to call back in the morning.

As he slunk closer to the house, he could see her car, still parked in the driveway. *That dame lied to me*, he thought, angry that he had been lied to, but relieved at being able to carry out his plan tonight after all.

Right after she had shown him the hole in the fence, he had made Patty describe the layout of the house to him. Now he was stealthily making his way to the back of the house, where she had said the kitchen was located. She had told him the lock on that door had seemed old and flimsy, and it was also the room furthest from the bedrooms. It was less likely anyone would hear him if he entered through here.

As he made his way to the door, he paused and waited, listening intently for any sounds inside or outside in the yard. The grass was already wet with dew, and his sneakers were soaked through. He knew it was likely he would leave footprints with the wet shoes and contemplated whether or not he should take them off. He had watched crime shows where they could measure footprints to find out your identity.

As he shimmied up to the door, he slid a small and narrow knife from his pocket. If there was one thing that Snake had taught all of them, it was how to break into a house quietly and with just a small and simple pocket tool. He crouched down, working on the lock, smiling when he realized that the lock was indeed flimsy and old. It took him less than a minute to get the door open.

Carefully easing his way into the darkened room, he let his eyes adjust before slinking across the door to the hallway. He was irritated that the girl had refused to come with him. It would have been faster and easier if she had. She could have shown him the way to the woman's office and also which room she would stay in.

He started searching the office first since Patty had told him it was opposite the bedrooms, figuring he might as well see what he could line his pockets with, and then head down to find the woman. After all, if things worked out the way he hoped they would, he would need to make a quick getaway after he dealt with her.

Just thinking about the woman put him in a vile mood again. She was the sole reason his stupid girl was messing with his plans. He had it all figured out. How they would break in, take whatever money they could find, and grab the files for Victoria Bannan. Then he would take the woman, force her to her ATM, and finish her off once and for all. With Patty right there next to him, he could make his getaway fast and be assured that she would work for him and not go back to Snake. He was counting on the baby she was carrying to bring in more money. There were lots of people out there willing to do anything, and pay well, for an undocumented newborn.

Now, because of this useless Social Worker, Patty had messed everything up. While they were waiting for everyone to go to sleep, he had gone to take a quick leak in the bushes. By the time he came back, she had been gone. He had to waste precious time driving around looking for her until he finally gave up and went in alone. Tonight was his last chance, and he wasn't about to miss it.

He had no illusions that Gabe wouldn't spill the beans, telling the cops everything they wanted to know, names and all. For all he knew, the cops were already looking for him. Unless he got in and out fast, and found Patty tonight, he would need to leave town without her. He wasn't about to risk staying around any longer than that, even if he did lose Patty and the baby. Either the cops or Snake were going to come looking for him sooner or later.

As quietly as he could, he checked through the files and drawers in Tessa's office. There was no file for a Victoria Bannan or anything even close. Patty had told him it had been there; she'd seen it right before she was caught and hadn't been able to take it. If the woman had already given it to the cops, they already knew Patty's name and her connection to Snake.

Digging through the desk and drawers only yielded him a few dollars, and he moved on to the office next door. There, he rummaged through the files as well, still not finding anything, and dug through the desk and drawers in that office. After he was done, he grunted in frustration, quickly counting what he had. It barely added up to $100. That wouldn't even get him out of the state, he thought angrily.

By the time he made his way down the hall, he was fuming and craving revenge on both the girl and the woman. He needed a drink badly, so he stopped in the kitchen to hunt around for anything that would satisfy his thirst. Unsurprisingly, his search turned up nothing more than a bottle of cooking wine.

As he slowly slunk out, utterly frustrated and angry, his eye caught a glimpse of a set of kitchen knives, neatly put away in their holder by the sink, glinting enticingly at him in the moonlight. Creeping over, he looked for the largest one, holding it up in the moonlight to admire its long sharp blade.

Unlike Gabe and most of the others in the gang, who preferred guns as their weapon of choice, he had a different preference. They slept with them strapped to their bodies, and he'd learned quickly that Gabe had a habit of pulling his out often, waving it around when he was angry. Ethan never felt the need for that. He had a skill he'd learned early on from his drunken father, a man who had never gotten enough money together to buy a street gun. He'd compensated by honing his talents with another weapon, making sure he taught his son the same skills. He explained to Ethan that guns were hard to buy and traceable, but a knife could be found anywhere and was just as effective, if not even more so.

Ethan had learned his lessons well and practiced hard, garnering the grudging respect of the others who had learned to stay well out of reach when he was mad if they wanted to avoid his blade. Now, as he admired his new weapon, he silently thanked his father for the lessons. The woman would either come with him quietly, or she would suffer the consequences, and it would all be done silently and quickly, with no one being the wiser until morning.

Slinking down the hallway, he hugged the wall, taking advantage of the deep shadows and stopping now and then to listen before continuing on. Since Patty wasn't with him to point out the right bedroom, he now needed to check each room painstakingly and soundlessly until he found her. The other women would all have children sleeping with them in the same room, and he was fairly certain once he found a room with just one person, he would have his target.

Quietly, he opened the first door that he came to, peering through the crack. Luck was on his side, and the clouds had given way to a moonlit night. He could make out the sleeping figures of two bodies in the bed and another on a small cot. Closing the door silently, he continued to work his way down the hall, checking each room until he reached the last one.

I should have just started here. This has to be it, he thought humorlessly. *It's always the last room!*

Opening the door, he peered in. Someone had drawn all the shades in this room, and it was pitch black. He could hear heavy breathing breaking the silence of the room, and a slight panic overtook him. *What if there was more than one person in here? What if she wasn't at the shelter after all?* His plans would be ruined.

Suppressing his rising panic, he stealthily eased his way along the wall, feeling his way towards the bed. As he got nearer, he could just barely make out a lone figure lying beneath the covers. He hadn't counted on it being so dark, and he couldn't see where her mouth was so he could muffle her before she could scream out. He felt the rage building up in him again. Things never seemed to go his way anymore, and right now, as he stared loathingly at the body lying in front of him, he didn't care who it was. They were about to feel the full brunt of his hate and resentment.

Soundlessly easing the knife high above his head, he tried to judge where he would hit the heart, or at least some major organ. He thought to himself, *I may not be walking out of here with the money I wanted, but I'll see to it she pays the price.*

CHAPTER 16

Beau picked up the call on the first ring, looking at the caller ID, and wondering who was calling him this late. As usual, he was ready to deal with any catastrophe.

"Tessa, what's wrong? Where are you?" he said, keeping his voice as calm as possible even as his adrenaline roared.

"I'm at the cottage, but I have to get to the shelter, fast. Something has happened." Tessa's voice was panicked. "Oh Beau, I think someone's been killed!"

Beau leapt to his feet, scrambling into his pants with one hand while he held the phone with the other. "I'm on my way over to you right now. Stay where you are until I get there, understand?" he commanded, grabbing a shirt and slipping into shoes all at the same time.

As he raced over to the cottage, he spotted a large form running towards him in the dark. *Cash,* he thought. *Good, he might actually come in useful tonight.*

Tessa was already at the door, running out as soon as she spotted him.

"We need to get there fast, Beau. I'm sorry I had to call you, but it's so dark, and I can't afford to get lost right now," she said.

He grabbed her hand, pulling her along behind him as he went down the hill at a fast clip, heading towards the path.

"It's a good thing that you called. Can you fill me in on what happened?" he asked, keeping up his pace as he talked. He maneuvered his way into the path, wishing he had thought to bring a flashlight.

"I got a call from one of the women at the shelter. She was terrified and panicked, and she said I needed to come right away. Something happened with Angela and a man. She was crying and just kept saying 'they're dead' and that I needed to get there now," Tessa explained. Her heart was racing, and she prayed with everything she had that she would find Angela alive. The woman had done so much for her during the last few months, and she couldn't even imagine the devastation to her children if something happened to her.

Stumbling on a root, she fell onto Beau, who thankfully caught her before she went down. Grabbing her tighter, he said, "I can't see much. I'm going to slow down just a bit so we don't end up breaking a leg in here."

"But we have to get there fast, Beau! There's no time!" Tessa exclaimed, feeling something large and hairy brush against her.

"Cash! Good boy! Lead on out," Beau commanded, wondering if the dog really intended to help or if he had just become impatient with their stumbling about.

Hurrying after the dog so he wouldn't lose sight of him, Beau was now convinced that Cash really was slowing down just enough for them to follow. He could just barely make out the reflective collar he wore in the scant moonlight, but it was enough to know where he needed to step.

After what seemed like an eternity to Tessa, they finally stepped out into the dark clearing, and Tessa could see that the lights in the kitchen window were all brightly lit up. She raced up the back lawn, making it to the door at the same time as Beau. Tearing open the door frantically, she saw most of the residents of Hope's Haven huddled together around the large table. Some appeared to be weeping, but they all had the same shocked look.

"What happened here? Where's Angela?!" demanded Tessa, the panic that had been simmering in her gut finally rising and exploding. Wordlessly, the woman pointed to the hallway in the direction of the bedrooms, and Tessa raced down without waiting for her to speak.

Overtaking her quickly, Beau saw that the last bedroom was lit up and the door was wide open. As he reached the door, he turned abruptly, pushing Tessa back. "I'm going in first to see if it's safe." She allowed him to enter before her but followed him in immediately.

"Angela!" she cried, rushing over to her. "Thank God you're alive." Angela was sitting on the bed, holding a heavy pan in front of her, and staring down at the lifeless body of the man lying in front of her.

When she saw Tessa and Beau, she rose slowly and handed Beau the large cast iron pan, saying, "I didn't mean to kill him, Mr. Beau. I just wanted to stop him."

Beau took the pan from Angela, setting it on the dresser before bending down in front of the man, checking him for any signs of life. Finally, he stood up, looking directly at Angela. "We have to call the police."

A voice coming from the corner of the room said, "I called 911 right after I called Tessa." The woman stepped up to Beau, holding out her phone. "They should be here at any minute now."

Tessa had sat down on the bed next to Angela and was cradling the distraught woman in her arms. Looking up at Beau, she asked, "Is he dead?"

Nodding, he told her, "That's the other man who tried to abduct you, the one that ran away. I'd recognize the little weasel anywhere."

Tessa paled and looked down at the man lying dead by her feet. Stepping away from the body, Beau turned to the woman who had been standing in the corner. "What happened here?"

"I don't know. I have the room next door, and I woke up to a commotion. I told my kids to stay put and raced over to see what was going on, figuring it was probably just a scuffle, or maybe that girl came back. But when I walked in, I saw that man walking towards Angela with a knife. He was bleeding, but he was clearly intending to stab her. I was still searching for some kind of weapon to hit him with when I saw her jump up and whack him with the pan." The woman looked over at Angela in admiration. "I never would have thought you could move like that!"

Tessa could hear the sirens from the police cars coming nearer, and she looked at Beau fearfully. "She had to defend herself, Beau. She didn't have a choice. You don't think she'll be in any trouble, do you?"

"No, Tessa, of course not," Beau replied. "But we need to find out who this guy is and what he wanted." Walking over to Angela, he crouched in front of her while avoiding the body. "I'm going to let the police in now, Angela. You need to tell them exactly what happened. Don't worry, you won't be in trouble. Tessa and I will be right here with you."

After Beau left the room, Angela put her head on Tessa's shoulder, wailing, "I didn't want to kill him, Miss Angela, honest. But he was coming right at me with that knife. I had to stop him. I need to take care of my kids!"

Patting the woman's back, Tessa said soothingly, "Shhh, Angela. I know. It's going to be okay. You did what you had to do, I promise you, everything is going to be all right."

She looked up to see Jack striding into the room, with Beau following immediately behind him. Jack looked at Tessa and Angela huddled on the bed, and then at the body lying in front of them.

Walking over to the body, he knelt down and checked for a pulse. When he stood up, he looked directly at Tessa.

"What happened in here?" he asked.

Before Tessa could speak, the woman who had been standing in the corner and made all the calls strode forward and explained what she had seen and how she had called for help. Tessa got the impression that the woman was enjoying her role in the limelight, but she was grateful to not have to explain the situation herself.

When the woman had finished speaking, Jack told her to join the other women in the kitchen, asking her to recount her story to an officer who would make the official recording. There were several officers already taking statements from the other residents.

After she left, Jack once again looked at the body, asking, "Has anyone touched or moved the body?"

Angela shook her head. "That's where he fell when I hit him with the pan," she answered.

Jack looked at the pan, and then at Beau.

"Angela handed me the pan when I walked in, and I'm the one who put it on the dresser," Beau said, answering Jack's unspoken question. "I also checked the man for a pulse and vitals, but other than that, no one has touched him since we came in the room."

Jack looked at Angela and Tessa, saying, "The coroner is on his way, and I'd like to move to the living room so he can do his job in here undisturbed. I need you to tell me exactly what happened tonight, Angela."

Both Tessa and Angela carefully stepped away from the body, and Tessa led Angela to the living room, sitting her down on the couch, staying close to the distraught woman the whole time. She could see that Angela was completely shaken and horrified at what had happened.

Jack walked in, sitting down opposite them, while Beau stood at the doorway, watching the entire proceeding without sitting. "All right, Angela, tell me what happened right from the beginning." He took out his notebook.

Angela straightened up, looked at Tessa for reassurance, and then began, "I was asleep, and something woke me up suddenly. At first, I didn't know what, but then I thought I could hear the floorboards creaking outside in the hall." She looked at Tessa. "You know how those boards always creak, even when someone is trying to stay quiet?"

Tessa nodded at her, while Jack prompted, "Go on, Angela, what did you do then?"

"Well, I assumed one woman was sneaking around, so I peeked out of my room to see. At first, all I could see was someone sneaking out of one room and into another, and I figured the woman was trying to steal from the others." Sniffling with slight indignation, she said, "No matter how careful we are, we do sometimes still get women who think they can steal from one another."

"I understand," Jack said patiently. "What did you do when you saw that?"

"Well, I figured I needed to confront whoever it was sneaking in and surprise them when they came out, but when they left the room, I could tell it was a man, not a woman... You can imagine my fright when I saw that." Glancing around at them, Angela continued, "I know you all think I should have called the police, and maybe I should have, but I've learned to rely on myself since I was young, and I guess instinct just kicked in."

Tessa stroked Angela's hand reassuringly. "It's okay, Angela. No one is blaming you." But even as she reassured the woman, she was finding it hard to ignore the slight buzzing in her head.

"Anyway," Angela continued, "since he was blocking the way to the living room, the only option I had was to go to the kitchen and find something to defend myself with. I crept down the hall, but it was so dark everywhere, all I could find was that big old cast-iron skillet. One of the women must have left it on the stove, so I grabbed it, figuring I'd try and sneak up on him." She paused then, looking out towards the hallway. "When I saw him go into the last room, I knew no one was in there, and I figured that was a pretty safe place to confront him. I didn't want to frighten any of the children," she explained. "He left the door open a crack, so I peeked in and saw him standing by the bed, staring down at the lump of bed sheets on the bed." She looked over at Tessa apologetically.

"I'd been in the middle of washing the sheets this morning, just like you asked me to, but I got distracted, and I guess I forgot to go back and collect them. I'm sorry, I know I told you I would take care of it."

"It's okay, Angela. Don't worry about that now," Tessa told her, wondering if it was the stress of the night causing the slight but incessant buzzing in her head.

"Well, I was wondering why he was staring at the sheets when I saw him raise his hand up, and that's when I saw the knife that he was holding." Angela shuddered at the memory. "He stabbed down at the sheets, and I think I heard him say, 'It's time you die, lady.'"

Tessa looked over at Beau, her eyes wide. He was gazing intently at her. She couldn't help but think if he hadn't convinced her to stay at the cottage, that would have been her lying in the bed, not a stack of bed sheets.

Angela continued, "As soon as he stabbed down, I rushed in and hit him with the pan. I figured it was hard enough to knock him out but easy enough to kill him or hurt him too bad."

"So you hit him harder than you thought you did?" Jack asked, looking at Angela.

"No, sir, I didn't hit him hard enough. He staggered a bit, but then turned around, shoving me away. He looked kind of shocked to see me at first, but then I could see him get furious, and he came at me with the knife. At first, I scrambled away, and I screamed for help, but then I tripped and fell. That's when he came right at me. He held that knife up high and ready to stab down on me. I knew if I didn't get away, he'd kill me." Angela looked at Jack. "I don't know how I managed, but I jumped up and whacked him in the head as hard as I could." Holding her head to her hands, she sobbed, "I have two kids and there's no one else but me to take care of them. I had to do something! I never meant to kill him, honest. I just wanted to stop him."

There was a commotion in the hallway, and they all looked up to see the coroner bustle by, followed by a man pushing a gurney.

"Looks like the coroner finally made it," Jack announced, standing up. "You all stay in here and out of the way. I'll be back to get your statements in a while," he said to Tessa and Beau, hustling after the coroner.

About two hours later, Tessa and Beau were finally free to leave and headed down the path back to the cottage. Tessa had seen that Angela was tucked safely into bed with her two children. Carmen, the woman who had called them and the police, had promised Tessa that she would check on Angela throughout the night and make sure she was all right.

They were only about halfway back when they were joined by Cash. Tessa reached out, ruffling the fur on his head. "I never thought I would say this, but I'm actually glad to see him right now."

"Yeah, so am I. I think I'll tell him to sleep outside your cottage tonight," Beau said. "Until we figure out what that creep wanted, I don't feel safe leaving you completely alone."

Shuddering, Tessa thought about the man lying lifeless on the floor. Even though none of them had actually said it aloud, the angry thrusts coming from the man's knife had been meant for her.

Trying not to focus on what could have happened, she said, "Poor Jack is going to have a busy night tonight. I doubt he'll get much sleep. I'm kind of surprised he still wants to interview Patty's mother tomorrow."

"I'm pretty sure he's as eager to find out what the connection between Patty and these men is just as much as we are. The sooner we figure out how the puzzle pieces all fit together, the better it is for you," Beau answered, carefully watching where Cash was going.

"Hopefully we find Patty soon as well," said Tessa. "These men are dangerous. I hate to think that she was forced to be with them."

Beau looked at Tessa doubtfully. "The signs are not pointing to her being forced to be with them at all, Tessa. I hope that you're right, and she did not know what they were really up to, but to be honest, I don't think Jack or I think she wasn't with them of her own free will."

"You're both wrong. I'm sure she did not know they were this horrible," Tessa said, convinced she was right. "I just hope that there's no one else out there looking for her."

"Are you ready?" Jack looked over at Tessa, sitting next to him in his unmarked sedan. They had just pulled up a few feet away from Victoria Bannan's house.

Letting out a breath of air, Tessa replied, "Yes, I'm ready. Are you sure that this is the right address?"

"Pretty positive. The local police verified it was her. Do you think she'll recognize you?"

Tessa shrugged. "I don't know. After last night, I don't know what to think anymore. But if she's involved in any of this, I should be able to tell right away," she said confidently.

The buzzing from last night had disappeared, and when she had checked on Angela earlier, there had been nothing but blessed silence in her head. "She should recognize me, though; it's only been a few years since I helped her. I don't think that I've changed that much."

Even as the words left her mouth, she thought about all that had transpired since she had so innocently helped a woman and her children escape. Could Victoria Bannan be the reason she had lost everything that was dear to her? Looking over at the nondescript ranch house where Victoria lived, she reflected aloud, "I just can't understand why she came right back to the city she'd been so eager to leave."

"You said yourself that it's not that uncommon for abused women to go right back to their abusers and what they know. According to the timeline, she went back to Harley Brinker before she finally married her current husband," Jack frowned. "I wonder if she ever told him your name when she went back."

Tessa was wondering the same thing. Had Victoria inadvertently given Harley the ammunition he needed to get his revenge on her for aiding his wife and children in their escape?

Taking one more look around, Jack opened his door. "All right then, let's get going. The sooner we talk to Victoria, the sooner we'll get our answers."

After they rang the doorbell, it took a few more minutes before they heard someone coming to the door. When it finally opened, they were surprised to see a large, surly-looking man standing in front of them.

"Yeah, what do you want? If you're selling something, I'm not interested," the man said gruffly.

Jack looked over at Tessa. According to the reconnaissance the local police had done, Wyatt Bannan should have been at work right now, not standing at his door. He could tell from the way Wyatt was looking at him that he already knew he was a cop, so Jack pulled out his badge, holding it in front of the man's face.

"We're not selling anything, Wyatt. We're here to get some information. I'm Sheriff Jack Lewis, and I'm looking for Victoria Bannan. Is she here?"

Wyatt's eyes narrowed. He looked at them suspiciously. "What do you want with her? Is she in some kind of trouble again?"

It was clear they had caught him off guard. Tessa suspected he had thought they were looking for him, not his wife.

"That depends," Jack said. "I'll need to talk to her first, and then I'll let you know."

Examining Jack's badge closely, Wyatt asked, "What's a cop from Tennessee want with Vicky? I don't think she's even ever been to Tennessee. Are you sure you got the right Victoria Bannan?" He stood in the door, still blocking their way, but Tessa could see he was deciding whether he dared deny them entrance.

Standing squarely in front of Wyatt, Jack pulled himself to his full height until he towered over him, looking at him coldly. "Our business is with Victoria and not you. After we talk to her, she can decide whether she wants to tell you what this is about."

Wyatt's face reddened in anger, and Tessa guessed he didn't like the idea of Victoria deciding what he was told or not told.

"Vicky, get your behind down here," the man bellowed, still not moving from the door. "There are some cops that want to talk to you. You better not have gotten yourself into trouble again."

"I'm coming, I'm coming," Tessa could hear a frazzled voice calling from the back of the house. "What do you mean there are cops looking for me? I did nothing. I barely even leave the house, you know that."

Victoria's face peered out from behind the man, looking at Jack in trepidation. She was holding a small boy, about 3 years old, on her hip. She was heavier than she had been when Tessa had first seen her and had dyed her hair a bright auburn color, but there was no mistaking that this was the same woman who had walked into her office seven years ago with two children in tow.

Jack glanced at her out of the corner of his eye, and Tessa nodded at him in affirmation. She was certain that this was the same woman she had helped. "Hi, Victoria," he said, pulling out his badge again and showing it to her as well. "I'm Jack Lewis, and I'd like to ask you a few questions about your daughter." He purposely didn't introduce Tessa just yet.

At the mention of her daughter, Tessa saw Vicky shrink back, and Wyatt immediately turned and glared at her, growling, "What's that girl done now?"

"We'd like to talk to you for just a few minutes, Vicky. As soon as you answer some of our questions, we'll be on our way," Jack said. As he was speaking, he took advantage of the space left by Wyatt and walked into the house.

The hall was cramped, and Wyatt waved his arm, motioning for them to continue further down the hall. "You might as well go into the living room now that you're in. You can tell us what that girl has done in there, where I have some more breathing space."

As Jack and Tessa walked down the stifling hallway, she could hear the man snarling at the woman to handle this fast and get rid of them. Entering the cluttered room, Tessa turned around and watched the woman slinking in behind her husband, still holding her toddler on her hip. Victoria Bannan looked at her clearly for the first time, her eyes growing wide with recognition. Tessa was certain that some of the color drained out of her ruddy face as well.

"Well, what do you wanna know?" Wyatt demanded, without offering them a seat. Jack looked at Vicky and then back at Wyatt. "Are you sure you want to talk in front of him?" he asked evenly, watching Vicky to see her reaction.

Ignoring his question, Vicky didn't seem able to take her eyes off Tessa, but Wyatt spat out, "I'm her husband, and whatever she has to say, she'll say in front of me, you got that?"

"Victoria?" Jack ignored the man, continuing to look questioningly at Vicky.

Finally, she turned to Jack, clearing her throat. "Ummm, yes, of course, Wyatt can stay. What is it you want to know? I haven't seen my daughter in almost a year. Did she get herself into some trouble?"

"A year?" Tessa said softly, looking at the woman. "Surely you've spoken to her in that year? Do you know where she is right now?"

Looking down at the floor, Vicky threw her husband a furtive look and said vaguely, "She's with relatives."

"I would need the name and number of these relatives." Jack pulled out a notebook, looking at her expectantly.

"I, uh, I'll have to go and get it." Vicky looked at her husband but didn't move, clearly waiting for his permission.

"That's okay, we'll wait while you get it," Jack prompted her.

Looking right at Tessa, Vicky said, "It's in the kitchen, right next to the bathroom."

Tessa understood immediately what Vicky wanted, and she looked over at Wyatt, plastering on a sweet smile. "Actually, it's been a long ride. Do you mind if I use your bathroom?"

Wyatt grinned, clearly delighted at the show of humility, saying, "I guess even cops gotta pee sometimes, huh? Yeah, you take care of business. Vicky can show you where it is while she gets that number you want. After that, it's time you two hustled your way back outta here."

"Thanks," Tessa gave Wyatt another demure smile, following Vicky, who had deposited her toddler on the couch, out of the room. As she walked out, Tessa could hear Jack asking Wyatt about the large screen TV that took over most of the living room.

When they reached the end of the hall, Vicky whirled around at her and whispered angrily, "What are you doing here? Why do you want to cause trouble for me? I've finally found some peace in my life!"

Tessa looked at her in shock. *This was peace?* she thought. "It's about your daughter, Vicky. I would think you'd want to help her. She may be in trouble and needs your help."

"I already told you; I haven't seen Patty in over a year. There's nothing I can do to help her or you." Vicky looked down the hallway nervously, as if she were expecting her husband to appear at any minute.

"Vicky," Tessa said gently, "Patty is only a child. I know that she's not with relatives like you say she is. I just saw her a few days ago, and she was very much alone and on her own."

"You saw Patty!" Vicky gasped, putting her hand over her heart. "How is she? Is she okay? Where is she now?"

"When I saw her, she was okay, just scared. She was at a shelter for a few days, but then she ran off. I don't know where she is right now. That's what I was hoping you could tell me. I thought she might come home to you, or you would at least know where she could have gone."

Giving Tessa a funny look, Vicky said, "I don't think she'll show up here. She never really thought of this as home, and Wyatt wouldn't let her stay even if she did show up." She shook her head resolutely. "I honestly do not know where she would have gone, but I'm sure Patty can take care of herself. She's pretty smart for a girl her age."

Tessa put her hand on Vicky's arm gently. "Vicky, Patty is pregnant. She's afraid, she's alone, and she needs your help right now. Please don't turn your back on her. Help me find your daughter."

Vicky's eyes widened as she stammered, "Pregnant?" Then she looked at Tessa sadly. "Of course, I don't know why I should be surprised." Vicky looked down the hall nervously and said in a hushed voice, "I can't talk right now, but Wyatt goes to work in about an hour. Come back then, and I'll talk to you."

"Of course," Tessa readily agreed. "We'll be back in an hour."

"Just don't park that car out in front of my house," Vicky cautioned. "It just screams cop car. Park on the other block and come through the back door. You can take the alleyway on the street behind ours and get to the backyard that way. Try not to be seen,

Wyatt has the neighbors watching the house. I want no more trouble than I already have."

Quickly pushing Tessa into the bathroom, she walked back down the hall to where her husband and Jack were still talking.

An hour later, Jack carefully locked the car, patting the holster holding his service weapon for reassurance. "Just in case this turns into an ambush, I'll go ahead of you, and you stay close behind."

"Relax, Jack. You're too paranoid. I'm sure this is no ambush. There was nothing deceptive about the way Vicky was talking." Tessa followed closely as he made his way through the alley and into Vicky's backyard. She was waiting for them at the back door, motioning them to hurry up and get inside, and then shut the door quickly behind them.

"Sit," Vicky pointed to the vinyl-covered chairs in the kitchen. "You have 45 minutes, and then Wyatt is going to call. I want you out of here before then. Little Wyatt is in the living room watching TV right now, and I think that'll keep him busy for a while, but make sure he doesn't see you. If he tells his Dad you were here, I'm in big trouble."

Trying to show some compassion for the woman, Tessa asked, "Vicky, what happened? I thought we helped you leave your abuser years ago. All the arrangements were made for a safe escape for you and for the children. They even sealed your records. Why did you go back?"

"Do you have any idea what it's like to start over in a strange city with two kids!" Vicky sat down heavily, her tone angry and accusatory. "Sure, they give you money for a few months, but then you're on your own. I did try to make a go of it, but I don't have a lot of marketable skills. I had two kids that no one helped me with. I couldn't get a job, and with no job, there's no money." Her eyes were flashing as she looked at Tessa. "What could I do? I had no choice but to go back to doing the only thing I've ever done, but at my age, and with two kids in tow, it was hard for me to find paying customers." She sighed, "I know you tried your best, but after a while, the only way I could think of to survive was to return to Harley. It wasn't safe for me in the new city alone. When you're in my line of work, you need someone to protect you."

"You went back to your abuser? The man who beat you?" Tessa was shocked.

"I didn't have a choice," said Vicki vehemently. "If I hadn't gone back, I would have been killed on the streets, and then what would have happened to the kids?!"

Looking her squarely in the face, Tessa said, "What happened to the kids, Vicky? The little boy in the living room is too young to be the baby you had seven years ago. What happened to him?"

Looking out the window, Vicky quietly said, "He's with a better family now."

Jack glanced down at his notes. There had been no mention of her adopting out her son in Victoria's records. "Where is the boy, Vicky? There's no record of an adoption in your records," Jack said.

"You looked me up?" Vicky's eyes were blazing. "I thought you wanted my help, not stir up trouble."

"When you commit crimes, that's what happens, Vicky," Jack said tersely. "Your life becomes an open book, and everything gets recorded. What happened to the little boy?"

Defiantly, Vicky retorted, "He was adopted, okay? By a really nice family! Harley made me do it as a condition of taking me back, and I'm glad he did! The kid is living a good life now, and we made some money in the process. It's a win-win for everyone!" She looked over at Tessa, almost defying her to say anything. "I should have let Patty go as well. She deserved to have a better life than I did, but now it looks like she's just following in my footsteps."

Jack was mulling over what to do about the illegal adoption that Vicky had confessed to. He doubted her parole officer knew about what happened to the boy.

Tessa could see that Jack wanted to pursue the matter of the boy now, but their time was running short, and her immediate concern was what had happened with Patty and where she was now.

"So, Patty stayed with you when you went back to Harley Brinker?" she asked.

Nodding, Vicky said, "Yeah, he knew she was his kid, so he let me bring her with me."

"When did you leave Harley and marry Wyatt?" Jack asked.

"A year or so after I went back, the abuse with Harley was getting so bad, I was forced to go into hiding again. I stayed with some friends of mine, but Harley found me. Even though he didn't want me for himself anymore, his pride wouldn't let me go." She paused, looking around her ramshackle kitchen. "Wyatt was still in the gang at that point, and he was one of the few people who was nice to me, even trying to intervene when Harley got too abusive with me. Some of the other members were also noticing that Harley was getting meaner to everyone." Vicky closed her eyes at the memory and continued to recite her story. "I think some of them were urging Wyatt to take over, promising him they would stay loyal to him. Of course, Harley got wind of the plan pretty quickly."

"Did Wyatt ever take over the gang?" Jack looked puzzled. If he had, it hadn't been known to the local police.

Shaking her head, Vicky fiercely announced, "No, but he could have," before she continued on, "If he hadn't been so afraid it would splinter the group, Harley would have probably destroyed Wyatt. But he was already having trouble keeping everyone in line. Since he wanted no more trouble, he made Wyatt a proposition."

"What kind of proposition?" Tessa asked, not so sure she really wanted to know the answer.

"Me," Vicky said simply. "He said that if Wyatt took me away, married me, and quit the gang, there would be no fights and no bloodshed."

Tessa looked over at Jack in disbelief. That was not what she had expected.

"You agreed to that?" Even Jack was dumbfounded.

"Of course I did. Wyatt had already wanted out of the gang and to start a normal life, and Harley offered him enough startup money to make that happen. I knew that if I stayed with Harley, I'd probably end up dead anyway, so I agreed to go with Wyatt and marry him. At the time, he really did seem to love me, and I figured that anything was better than the life I was living. I thought that living the suburban housewife life could be fun."

"And is it?" Tessa asked, looking around the dirty kitchen.

"I guess at first it was," Vicky said, "But life gets hard and men drink. That always seems to be the problem."

"Is that why Patty left?" Jack asked.

"No, Patty was pretty happy at her school. She didn't want to leave, but she was acting out." Vicky looked to Tessa, sure at least she would understand. "You know, like teenagers will at times."

Tessa just nodded, waiting for her to continue.

"Patty started back-talking to Wyatt, so he started slapping her around as well. I tried to tell her to keep her mouth shut, but she just wouldn't. The more he slapped her, the more she acted out, making him even madder. It was like this endless cycle, and I just couldn't take it anymore."

Vicky paused in her narrative, looking at Tessa. "I finally tried to get away from Wyatt, just like I did with Harley. Of course, I took Patty with me, and I went back to the same place I went when you first helped us. This time they weren't so eager to help though because I went back to Harley. I asked for you because I knew you wouldn't refuse to help us."

Jack narrowed his eyes and watched Tessa's face pale.

"What did they tell you?" Tessa asked.

"That you didn't work there anymore… Then they gave me the address of your shelter. I was going to get there, but before I could, Wyatt came after me. He was furious, telling me he would not let me run off the same as I had from Harley." There was a very tiny, prideful smile on her lips as she continued, "He told me when I ran away from Harley, a lot of the guys lost respect, thinking he was weak because I got away and he couldn't find me. That's why Harley was so furious, I guess, and he lashed out at anyone around, including him. Wyatt said there was no way that I was going to disrespect him the same way that I had disrespected Harley."

"Did he threaten you?" Jack asked, "You know the police can protect you if you're in danger."

Vicky laughed at him bitterly. "Yeah right. I've heard that one before. They slap a restraining order on him that's just a worthless piece of paper, and it leaves me an angry husband, and no one to provide for me and the kids. No thanks."

"Why did you take Patty out of school?" Tessa asked.

"Because Wyatt was sick of her. He said if I didn't get rid of her, he'd make my life hell. He told me I should send her back to her father where she belonged, and so I did."

"You sent her back to your abuser?" Tessa gasped.

Vicky squirmed around uncomfortably, before saying, "It's not like Harley ever abused her. She was his kid after all, and he never laid a hand on her. I figured it would be better for her with him than it was here, with Wyatt slapping her around and all."

Vicky looked triumphantly at Tessa, "Besides, I gave her your information and told her that if things ever got bad with her father, she should contact you for help." She glanced back at Jack who was busy jotting down notes in his pad. "I contacted Harley to come and get her. That was about a year ago, and it's the last I saw her or talked to her. I figured since I had heard nothing, she was safe, and learning the ways of the street and how to survive."

Looking up at the clock, Vicky jumped up abruptly. "That's it, you need to go now. Wyatt's going to call any minute and he's going to want to talk to little Wyatt. I've got nothing more to say to you. I have no idea where Patty would have run off to, but if she went and got herself pregnant, then that's on her. I told her to stay out of trouble." She opened the back door, peering around outside. "You have to leave now. And make sure no one sees you."

Jack and Tessa stood up, both knowing that the interview with Patty was over, and that was all the information she was going to give them. As they were walking out, Jack paused. There was one more thing he wanted to know.

"Vicky, when you went back to Harley the first time, after coming out of hiding, did you give him Tessa's name and tell him she was the one who helped you?"

Vicky looked out the door nervously, giving him a light shove and trying to hurry him out before she answered, "I don't know, maybe. I probably did tell him. He wanted all the details. He was pretty mad that some woman had bested him." With that, she pushed him out and shut the door firmly behind him. Jack heard the distinct click of the deadbolt sliding in place as he hurried after Tessa.

It wasn't until she was seated back in Jack's car that Tessa finally allowed herself to take a deep breath. Sinking into the hot plastic seat, she watched silently as Jack maneuvered the car away from the curb and back on the road.

As the distance between them and the shoddy ranch house increased, she felt the tension in her back and shoulders slowly fading, wondering if poor Patty had felt the same whenever she had left her house.

Glancing at the houses slipping by them, she finally broke the silence. "Poor Patty… It's no wonder she ended up in such poor company. She never stood much of a chance."

"Yeah, poor kid. I'm not sure who was worse at that house, Wyatt, or the mother that was supposed to keep her safe." Jack was watching traffic as he spoke, contemplating what he should do with all the information they'd garnered from Vicky.

At the very least, he needed to see that the little boy she had given up was indeed safe and with a good family. Vicky's revelation that she had indeed provided Harley with Tessa's name put him at the top of the list of suspects for the attack on her family, as well as the recent attempt at her kidnapping.

"It's not all Vicky's fault, you know." Tessa felt the need to defend the woman. "Her life probably started out like Patty's. She was on the streets at a real young age too, and she's just doing what she learned to do." She chewed her lower lip, feeling an overwhelming sense of guilt. "The system, and that includes me, failed them both. If we would have done more for them, they wouldn't be in the situations they're in."

Jack looked over at her and said, "Don't go blaming yourself, Tessa. You did what you could do and gave her all the help and resources you had at that time. If she ended up not using them, then she has the responsibility for that, not you."

"You heard her, Jack. We didn't give her the right tools. Instead, we left her and her children high and dry, with no skills and no way to earn a living except to go back on the streets. We're responsible for her failure, and we owe her, Patty, and her little boy help."

Now that she was away from the depressing, ramshackle little house, Tessa was determined to see what she could do to help Vicky and Patty. She couldn't imagine the poor woman living in her little ranch prison for any longer than she had to.

"You know that we're not done with her yet, right?" Jack asked, glancing away from the road to look at Tessa.

"What do you mean?" she asked. "Do you mean you and I, or the police?"

"I mean the police," he said resolutely. "She can't just go giving her minor children away the way she has, even if she does say it was better for them. Right now, we do not know where either of them are, and I don't intend to just take her word for it that the little boy is safe. I need to find out who has that little boy, and if she doesn't know, then that will be a question for Harley Philipps. You can't just sell off your kids because you don't want them anymore."

Rubbing her forehead, she replied, "I know that, Jack, but if you contact Harley Philipps, he will cause trouble for Vicky again, and then Wyatt is sure to hear about it as well. Let's at least try to get her away from them first."

Jack was silent for a minute, and Tessa was anxiously hoping he would agree when her phone started ringing. Glancing down at it, she quickly turned it off.

"Who was that?" Jack asked, surprised. Tessa was not usually one to ignore her calls.

"Carter," she replied, sighing. "Before we left this morning, I filled Stephanie in on everything that happened last night at the shelter. I'm guessing she probably told Carter by now. He's probably calling to scold me for not notifying him right away myself."

Curious, Jack asked, "Why didn't you call him last night?" It was apparent to anyone who spent time around the two of them that Carter Williams' interest in Tessa went beyond just a friendship.

"Because he would start badgering me to stay with him in the city again. He believes I spend way too much time and energy at the shelter already, and I'm sure this incident only fuels his argument for me to step back from it."

"He wants you to step back from running the shelter?" Now Jack's interest was really piqued. "I thought he was helping you and Stephanie manage things from the financial side?"

"He does help us, and he's great at that. I honestly don't know what we would do without his help. Steph and I are both helpless in the bookkeeping part of things. But I think that's part of the problem."

"How so?" asked Jack, merging onto the freeway heading back to Tennessee.

"He can see what a financial mess we're in," Tessa admitted. "It's not easy to run a shelter, and neither Stephanie nor I are very good at soliciting donations. If it weren't for the one anonymous donor who periodically gives us money, we wouldn't be able to stay open."

This was the first time that Tessa had ever opened up to him about the finances of the shelter, and he had never heard about an anonymous donor. When Tessa had asked him to look into the investigation on the murders of her family, he had asked her for a list of people that could be suspects. In his book, an unknown person handing the shelter money fit into that category.

Letting that drop for now, he said, "I'm ashamed to say that I never thought about how you kept everything running, but I'm sure the town could help with some of the fundraising efforts. Everyone is well aware of all the good that you do, and I'm sure that there are many people who would be eager to help."

"That's kind of you, Jack. We really could use some help in that area," she admitted.

"You were kind enough to donate some of your best paintings to help us in our fundraiser. The least we can do is help the shelter out as well," he answered.

At the mention of her paintings, Tessa groaned. "Most of my paintings went up in smoke in that fire. There isn't much left to donate at this point."

"Luckily, you already delivered quite a few of them. I'm sure that once you're settled again, you'll have the chance to paint more. You garnered quite a few fans among the police force. I know several officers who want to purchase your paintings," he informed her.

Smiling, she said, "That's really kind of you to say, and it is nice to know. Anywhere we can make some money to help these women is helpful. But until then, I guess I have to hope that our donor comes through again."

"Have you ever tried to find out who this secret donor of yours is?" he asked.

"Of course, we have. Carter has tried hard to find out who it is, but whoever it is seems to be very good at covering their tracks. All I know is that somehow, whenever I think we can't continue on anymore, enough money comes through to keep us going."

Perplexed, Jack shook his head. Strangers didn't just dole out money for no reason, in his experience. "Do you think it's Carter? He, of all people, would know when you have money issues."

"No, I'm certain it's not Carter. He's pretty comfortable, but not at the point he can afford the kind of money that we sometimes get. Besides," Tessa smiled, "despite being extremely generous to all of his friends, Carter does like to take credit for it."

Jack didn't like the idea that some unknown person could find out about the money issues at Hope's Haven. Even though he did not know what her financial situation was, and she confided in him about most things. "Do you or Stephanie have any ideas who it could be?"

She bit her lip, contemplating. "We found out shortly before Hope was killed who her birth father really was. Stephanie thinks it could be him or Hope's grandmother from his side. Turns out they were pretty wealthy, and he did try to pay me off to stay quiet about who Hope's mother was."

"He tried to bribe you. That seems odd. Why?" This was all new to Jack, and he didn't like what he was hearing.

"Let's just say he's a man with a lot of power in the Atlanta area, and he didn't want it getting out that he had an illegitimate child with a stripper."

"Hope's mother was a stripper?"

"Among other things, yes. She was a young girl who was being exploited by everyone around her. Hope's mother had learned to do whatever she needed to do to survive. Apparently, this man decided he was also next in line to exploit the poor girl."

Jack looked back into the file he had on the murders of Tessa's family. He wondered if anyone had ever looked into this "man" as a suspect in the murders.

"What about the grandmother?" he asked. "Why would she want to give you money?"

"She wanted to buy my silence as well. She wanted nothing to tarnish her son's reputation. I guess that's understandable in a way. Stephanie thinks it may also be guilt on their parts for not being more active in Hope's life while she was still alive. I'm not sure what to think, but honestly, I wouldn't know who else has the money that's been coming through."

Before Jack could ask Tessa any more questions, the computer on his dash lit up. Glancing at it quickly, he said, "Looks like Sleeping Beauty is finally up."

CHAPTER 17

Gabriel Rogers is finally awake and able to answer questions?" asked Tessa.

Jack nodded affirmatively, and she eagerly announced, "I'm coming to the hospital with you. I want to hear what he has to say."

Jack nodded again, saying, "We may as well head right over to the hospital right now then. I've been waiting a long time to ask this guy some questions."

Finally arriving at the hospital, Jack showed the cop stationed outside Gabe's room his badge, and they entered his room. They found him sitting up in bed, staring morosely out of the window.

"Gabriel Rogers?" Jack asked, walking over to the bed and standing directly in front of the man. "I'm Sheriff Lewis. I have a few questions I'd like to ask."

Looking up at him with red, tired eyes, Gabe let his gaze drift towards the door, where Tessa had remained after Jack strode in. His eyes widened in recognition.

"You," he said tersely. Turning back to Jack, he said, "What's the dame doing here? She's supposed to be a social worker, not a cop. What did you bring her for? She's caused enough trouble for me already."

""I see you remember Mrs. Graves," Jack said, without answering him directly. "You were the one causing the trouble, Gabriel, and unless you want to take the heat for all that trouble by yourself, I suggest you answer my questions."

"I think I have a right to a lawyer," Gabe jutted out his jaw, looking at Jack sourly.

"That's right, Gabriel. You would have a right to a lawyer if I had placed you under arrest. For now, though, I'm only asking you a few questions."

Gabe looked at Jack in surprise. "I'm NOT under arrest?"

"No, not yet, anyhow. I just thought that you and I could have a nice, friendly little chat, just between us, and clear up a few things."

Tessa observed Jack, wondering what he was up to.

Jack continued, keeping his gaze evenly on Gabe, "I'd hate to see you go down for all of this on your own, Gabrielle. You seem like a decent enough fellow." He settled easily on the side of the bed. "While you were snoozing, I looked you up and found out some information about you. Your parole officer told me what a great guy you really are, and from what I gathered, you did your time in prison without causing any trouble."

Gabe nodded his head, wincing slightly at the movement. "Yeah, that's right. I am a pretty decent guy. You got that right. I shouldn't have to go back to jail. None of this was my idea."

Giving him a sympathetic look, Jack said, "See, that's exactly what I figured, Gabriel, that none of this was your idea. You were just following orders, right? I'd hate for you to take the fall for a kidnapping all by yourself. I doubt that you have anything against Mrs. Graves here personally, am I right?"

Gabe looked over at Tessa. "No, I don't. I didn't even know the dame existed a week ago. I was just minding my own business and staying out of trouble. That's all I was doing," he said.

Jack glanced at Tessa. "See, I told you he was a pretty decent fellow, didn't I?" Then he shifted his attention back at Gabe. "So someone had to have put you up to this kidnapping, right? Or else you would have never been involved in something like this."

Gabe nodded again. "That's right again, Sheriff. I was put up to it. None of it was my idea."

Jack looked at him, his gaze unwavering. "So all I need is for you to tell me now, who it was that put you up to it, Gabrielle. Let's figure out how we can get you the best deal possible."

Gabe narrowed his eyes at Jack, trying to figure out his best option. It was clear to Jack that he wanted a deal badly and didn't want to go back to prison. But if it had been Harley Brinker who had been behind the kidnapping, Jack knew Gabe would know the risks of snitching on his boss.

"I don't snitch on nobody, Sheriff. That kind of stuff can put you six feet under," Gabe finally said.

Jack kept his demeanor casual. "I don't want you to snitch on anyone. We're just having a friendly little chat here, Gabrielle. I'm just trying to help you out. See, if you go down for this kidnapping all on your own, you'll be back in prison, and I can't help you there." Looking over at Tessa, he continued, "It's just like I told Mrs. Graves earlier. I don't think you're a bad guy, and I don't think you meant her any harm. That just isn't the same guy that your parole officer was describing. So I said to Mrs. Graves, we've got to find out what, or who, would have made a decent guy like Gabrielle Rogers, a man who's clearly trying to keep his nose clean, attempt a kidnapping."

Gabe now turned his full attention to Tessa. "The sheriff here is right, lady. I have got nothing against you. Like I said, I didn't even know who you were until a week ago."

Nodding at him slowly, trying to keep her voice sympathetic, Tessa spoke, "I believe you, Mr. Rogers. The Sheriff already told me how highly everyone speaks of you. I'm convinced that you wouldn't want to hurt anyone." She looked at Jack for confirmation, and when he gave her a slight nod, she continued, "I just want to know who it is that would want to kidnap me, Mr. Rogers, and why. I don't want you to take the blame for something that's not your idea."

Now, Gabe was watching Tessa in a much more relaxed manner. He was feeling the camaraderie she was extending to him and was flattered at the way she referred to him as Mr. Rogers. This woman knew how to defer to a man like him, he thought.

"Like I told you, I have nothing against you, lady. Heck, I'm even starting to like you. But you sure got under the skin of some really powerful people, lady. I can tell you that much."

Gabe figured he could tell her, at least throw her a little bone without getting himself into trouble. "These powerful people," Jack asked, "are these the same people who instructed you to kidnap Mrs. Graves?"

Chortling, Gabe said, "Heck no. That was all that punk Ethan's idea. He figured if we kidnap the dame, he could force her to tell us where the money's at, and we could hand her over to the big guy."

Tessa's head was whirring. So far, he was telling the truth, she thought, but the faint buzzing in the back of her neck told her he was still holding something back. "What money, Mr. Rogers? Why would you think I was hiding any money?" she asked.

Looking away from Tessa, Gabe instantly grew wary. Now they were heading into dangerous territory, and even though the woman was respectful, he wasn't about to rat out Snake. He knew that no jail was going to keep him safe if he did that. "The kid said that you had money," he said, "I was just helping him and his little girlfriend out. To be perfectly honest, Sheriff, I don't even know who the two of them were working for."

Tessa's head was buzzing again, and she looked at Jack, shaking her head and wondering how he would proceed now.

"So you're telling me a scrawny kid was calling the shots for a grown man like yourself?" Jack widened his eyes, looking at Gabe in disbelief. "Why would you risk getting yourself into trouble for a kid, Gabrielle?"

"I felt sorry for him, Sheriff. That's the honest truth. He told me it wouldn't be a big deal, that the dame had lots of money and he'd give me a cut." Looking back at Tessa contritely, Gabe said, "I did not know he was going to burn your place down, lady, and that's the God's honest truth too. I yelled at him for that, but he said that it was your own fault. He said you must have stashed the money in that big old safe you had up there, and he burned the place hoping it would crack it and he could get at your stash." Looking back at Jack, his expression was curious. "Did you catch the kid yet? You can't believe a word he says, he's the one that caused all the trouble, not me. That kid has a temper on him like you wouldn't believe. I've seen him slice up a man with that knife of his just for looking at him funny." Leaning back on his pillows, Gabe was enjoying his moment of attention. "Now, if you want to get a dangerous criminal off the streets, he's the one you're after Sheriff, not me."

Jack nodded at Gabe conspiratorially, "Yeah, we got him Gabrielle. Just for the record, what did you say the kid's name was?"

"Ethan Turner, Sheriff, that's his name. And let me tell you, that's one dude I don't mind snitching on. He's been nothing but trouble since I laid eyes on him."

"And when exactly did you first lay eyes on him, Gabrielle? I'm just wondering how a decent guy like you ends up in the company of such scum?" Jack's gaze never wavered from Gabe.

Gabe pursed his lips, thinking for a few minutes before answering. *Let the kid be the one to snitch on Snake*, he thought.

"Yeah, well, I kind of got to know the girl he was with, his girlfriend, and she introduced us, you know. Like I said, I felt sorry for her and all. She seemed like a nice kid, and I just wanted to help her out."

"Because she was pregnant?" Tessa asked.

"What?!" Gabe sputtered.

It was clear from the shock on his face that he hadn't known, and Tessa immediately regretted her question, vowing to stay quiet before she revealed anything else to the man.

After throwing her a warning look, Jack looked at Gabe. "I take it that Ethan never told you his girlfriend was pregnant?"

Gabe was shaking his head slowly, trying to get things straight in his mind.

"Nah, never said a word to me," he admitted. "But it doesn't surprise me that much either. The kid did seem to have a way with the women, although that one seemed awful young,"

"Who did the kid work for, Gabrielle? Was the girl working for the same guy?" Jack leaned forward, his gaze growing intense. "Remember, I'm just trying to help you out here. They're blaming this whole kidnapping scheme on you, and they're willing to deal, Gabrielle. What about you? Do you want a deal, or are you going to take the whole blame?"

Gabe's stomach was clenching in anger at what the Sheriff was saying. *Figures the kid would try to rat him out first,* he thought bitterly. He'd had a suspicion that Ethan had been planning to betray Snake and make a run for it with the girl, and now that he'd found out she was pregnant, he knew he'd been right. They would have left him to face Snake on his own, and now they were trying to make him take the fall for everything.

As Gabe was still racking his brain for a way to lay the blame on Ethan, without ratting out Snake, his thoughts were interrupted by a knock on the door.

Annoyed, Jack looked at the uniformed officer walking in. "What?" he growled.

"Sorry to interrupt, sir, but the coroner is finished with Turner's body, and he wants to wrap it up. He asked me if you wanted to come and look at it before he puts the kid on ice?"

Gabe's face lit up while Jack scowled at the officer. He knew the officer was just doing his job, but right now he wanted to fire him.

"Tell him to wrap it up," Jack instructed tersely, trying to hide his aggravation.

After the officer left the room, he turned back to Gabe, hating the smug look on the man's face. "So the kid bit the big one, huh? Tell me, did he run into the same brute that laid into me?" he asked gleefully.

"No, he ran into a lady with a frying pan," Jack said, taking some satisfaction in the surprised look on Gabe's face.

"Well, can't say as I'm sorry to hear of the kid's demise. He was a no-good punk." Gabe smiled happily. "I guess unless the girl has something to say, we're just all never gonna know who the kid was answering to, are we?"

A short while later, Jack glanced over at Tessa. She had been silent ever since they'd gotten in the car. Jack had offered to stop for coffee, but Tessa had insisted she needed to get back to the shelter and check on Angela.

It was hot outside, and he had the air conditioning on full. Watching as the air blew the hair back from her face, exposing her flawless chin line, he couldn't help noticing how forlorn and defeated she looked.

"We might still get some answers from Patty when we find her," Jack offered, trying to give her some hope.

Once Gabe had realized there was no one left to contradict him, he had spent the next half hour putting the blame for every occurrence on Ethan Turner. He had steadfastly refused to connect Harley Brinker to either of them or even admit that he had seen Harley since his release from prison.

Tessa just nodded absently, asking quietly, "Do you really think we still have a chance of finding her?" Jack remained silent, knowing it was useless to try to tell Tessa anything but the truth. He had sent officers to question Harley Brinker right after they had left Vicky Brennan, hoping if he truly had gone back to seek refuge with her father, they would find her. But Harley had denied having seen her in weeks, and they had found out nothing.

"It's possible she could still surface somewhere. She will need money and help. We'll keep Brinker's place under surveillance for a while just in case she does end up back there. And we'll watch the Bannan house as well, of course."

Despite the blistering heat outside, Tessa hugged her arms around herself, thinking of how Ethan had been creeping around her house just the night before.

"It's terrifying to think that such a dangerous man like Ethan Turner was around the women I promised to protect," she said. "If Angela hadn't been so alert, I can't even imagine what could have happened. And it's all my fault for not following my own protocol and allowing the danger into my house."

"I don't think that anyone else in the house was in danger, he was after you, not any of the other women. You can't keep blaming yourself for everything Tessa. You have a good heart, and you were just trying to help the girl. No one is faulting you for that." Jack looked at her compassionately.

She knew Jack was trying to comfort her, but despite what he said, she had placed everyone around her in grave danger. The worst part was that even though they now had a new suspect in the murders of her family, they were no closer to solving the crime. Now, there were even more questions and no answers.

"What if Harley came to the house to take his revenge out on my family, Jack? That would mean that Hope and Luke are dead because of me."

Jack pulled to the side of the road, turning to look at her sternly as soon as he parked. "Is that how you want to live the rest of your life, Tessa? Blaming yourself for what happened?"

She was looking at him with tragic eyes, and his heart melted, but he knew he had to continue.

"What if it was Harley Brinker who attacked you that night, and what if he was seeking revenge on you for hiding his wife and children? What would you do differently, Tessa? Send Victoria, her son, and Patty back into an abusive household?"

"They went back anyway, Jack! It was all for nothing," she wailed. "And Vicky is the one who told Harley my name. She's the reason he found out about me."

Jack nodded. "True, but she didn't know he was planning to do anything with the information, Tessa." He took her shoulders firmly in his hands, making her face him, "We don't even know if Harley is the one responsible for the murders. All we know is, he was more than likely the one who sent those goons after you. We just need to prove it."

She put her hands to her face, sobbing. "No one is safe around me anymore. I cause pain for everyone who comes near me."

Jack leaned over, taking her in his arms and holding her tightly until her sobs finally subsided.

When she had cried herself out, he brushed the damp hair from her face and looked at her sternly.

"If Harley Brinker handles your kidnapping or the murders of your family, I'm going to get him, Tessa. He made a big mistake coming after you, and now he's on my radar. We'll be watching him day and night until I can lock him up." He laid her head on his shoulder as he leaned against the back upholstery of the sticky car, continuing to brush her hair back from her face carefully. "No matter what happens though, none of this is your fault. If Harley Brinker is behind any of this, he's the one to blame, not you, and he will pay the price." Tessa started shaking her head in denial, but Jack took it firmly in his hands to stop her. "Shhh Tessa. Be honest with yourself, once and for all. If you really believe that you're a danger to everyone around you, then the right thing to do is quit. Just leave."

Tessa bolted up, staring at him through her tear-stained eyes.

"What? Leave Hope's Haven?" she was shocked that he would even suggest that.

Gazing at her steadily, he said, "Why not? If you believe you're causing more harm than good, then that's what you should do."

Stroking her wet cheek, he continued, "If you would truly go back in time and change anything you've ever done to help anyone because you think something bad could happen because of it, then you shouldn't be in the business you're in Tessa."

Tessa sank her head back against Jack's shoulder. She hadn't felt this exhausted and overwhelmed in years, and the whirring in her head became incessant as she mulled over what Jack was saying.

She finally opened her eyes and sat up, looking Jack directly in the eyes.

"You're right, Jack. I wouldn't go back and change anything that I've done to help anyone. These women need me, and if I don't help them, then who will?"

Jack smiled at her, satisfied. "You can't change who you are inside, Tessa. None of us can. We all have a destiny to fulfill, and yours is to help these women."

Finally arriving back at the shelter, Tessa saw that Carter's car was parked in the driveway. She groaned inwardly, wondering how much he knew about the night's events, and if he was going to lecture her about breaking their protocol.

On the rest of the drive home, she had also texted Stephanie some of the relevant information they had learned today from Gabrielle, and there was no doubt in her mind that Stephanie had wasted no time talking to Carter.

Helping her out of the car, Jack excused himself, saying he was heading over to talk to Beau next door and find out if he had learned anything from his sources, and then he needed to get back to his station to catch up on other things.

Reluctantly opening the front door, Tessa expected encountering a very irate Carter. Instead, he came running towards her, enveloping her in his arms as soon as he reached her.

"Tess, my dear Tess. Thank God you're all right." Holding her back at arm's length from him, he looked at her carefully. "You are all right, aren't you? He didn't hurt you?"

Tessa shook her head. "I'm fine Carter, really, just fine. I never even saw him last night. Well, not alive anyway. I was at the cottage when he broke in. Poor Angela had to deal with him all by herself."

Pulling her in again, Carter hugged her closely and continued stroking her back. "I can't believe how close I came to losing you, Tess. I don't even want to think about what might have happened here last night!" Hugging her even closer, he said, "I don't think I could go on if I lost you!"

Tessa nestled into his familiar arms, letting herself be held gratefully. It had been a very long, traumatizing night, and the conversation with Gabrielle Rogers had left her drained. Having Carter's arms around her felt so safe, and him telling her how much she meant to him just felt good. She nestled in further, just relishing the comforting feeling for a while.

Carter continued to just hold her quietly for a few more minutes, until she finally drew back, saying, "I really should check on Angela. As nice as it is to have you hold me right now, she's the one who suffered the most trauma last night. I need to see how she's holding out."

"You're right, of course. I think she's in the kitchen. Let's check on her together." He led the way, still holding Tessa's hand as if she were the most precious commodity on earth.

They found Angela sitting at the kitchen table by herself, staring down into a cup of coffee. As soon as she noticed them, she rose to her feet quickly.

"Miss Tessa, Mr. Carter, please sit down. Let me get you some coffee."

Tessa smiled at how naturally Angela was treating the kitchen as if it were her own little domain.

"No, Angela. You sit down. I'll get us the coffee. There's no need to serve us. I just wanted to see how you were doing," Tessa replied.

Angela sat back down, watching as Tessa gathered mugs for her and Carter, filling them both with the steaming brew from the pot on the stove.

After she sat down, Tessa looked around curiously. "Where are your children Angela? I also thought that some of the women might be here with you, I don't think you should be all alone right now."

"Maria took the kids outside to play. After all the questioning from the police, I got little sleep last night." Looking at Tessa with compassion she said, "I can see you got little sleep either." She looked out the window. "Anyway, like I was saying, Maria took the kids outside so that I could get some sleep, and the other women took over most of the chores for me today. I tried to sleep but I couldn't, so I just figured that I would get up and wait until you came back."

Tessa gave Angela a curious look. She had the feeling that Angela had something on her mind she wanted to talk to her about.

"What's troubling you, Angela? Do you need to talk to me about something?" she asked.

Tessa prayed fervently that there wasn't something about last night that Angela was hiding from the police. They had all agreed that Angela had acted in self-defense, but she wanted to be sure there were no secrets that could still get Angela into trouble.

Nodding at her, Angela looked at Tessa miserably. "It all just happened so fast, Miss Tessa. I acted because I knew I had to, but there is something I still need to tell you, and I'm scared."

Tessa looked at Carter and then back at Angela. "Do you want me to ask Carter to leave? Is it something you need to tell me in private?"

Angela looked at Carter, and then back at Tessa, unsure of what she should do. "No, I guess it's all right if Mr. Carter hears it. Maybe he can even advise me, him being a lawyer and everything."

Carter sat forward attentively. Just like Tessa, he too had hoped that Angela had told the police the entire story last night. It wouldn't bode well for the woman if she kept secrets from them, and he wanted to do what he could to keep Angela safe and out of trouble.

"Okay, Angela. I'll do whatever I can to help you. Tell us what's bothering you. What did you not tell us last night?" he asked.

Slumping back in her seat, she looked at the two of them, her eyes sad and resigned, as if she were submitting to a terrible fate.
"I knew that the man was going to enter the house last night. That's why I was ready and waiting for him."

CHAPTER 18

Tessa looked at Angela, stunned.

"You knew he was going to break in? But how? I don't understand. You said you'd never seen him before."

"That's true, Miss Tessa. I didn't know him before last night. Most everything happened just the way I said it did. The only thing I didn't tell the police was that I'd been forewarned and that I set up the bed to look like someone was sleeping in it."

Tessa looked at Angela in disbelief, trying to process what the woman was saying. She remembered the buzz in her head last night, but she'd convinced herself it was due to all the trauma and events of the night. It had never entered her mind that Angela was lying to them.

Carter was sitting forward in his seat, wearing his professional lawyer demeanor. "Tell us exactly what happened last night, Angela, right from the beginning. This time, leave nothing out. I can help you, but only if I know exactly what really happened."

Guiltily avoiding Tessa's gaze, Angela instead focused on Carter as she spoke. "Last night, while I was getting ready to put the kids to bed, I got a call from Patty."

Tessa gasped, "Patty called you? Do you know where she is?"

Carter put a hand on Tessa, cautioning her to stay quiet, and looked evenly at Angela. "Go on, Angela. What did she say to you?"

Looking down at her coffee cup, Angela swirled the now cold brew around with distaste, and then continued talking, not looking at either of them. "She told me she and her boyfriend had been parked outside of the house all evening. He planned to come in and kidnap you, Miss Tessa." Looking at Tessa directly, she said tragically, "She told me he was trying to force her to help him, but she didn't want to hurt anyone. He forced her to tell him how she had snuck out through a hole in the fence, and when he went to check it out, she grabbed his cell phone and ran down the street to hide."

"So she called you from his cell?" Carter prompted.

"I guess so. I gave her my number when she was here, and I told her to contact me if she needed help."

She said to Tessa, "You know that I really felt for that little girl. I knew that deep down she was a good girl. She just got mixed up with a bunch of bad people. It wasn't her fault that she was raised the way she was. I just wanted to give her a chance at a better life."

Remembering her visit with Victoria and what the woman had told her about Patty's upbringing, she knew Angela was right. Patty had never stood a chance with parents like Harley Brinker and Victoria Bannan.

"I know, Angela. I felt the same way about her."

Angela looked up and out of the window, gathering her thoughts. "Anyway, after she told me what that man Ethan was planning, I asked her if he had a weapon. She said he just had a little pocketknife, something he carried with him everywhere, but other than that, he didn't have a gun or anything." Angela started wringing her hands in distress. "The poor child was so terrified that she was going to be put in jail for helping him, and she told me she didn't want her baby to be born in a prison cell."

Tessa thought about what Patty had already gone through in her life, and she still found it within her to warn them, despite any fears she had for herself. Blowing her nose first, Angela said, "I told her that she'd done the right thing by calling me and warning us, and then I told her to hide until a woman I know could come and get her."

"What woman, Angela?" Carter asked.

"A friend of mine who had escaped from an abusive husband a few years ago. I told Patty I was going to call the woman and tell her to pick her up, and that she should stay hidden until the woman called her. Then she should go with her and do what she says."

Carter leaned in, asking, "Did you call your friend last night, Angela?" Angela nodded silently.

"Did Patty go with your friend?" Tessa asked, hoping that Patty might be safe after all.

Angela looked at her hands. "I guess so. I haven't heard from Patty since she hung up. I tried to contact my friend today to find out what happened, but all she could say was that Patty was safe."

"Why didn't you call the police after you called your friend to pick up Patty? You knew what Ethan Turner was planning," Carter asked.

Angela shrugged her shoulders. "I wanted to give Patty a chance to get away first. I figured it would take a few hours for someone to collect her, and I was worried she wouldn't get away before the police came and found her."

Taking Angela's hand gently, Tessa said, "Angela, the police aren't the bad guys. They would have helped Patty as well." Angela looked at Tessa reproachfully.

"Really, Miss Tessa? The child was involved with someone who was planning to rob you, kidnap you, and had already attempted it once. Patty was the one who more or less opened the doors for him. Do you really think the police would have just said thank you, ma'am, and sent her on her way?"

Rebuffed, Tessa looked away. Listening to how Angela described it now, she did wonder how Patty would fare if the police caught up with her.

Angela continued, "At worst, she would have been sent to jail for her part in all of this, and at best, she would have been sent to a juvenile halfway house. Either of those places is no place for a girl to get a second chance, and she would have lost the baby to the state." She looked at the two of them miserably. "I just couldn't let that happen to her, especially not after she called to warn us. She could have just as well run off and worried about herself. I felt we owed her that second chance."

Neither Tessa nor Carter could really blame Angela for what she had done. "Anyway," Angela continued, "after I called my friend, I thought I'd better keep a watch out for the young man, in case he really did try to break in." She looked at them pleadingly, "Now mind you, I didn't know how dangerous he really was. I kind of figured that when he found out Patty had run off, he would just take off anyway, trying nothing, but just in case, I stuffed the sheets under the covers in Patty's old room, thinking he'd believe that someone was sleeping in there. I even left the door open a bit, hoping that he would look in there first. Then I grabbed the heavy frying pan to protect myself, and I just waited in the living room."

Tessa shook her head in wonder at Angela's cunning. Even though she knew the woman had to have some street smarts to have survived in her marriage for as long as she had, this was a side to Angela she hadn't seen before.

"I waited for hours, but when nothing happened, I figured he really had given up and went on his way. I was planning to call Mr. Beau in the morning and let him know what Patty and the boy had been planning, and I wanted him to fix the hole in the fence. I figured that would give her enough time to get away, and he could tell me what I should do." Angela looked at the stove where the cast iron pan usually sat, shuddering. "I was still in the living room, just about to head to bed when I heard someone in the kitchen. I crouched behind the couch and I watched him go to your office, then Miss Stephanie's office, and then he walked into the kitchen." Looking at them with large, fearful eyes, she told them, "When he came out, I could see that he was carrying a large butcher knife at his side, and I was terrified, Miss Tessa. I realized that I had stupidly left my cell phone in my room earlier when I had gone to check on my kids. I was so afraid that if I made any noise and he thought someone was up, he would hurt one of us. So, I just stayed crouched down and watched him sneaking in and out of the bedrooms. I didn't know what to do."

Tessa saw how Angela was looking down the hallway in fear, reliving the nightmare of the night before.

Angela continued, "I thought he had noticed that no one was in that last bedroom, and he would come looking in the living room with that big knife and find me. I needed a better place to hide, so when he crept into one of the other bedrooms, I snuck into the empty bedroom and hid in the closet. When he came in and started stabbing at the sheets, I panicked and hit him with the pan." She looked at Carter again, as if pleading her case. "I really just wanted to stop him, Mr. Carter. But after I hit him, he looked at me with such hate, I was terrified. I've never seen a look like that in anyone before, not even my ex-husband. I tried to get away from him, but then I tripped, and he came at me with that knife in his hand. I knew that if I didn't stop him, he was going to kill me. Somehow I got up, and I whacked him as hard as I could, and he just fell down and didn't move anymore."

While Angela had been speaking, the whirring in Tessa's head had continued, letting her know that this time she was telling the entire story as it had really happened.

Carter looked at Tessa, waiting to see what she thought of Angela's story, and she nodded absently at him, still trying to envision the scene that Angela had described. He then looked with compassion at Angela but said to Tessa, "We have to let the police know."

"I know, Carter. I'll call Jack and ask him to come over," Tessa said. Seeing the panic on the woman's face, she took Angela's hand, trying to calm her. "It's going to be okay, Angela. You did nothing criminal last night. Jack will not take you to jail, and you won't be in any trouble, I promise."

Angela tensed, and for a minute, Tessa was convinced that she was going to jump up and run, but she suddenly slumped back in her chair, her face dejected and resigned.

"Okay, Miss Tessa. I trust you. I'll do whatever you say."

Hours later, Tessa finally found herself alone on the veranda of the little cottage. The session with Jack and Angela had been grueling, but in the end, Jack had agreed to let Angela go with only a reprimand. He said she should have notified him and the police immediately, but as far as he was concerned, her behavior hadn't been criminal.

Sinking into the oversized chair and looking out at the mountains, she wished for the sunset to hurry. After all the ugliness she had seen over the last few days, she needed to see something beautiful again. She held the icy water glass up to her fevered forehead when she felt a cold nose nudging her.

Looking down at two dark, soulful eyes gazing up at her, she said, "Oh, hey Cash. How're you doing, boy? You got out of your kennel again, huh?" Wagging his tail, the large dog sat on her feet, watching her face as if he understood every word.

Sighing, Tessa patted his head absently. "I don't know why anyone even bothers locking the door to your kennel. If you want out, you always seem to find a way anyway, don't you?" Laying his head on her lap, Cash whined, staring at her mournfully and looking every bit the part of a neglected and misunderstood puppy.

Hearing a soft cough coming from beside her, she looked up to see Beau standing just off to the side of the veranda. As usual, her stomach fluttered in excitement.

"Sorry to bother you, Tessa," Beau said. "Ellie just called me to tell me that Cash got out again. When she went to feed him, she found his kennel empty. Something told me he might be over here with you."

Tessa looked down at the dog, who still had his head on her lap, smiling at him fondly. "Yes, Cujo found his way over again."

As Beau stepped forward, leash in hand and ready to attach it to the dog, Cash buried his head further into Tessa's lap, flashing Beau a warning look.

"Sorry about that. As soon as I can get this leash on him, I'll drag him back," Beau said, looking apologetic. "I really need to get this dog under control."

Tessa stroked the dog's soft head, and he whined in pleasure. "That's okay, just leave him here. He always seems to find a way out, anyway."

"You sure?" Beau asked doubtfully, surprised at her sudden change of heart when it came to the dog.

She watched out of the corner of her eye as Beau walked over and sat down across from her, the chair squeaking softly as he settled in.

"I guess it's been a rough couple of days for you, huh?" he asked, noticing the sun glinting on her dark hair and casting a shadow over her sad and tired face.

"Yeah, it really has." She looked down at the soulful eyes still staring up at her. "Do you want to talk about it? I'm a good listener."

Tessa relayed to him all that had transpired that day, including what Angela had confessed upon their return to the shelter and how Jack had handled it all. When she was done, she sat back, exhausted, waiting for him to comment. All he said was, "I see." She waited for the familiar buzz she should hear, knowing he was keeping something from her. When she didn't hear it, she let out a sigh. It sounded almost deafening to her in the stillness in her head.

"You already knew Angela didn't tell us everything last night, didn't you?" she finally asked.

Looking at her evenly, he admitted, "Not until this morning. She called me to tell me about the hole in the fence, the one that Turner must have snuck through to get in. I think she was panicky that if it didn't get fixed, someone else could find it and sneak in. I persuaded her to tell me how she knew about it."

"Were you ever planning to share any of this information with Jack or myself?" Tessa was irritated at him, without really understanding why.

"I hoped that I'd convinced her to tell you herself, and I wouldn't need to. I thought it would be best if she told you and Jack herself," Beau answered.

Knowing how she felt about duplicity, his gaze never left her face, trying to gauge her reaction. She just closed her eyes wearily. It seemed even with her heightened senses, she could still be deceived, and the sense of betrayal stung.

Moving over to sit next to her, he settled his muscular legs over the side of her chair and took her hand, causing her heart to quicken at his nearness and his touch. "Look Tessa, I promise I would have told you if she hadn't told you by tonight. You can trust me. I only wanted to give Angela a chance to come clean herself. She has a hard enough time trusting men. I didn't want to betray her unless I had to."

Nodding silently, Tessa kept her eyes closed. With all the ugliness and deception in the world, was trust even a possibility anymore. Finally, she broke the stillness, "It's okay. At least Patty and her unborn baby are safe now."

He got up, and she heard him rustling around the kitchen, coming back with two glasses and handing her one. When she took a sip, she almost choked.

"What is this?" she gasped. "Are you trying to poison me?"

"Scotch. On ice," he replied, taking a sip. "You looked like you could use one."

Feeling the hot liquid coursing through her veins and making its way to her stomach, it left a warm and soothing feeling inside. She risked taking a small sip, this time without choking. "I think maybe you're right. I did," she admitted.

Cautiously, he asked, "You're worried about the baby, aren't you?"

She shrugged her shoulders, trying to act indifferent. "Of course, I am. Patty is so young. I just hope that she makes the right choices when it comes to the child."

"What, in your opinion, are the right choices, Tessa?"

Letting me adopt the baby! Giving me a second chance! she wanted to scream out. Instead, she quietly said, "I don't know the answer to that. I guess it will depend on where she ends up and what she herself decides is the best choice."

"Is there any way that you can check on her? Find out that she's all right. Angela's friend must know where she is, and I'm sure that Jack still wants to question her."

Tessa smiled sadly, staring at the glass in her hand. "She's in a safe house now, Beau, hidden away somewhere until she decides it's time to come out. I've used them myself a few times to help women disappear from their husbands. There's an extensive network of them all around the country, and they operate in complete secrecy. At this point, she could be anywhere, and there is nothing Angela, her friend, or even Jack can do to find her."

"I see," he said thoughtfully, staying silent for a while and watching the sun reflect off the woman sitting in front of him. He admired her strength and fortitude.

Tessa was lost in thought as she gazed at the red and pink colors reflecting off the distant mountains. She marveled at the beauty that nature could still provide, in spite of all the heartache.

"It's beautiful," she whispered. "Even at the worst of times, nature has a way of reminding us that there's still beauty and wonder all around us, doesn't it?"

Beau just nodded silently, ignoring the sunset and watching her instead.

"I'll miss this view," she said wistfully. "Before I leave, I'll need to take some pictures. I'd like to paint this scene, although I doubt I could ever do it justice."

Beau frowned, and the soft look he'd been watching her with disappeared. "What do you mean when you leave? You can paint it right here, without a picture. Just set your paint stuff up and paint," he said.

"Carter let me know that Charly was being released from the hospital today. The family still needs to quarantine for a few more days, but everyone finally seems to be on the mend, and I should be able to move in with them by the end of the week."

"Why not just stay here till you can get back into your apartment? I told you that you can stay here as long as you like."

"I'm afraid I won't be going back to my apartment at all," Tessa informed him. "Turns out the damage was extensive, and my landlord has torn the entire building down and used the money to buy a condo in Florida."

Looking around her, she said, "I can't say as I blame him. He's been talking about retiring to Florida for years, and I guess now he'll finally get his opportunity. I guess it's time for me to look for a new apartment and start all over again."

Beau relaxed, sitting back in his chair, and watched as the last tendrils of red disappeared in the sky. "It's actually perfect. You'll just live here permanently. We can draw up the rental agreement tomorrow," he announced.

"I don't think so, Beau. I could never afford this place. Besides, you said you don't want to rent it, remember?" she replied.

"I believe I said I don't want to rent it to strangers. You're not a stranger," he countered.

Looking around her wistfully, she wished Beau's suggestion would be a possibility. Even though she'd only been here a few days, the little cottage was already feeling familiar and homey to her.

"I really wish I could, Beau. But I need to stay within a budget. I can't take more money out of the shelter than I already am, and Stephanie and her husband will need a bigger house soon too. Any extra money needs to go to help them get a bigger house, not a luxury cottage for myself."

"I never asked you for any rent," he said curtly.

"I don't want charity, Beau. I can pay for my own housing," she countered vehemently.

He sat silent for a minute, pondering. Finally, he looked up at her, taking a sip from his drink. "You're right, pay rent. It's only fair. Truth is, I do not know what you can afford to pay, and the rent to this place really might be too steep for you."

Even though she had been arguing this point all along, Tessa couldn't help feeling disappointed. "Well, good then, that's settled. I'll start looking for an apartment as soon as I can and probably move in with Stephanie by the end of the week."

Beau just continued to sit back, watching her, nursing the drink in his hand. "It is a shame to keep the place empty though," he noted. "There is such a housing shortage around here, I hear."

Tessa frowned. He was right. It had taken her forever to find her little apartment above the garage. Most of the places she had looked at had either been rundown or too expensive for her. "Well, you're right, I think you should rent it. It is a shame for such a nice place to sit empty. There are certainly enough people in town who are desperately looking for a place to rent," she agreed.

He nodded congenially. "I guess you're going to be one of them now too," he said, slightly amused.

Groaning loudly, she said, "I guess I am one of them now." The thought of apartment hunting again was depressing her more than she cared to admit.

They sat in silence for a few more minutes, the darkness slowly encroaching on them. Cash had nestled himself at her feet, and she wondered how he would act with the next person who moved into the little cottage.

Beau was sitting complacently in his chair, staring out into the darkness, when she finally asked, "Just out of curiosity, how much are you going to ask for rent?"

Glancing at her casually, he asked, "Why? You said you couldn't afford it?"

"I know what I said. I'm just curious, that's all. And I'm worried that Cash might not get on with just anyone."

"That's definitely something I'll need to take into consideration when I consider any future tenants." Beau looked down at the sleeping dog. "If they don't like him, or he doesn't like them, I'll have to reinforce his kennel."

"Will you be vetting any future tenants?" she asked, wondering if there were any reinforcements strong enough to keep Cash from escaping.

"Of course I will. Like I said, I like my privacy, and I promised you I'll do whatever I can to help the women at the shelter stay safe. Anyone that lives here will have to go through a very rigorous vetting program." He sighed, somewhat loudly and exaggerated. "To be honest, that's why I was excited when you said you were looking for a new apartment. You've already passed the vetting process and passed it. If you could afford the place, I could have saved myself a lot of time and trouble."

Bristling at his tone, Tessa glared at him. "Well, good to hear you've checked me out and I checked out okay."

He gave a casual nod in her direction, but other than that, ignored her comment.

"All right, fine, so are you going to tell me what the rent is, or not?" she finally said.

"I could, I guess. Although, does it really matter? You don't seem to want to move in any way," he said noncommittally.

"I never said I didn't want to move in!" she retorted. This man was driving her crazy.

"You didn't?" he asked, giving her an innocent look. "I'm pretty sure that's what I heard?"

Tessa let out an exasperated breath. The entire day had been exhausting and emotionally draining. All she'd wanted to do was watch the sunset and go to bed, but instead, she'd gotten a message from her landlord informing her he would tear down her building. The realization that she was now truly homeless and would need to search for a new place was exhausting. She was in no mood to have Beau tell her what she had and hadn't said.

"I NEVER said I didn't want to live here! I love it here, it's amazing!" she argued loudly.

"Well, I agree, it's nice. You don't need to yell at me," he replied, smiling slightly.

"I'm not yelling," she said, clenching her teeth. Cash lifted his head, watching with concern and looking around, wondering what was upsetting her.

Patting his head to reassure him, she said, more calmly, "I was just trying to explain that I NEVER told you I didn't want to live here."

"Oh, then what was it you were saying?" he asked serenely.

"I said that I couldn't afford to live here," she explained again.

"How do you know that? You don't even know what I'm asking for rent," he countered.

Expelling another exasperated sigh, she said, "What are you asking for rent?"

"$300.00," he said.

"What? That's it? That's not possible. This place would go for at least 5 times that. You're crazy!" she exclaimed.

He shrugged. "Maybe I am, but that's what I'm asking." Looking at her slyly, he asked, "I guess if someone can get through my rigorous vetting process, they'll be getting a pretty good deal then, won't they?"

"You're really going to rent this cottage for $300.00?"

He nodded and added, "Only if they pass my background checks, of course."

Tessa patted Cash's head, resigned. Her head was silent, no buzzing and no whirring, nothing to let her know what was in his head. She had the feeling she'd just been played, and frankly, she didn't care. The stillness in her head was as welcoming to her as the tranquility of the night.

"All right, I'll take it," she said.

"Take what?" he asked, grinning triumphantly.

"The apartment," she said, grinning back at him. "You can bring over the rental agreement tomorrow. But I'm warning you, I'll have my lawyer looking over them."

A week later, Tessa sat back, surveying the painting sitting on the easel in front of her. She'd just completed an outline of the mountains greeting her every day from her little veranda. Maybe tonight she would get the chance to fill in the color as she watched the sunset live. The past week had been hectic, and she was happy to have even a little time to devote to her painting.

She had salvaged what she could from the garage apartment, right before the wrecking ball had come and obliterated what had been her life for the last five years. Although there had been little to salvage, the old safe that had caused Ethan Turner so much trouble had withstood the unrelenting flames. Upon its opening, Tessa had discovered that she had indeed had the foresight to store her photos and keepsakes in it.

Stretching, she got up from in front of the easel she'd been working at. It was a gift from Stephanie and Carter, who'd been urging her to get back to her painting. This morning had been warm and bright, and Tessa had finally felt the urge to put the amazing views she saw on her canvas.

Strolling into the little kitchen to refresh her ice water, she stopped and picked up a newly framed picture of Hope and Luke. Although she'd lost the picture of Luke and Hope in front of the treehouse, this one showed the three of them hamming it up for the lens, Hope's radiant smile the same as it had been in life.

She blissfully looked around her little cottage. She had filled the previously bare walls with more pictures of Hope, along with several of her art pieces. It now exuded warmth and happiness, and she once again thanked God for her good fortune to live here.

She still worried about how Patty was faring, feeling a slight sense of loss when she thought of the small little human growing inside the teenager. But she realized all she could do now was pray that it would be safe and grow up in a better environment than poor Patty had.

The shelter's anonymous donor had come through just in the nick of time once again. Stephanie and Tessa had spent the better part of yesterday stocking up on the many supplies it took to house the women and children currently living there. They had asked Angela to stay on with them full time and help run the shelter, an offer the older woman had gladly accepted. Some of the money would build out a portion of the house into a small apartment for her and her children.

Jack had asked her to come by the station and listen in on another interrogation. Afterwards, he informed her that Gabrielle Rogers was safely tucked away in a jail cell. Although he had confessed to his part in the kidnapping, he had refused to implicate anyone other than the deceased Ethan Turner. For the time being, Harley Brinker was still a free man. She knew Jack was still desperately trying to find out what had happened to the little boy that Victoria and Harley had given away, but so far, that had led to a dead end for him.

Taking a drink of the cold water she had just poured herself, she smiled. Just before she had left the station, Jack had turned to her with an awkward smile and asked her to accompany him to the policeman's auction she'd donated her paintings to. He had been quick to assure her it wasn't a date; he thought she might enjoy watching how well the bidders received her paintings. She had accepted, agreeing that it would be nice.

When Tessa had told her friends her plans for the weekend, Stephanie had thrown her a knowing glance, and Carter had given her a sour look. But Tessa was just excited to get out, enjoying some time away from the shelter and her worries, even if it was only for an evening.

Taking her glass, she walked back outside and sat down again, closing her eyes so she could fully feel the warmth of the sun on her face. She heard the familiar pad of paws on her veranda and felt the now familiar nudge on her arm, opening her eyes to see his dark, soulful eyes looking up at her.

Smiling, she said, "Hey Cash, I see you got out again."

The dog thumped his tail, laying his head on her lap. Although it had become a daily routine for him to come and see her in the evenings when he had the run of the estate, during the day he was supposed to be in his kennel, staying safely away from the delivery men and maintenance workers.

Stroking his head, she said, "Don't worry, I won't turn you in as long as you don't bother anyone. You can stay here with me for the afternoon."

The dog looked at her gratefully, settling down at her feet, after circling a few times first to find the perfect position.

Feeling safe with the dog at her feet, she allowed her eyes to close, giving most of her senses a well-deserved rest. The blistering sun soaked into her dark hair, while the breeze coming off her beloved mountain helped keep her cool. She listened to the birds twittering in the bushes all around her, and Cash's easy breathing at her feet tickled her bare toes. Deep inside her head, she listened, but the buzzing and whirring that had become such a normal part of her were thankfully absent today.

Once she had asked Luke how he could come home to them, being so at peace, when he dealt with so much evil and turmoil every day. He had kissed her nose and said, "I focus on what I choose to focus on. And when I'm home with you and Hope, you're what I choose."

She looked at the horizon, the mountains shimmering in the red glow of the evening's setting sun, knowing that tomorrow would bring new problems and new women to help. But for tonight, she would follow Luke's advice, and focus on her beloved mountains.

ABOUT THE AUTHOR

NOTE FROM SAGE PARKER

Hi lovelies.

I love writing sweet and clean contemporary romance novels. I was born and raised in a small town in South Carolina, but you can almost always find me at the beach...usually reading a book. I hope my writing brings joy and inspiration to everyone that uses their precious time to read my stories.

Thanks for stopping by!
Stay safe and happy x

Keep in touch. If you would like to say hello, you can e-mail me at: hello@sageparkerauthor.com or
Follow me on Amazon [Sage Parker] to get updated whenever I release a new book!

MORE BOOKS BY SAGE PARKER

HIDDEN IN THE KEYS *Longboat Key Series*

LAST SEEN AT LIGHTHOUSE LANE *An Outer Banks Mystery Series*

THE HAMPTON BEACH CAFÉ *Starting Over Series*

THE LIGHTHOUSE SISTERS *Tybee Island Series*

THE HOLIDAY REUNION *Pine Lakes Series*

HOUSE ABOVE THE BOOKSHOP *A Rockport Secret Series*

SEARCHING THE HARBOR *Bar Harbor Series*

STARTING OVER IN BOOTHBAY *A Second Chance Mystery Series*

SECRETS AT THE OLD HOTEL *A Cozy Mystery Romance Series*

IN THE SHADOWS OF PARADISE *A Bahamas Mystery Series*

NEW IN CLIFFS POINT *Cliffs Point Series*

LAST RESORT ON THE COAST *Search for Truth Series*

A COASTLINE RETREAT *Feels Like Home Series*

THE BEACHSIDE CAFE *Saltwater Secrets Series*

Made in United States
Troutdale, OR
12/07/2023

15507774R00170